"I know I should let you go,"

Miguel said with an effort. "But, oh, my *querida*, ever since I saw you last I have wanted to be with you every minute. I have yearned to have you next to me, longed to have you share my bed at night. I have tried, tried like hell, to hold back, tried not to call you again, tried to let you go. I have told myself that once I go back to Arucas and become swamped in my work, once you start your research and become equally involved in your own affairs, we will soon forget about each other. And then this . . . this thing that has blazed between us . . . will simmer down. But I don't truly believe that. Do you?"

Pamela moistened her lips. "No," she whispered.

Dear Reader,

When was the last time your heart ached over an epic story, thrilled to a romance that spanned generations? This month in Special Editions, the ever popular Nora Roberts will satisfy that craving. The saga of the irrepressible MacGregor clan, introduced to you with *Playing the Odds* (#225) in March 1985, finally reaches its poignant conclusion in *For Now, Forever* (#361).

With the publication of *For Now, Forever*, we are also reissuing the entire award-winning series, *Playing the Odds* (#225), *Tempting Fate* (#235), *All the Possibilities* (#247) and *One Man's Art* (#259), in a special Collectors Edition. Look for them, with their tartan covers, at your local booksellers, along with this month's Special Editions.

Don't we all dream of finding that one great love? Nora Roberts's fifth book in the MacGregor Series goes back in time to tell how Daniel MacGregor, founder of the MacGregor dynasty, first wooed and won unflappable Anna Whitfield. You've seen Daniel as an inveterate matchmaker when it comes to marrying off his three children—but in *For Now, Forever*, Daniel is the one who's met his match! Whether standing alone or read with the other four, Daniel and Anna's story will capture your heart, for theirs is undeniably the love of a lifetime.

One reader wrote, "When you bring Daniel into any story, the pages truly come alive!" Come share in the MacGregors' joy and drama, and let them make your romantic dreams come true.

Warm wishes,
The editors

MAGGI CHARLES
Shadow on the Sun

Silhouette Special Edition

Published by Silhouette Books New York

America's Publisher of Contemporary Romance

To the Spirit of Carnival . . . and the Canaries

SILHOUETTE BOOKS
300 East 42nd St., New York, N.Y. 10017

Copyright © 1987 by Koehler Associates Ltd.

ISBN: 0-373-09362-4

First Silhouette Books printing February 1987

America's Publisher of Contemporary Romance

Printed in the U.S.A.

Books by Maggi Charles

Silhouette Romance

Magic Crescendo #134

Silhouette Intimate Moments

My Enemy, My Love #90

Silhouette Special Edition

Love's Golden Shadow #23
Love's Tender Trial #45
The Mirror Image #158
That Special Sunday #258
Autumn Reckoning #269
Focus on Love #305
Yesterday's Tomorrow #336
Shadow on the Sun #362

MAGGI CHARLES

is a confirmed traveler who readily admits that ''people and places fascinate me.'' A prolific author, who is also known to her romance fans as Meg Hudson, Ms. Charles states that if she hadn't become a writer that, having studied the piano and harp, she would have been a musician. A native New Yorker, she is the mother of two sons and currently resides in Cape Cod, Massachusetts, with her husband.

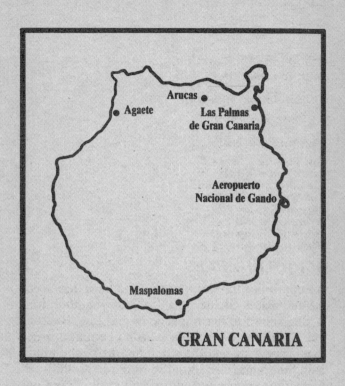

Arucas

Agaete

Las Palmas
de Gran Canaria

Aeropuerto
Nacional de Gando

Maspalomas

GRAN CANARIA

Chapter One

Pamela took a deep breath, then forced herself to exhale slowly. It was a trick that usually worked when she felt her nerves approach the screeching point.

The departure lounge at Boston's Logan Airport was a scene of mass frustration. The steadily mounting tension, built on uncertainty and disappointment, was aggravated by the overabundance of man-made heat that was being generated in this normally spacious area, now crammed with nearly three hundred people.

Pamela inhaled again, meanwhile keeping a watchful eye on the bank of telephone booths lining the far wall. All of them were occupied at the moment, as they all had been since the pilot's announcement that the flight would be delayed for at least an hour, so the passengers might as well disembark.

"But please remain nearby," he'd added before paraphrasing the slogan of a rival airline. "We want you to be ready when we are.'' The attempt at humor struck little response from the passengers.

The estimated hour had already stretched to an hour and a half, and now Pamela knew there was no way she could keep her cocktail rendezvous with Charles Evans at Kennedy, even if she raced back to the ticket counter and tried to get a seat on another flight to New York.

She consulted her watch for perhaps the hundredth time. It was not quite four o'clock. In just a few minutes, Charles would be leaving his downtown Manhattan office and cabbing it out to Long Island. Unless she could reach him and inform him that she was still earthbound in Boston, he was going to be very annoyed. This New York meeting would be their last time together for a long while.

In a way, that was just as well, Pamela conceded. Charles was becoming more and more insistent about setting a wedding date. She wasn't ready to even start thinking about marrying him. Still, she was fond of Charles, and she wanted to keep things on an even keel between them.

In the center phone booth, a plump blonde suddenly hung up the receiver with one hand and began collecting her bright-red tote bag with the other. Pamela wasted no time. She actually sprinted around the people in her way, and was within a few feet of her target when she saw she was about to be cut off.

A tall, dark-haired man quickly approached from her left, his long strides demonstrating a determination that was not about to suffer interference. Pamela made a last-ditch effort to get ahead of him, but failed. She saw a slender, deeply tanned hand reach out to grasp the hinged door of the booth, while its owner waited politely for the blonde to emerge rather awkwardly from the confined space. Then he slipped inside with an easy, fluid motion.

Pamela pulled herself up short, choking back the furious words she yearned to hurl at this man. Only at the last instant, as he was about to pull the door closed, did he acknowledge her. It was, at first, an impassive look. He stared at her with eyes as dark as midnight, and just as emotionally opaque as the rest of his face. Then there was a change, as if the film of an inner camera had shifted from one frame to the next.

"I will not be long," he promised with a smile, then politely shut the folding glass door in her face.

Pamela froze. She was twenty-eight years old, successful in her career, and well adjusted to the modern world. A friend who was a clinical psychologist had assured her of *that*. Chivalry was the last thing she expected in her daily encounters with the opposite sex. But this man was . . . something!

He left the door open a crack, so she could hear him speaking into the mouthpiece, but she couldn't understand a word he said. He was conversing in Spanish far too rapidly, no way could her recently completed crash course in that language help her with his conversation.

He was facing the front of the booth, glancing downward as he spoke, giving Pamela a perfect opportunity to study his face. It was an interesting face, handsome and intense. He had a broad forehead, a classic straight nose, high cheeks and a proud chin. His hair was thick, black and neatly trimmed, with a slight sprinkling of silver over each temple.

He was taking his time with the phone call, despite having said that he wouldn't be long. Pamela couldn't ignore the ebb and flow of his melodious Spanish and, though his expression remained unchanged, she sensed his displeasure.

Another glance at her watch revealed that it was definitely too late to intercept Charles. He would be on his way to Kennedy by now, unless something had detained him at the very last minute. To vent her displeasure, she swore softly, just as the phone booth door opened.

Dark eyes swept her face inquiringly, and read her correctly. "I am sorry," the man said. "The conversation took longer than I thought it would."

He spoke with a slight accent—a disarmingly charming accent—but his English was fluent. Pamela wished her Spanish was a thousandth as good.

He stood very erect, and gestured toward the phone booth. "Please," he invited, holding the door open.

Pamela slid into the space the tall Spaniard had just vacated and, despite her conviction that Charles would already be en route, dialed his office number.

His secretary's "Mr. Evans is on his way to Kennedy to meet a flight, Miss Merrill," only confirmed what Pamela already knew about Charles. She doubted if he'd ever been late for anything in his entire life.

"*My* flight," she informed the secretary, letting her bitterness sour her tone. "If he checks in with you, will you please tell him my plane was delayed in Boston."

She hung up, both annoyed and depressed over this turn of events. For the next four months she would be on distant Grand Canary Island, immersed in work that she hoped would yield material for a doctoral thesis. She had wanted to leave matters with Charles on a relatively pleasant note.

A voice at her elbow said urgently, *"Señorita!"*

She turned to face the man who had cut in front of her.

"Señorita," he repeated, "I wish to apologize. My call was important, true. But evidently, because of me, you missed whomever you were trying to contact."

There was no point in denying it. "Yes," Pamela said evenly. "Yes, I did."

"I'm very sorry," the tall Spaniard said. He hesitated, then shrugged slightly. There was an eloquence to the shrug that made Pamela suspect that all his body language would be equally eloquent. Though he was definitely slim—actually a shade too slim—he was well built, and his charcoal suit could not have fitted him more perfectly. Custom-made to the last inch, and obviously expensive.

"Look," he said, "this is not just to make amends. I realize it is impossible to do that. It is already too late. But may I buy you a drink? There is a small lounge not too far up the corridor. I imagine we could both use something to settle our nerves."

Pamela shook her head. "I don't think so, thank you."

He grinned, and the effect was electrifying. It lighted his dark features and brought a spark to his midnight eyes. "You must have a thirst," he teased gently. "Even a small thirst?"

It was much too easy to smile back at him. "I do," she admitted. "But we really shouldn't leave this area."

"Let me find out how much longer we are apt to be kept waiting," he suggested, and left her side so quickly, so smoothly, that she blinked.

She watched him cross the crowded room, liking the way he walked, liking the grace of his movements and the assurance he projected as he worked his way around the people huddled in groups.

Her green-gray eyes widened in surprise as she saw him nod to a uniformed man at the jetway entrance and then disappear down the ramp.

Nothing like hearing the news right from the horse's mouth, she conceded, amused. Evidently he was going straight to the pilot for his information.

He returned a few minutes later. "There is no way we are going to move from here for at least another hour. So, we definitely have time for a drink. Agreed?"

"Why not?" Pamela asked rhetorically.

The cocktail lounge was filled with frustrated passengers like themselves, passing the time. When a couple at a corner table rose, Pamela's companion was quick to claim the vacated space.

"Would you like a cocktail?" he suggested, as a waitress approached.

Pamela shook her head. "No, thanks. I don't think I could tolerate anything strong at the moment. Perhaps just some vermouth on the rocks."

"Two Cinzanos, please," he requested pleasantly, and added, "with twists of lemon."

The order given, he leaned back, letting his own frustrations show briefly as he muttered, "What a mess! If we're not on our way in an hour, we'll miss the Iberia flight from Kennedy." He smiled apologetically. "That does not concern you, of course."

"What does not concern me?"

"I must make a connection in New York with an Iberia flight to Madrid," he said.

"I'm in the same predicament," Pamela confessed. "I'm supposed to make the Iberia connection in New York, too."

"You are going to Madrid?"

"Actually, I'm going to the Canary Islands," she volunteered. "When I checked with a travel agent about how to get there, going via Madrid seemed my best route."

"That depends," the Spaniard said. "But, yes, to go via Madrid is probably as good a way as any." He paused. "Where are you going in the Canary Islands?"

"Grand Canary."

He chuckled. "I am apt to start believing in that long arm of coincidence," he said. "I am from Gran Canaria. My home is on the island."

The Canaries, a group of islands owned by Spain, are situated off the northwest coast of Africa. Some historians claimed they were the remains of the fabled lost continent of Atlantis, lending them a mystical quality. In any event, they happened to be the perfect locale for Pamela's research, especially since she had a place to stay in Las Palmas, Grand Canary's capital.

"That *is* quite a coincidence," she murmured.

"And a very pleasant one, I must say," her companion told her. "Forgive me," he added, "I haven't even introduced myself. I am Miguel Rivero y Fonte. Miguel Rivero, that is."

"Pamela Merrill," Pamela responded absently, her concentration lingering on each Spanish syllable of this man's name.

"Would it be too curious of me to ask what takes you to Gran Canaria?" he queried. "A vacation, I suppose?"

Pamela shook her head. "No. I'm going there on business, as a matter of fact."

"Business?"

"Research."

"Again, would I be too curious if I asked you the subject of your research?" he persisted.

"Water," Pamela replied.

Miguel Rivero sat back and surveyed her with frank astonishment. When the waitress brought their drinks, he remained still, making no move to touch his glass, filled with ice cubes and an amber liquid.

"Water," he echoed. He said something in Spanish too swiftly for Pamela to understand. Then he laughed. "I confess," he admitted, "you have staggered me. What is it about water that concerns you, Miss Merrill?"

"I'm a hydrologist," Pamela informed him, and saw that if he'd been "staggered" before, he was doubly so now.

He rallied, his smile returning. "So," he suggested, "you are coming to the Canaries to solve our problems, is that it?"

He was probably teasing, but Pamela decided to take him seriously. "I doubt I could do that," she answered. "I've heard enough about the Canaries' water plight to appreciate that it's far beyond my ability to solve. As an area for study, though, Grand Canary will be fascinating. There are so many aspects to consider, from the effects of long-term deforestation upon annual rainfall to..."

She spread her hands wide, and favored Miguel Rivero with a smile that, though wry, lit up her features in a way that made him even more aware of her attractiveness than he already was.

It had been a shock, while standing in the phone booth, to look up and see hostility blazing in a pair of eyes almost the color of Spanish olives. Her dark-gold hair had reminded him of the gilded picture frames in his home on Grand Canary that held oil portraits of his ancestors. Her hair was the same rich gold color, and as full of unexpected glints.

As they'd walked down the airport corridor together, Miguel had been able to appraise Pamela fully. She had the stunning long legs that he considered something of an American trademark. Her rather boxy green jacket obscured another area of interest, but he had every reason to believe that hers would be everything he admired in a woman's figure—gently rounded, the curves in exactly the right places, not too thin, not too fat.

And her face . . . her face was arrestingly lovely. Clearcut features, a wide and generous mouth, a tilt to her nose, and skin the color of ivory, her cheeks flushed a rose tinge.

Now he had just discovered that not only was she a beauty, she was also a brain. Perhaps too much of a brain, he thought, and was at once irritated with himself. Still, he seldom related well to career women, especially scientists and engineers. To date, he had found most of them brusque and more overtly masculine than feminine.

Miguel Rivero nearly laughed aloud at this reflection. Possibly Pamela Merrill could be brusque upon occasion, but she certainly was not masculine in any way. She was, in fact, quintessentially feminine.

Curious, he asked, "Where will you be staying on Grand Canary?"

Pamela frowned slightly before she answered, and Miguel got the impression that she didn't want to be rude, but wasn't in the habit of giving out information to strangers.

She said, rather cautiously, "I'll be staying in Las Palmas."

"Las Palmas is a big city," Miguel reminded her. "About three hundred and fifty thousand people, at the last count."

Pamela nodded. "So I've heard."

"Have you booked a hotel room?"

"No."

It was his turn to frown. "Then you may have a problem," he said. "You will be arriving in Las Palmas at the height of carnival time. We have quite a carnival, you know. Comparable, some say, to the celebrations in Rio and New Orleans. As you can imagine, accommodations are at a premium."

"I'll be staying with friends," Pamela stated.

"Spanish friends?"

"Yes. That is, one of them is Spanish. Juan is from Grand Canary. His wife is American."

"Juan?"

Miguel was persistent in a pleasant way, but Pamela disliked the gentle inquisition. She was tempted to tell him that Juan's identity was really none of his business. Then, sizing up Miguel Rivero y Fonte, she began to suspect that he and Juan might very well travel in the same circles.

"Juan Basilio y Marrero," she added.

Miguel shook his head disbelievingly. "Such a small world," he mused. "I know Juan Basilio. As a matter of fact, his sister and my sister are close friends. They attended school together, and got married at about the same time. Their husbands even died within six months of each other. Doña Carmen—Juan's sister—lives not far from my home in Arucas, just a few kilometers up toward the mountains from Las Palmas. Dolores, my sister, keeps house for me. The two ladies are now in their late forties, and very much immersed in their respective lives. Of course, they share many interests. Juan is a few years older than I am."

"I see," Pamela said, and added slowly, almost reluctantly, "I met Juan when he was teaching hydraulic engineering as an exchange professor in the States. I was one of his students. His wife, Grace, is an American. She and I were . . . thrown together."

They had, indeed, been thrown together in the aftermath of an accident on a rainy night when, after class, Pamela had let Juan drive her home. She'd just broken up with Glenn Babcock that afternoon, after a three-year relationship that had taken a tremendous emotional toll.

Juan had come upon her crying quietly in a corner of his classroom. She'd thought that everyone had left for the day, but Juan had returned to retrieve a notebook.

That had been seven years ago, when Pamela was twenty-one and Juan in his mid-thirties. He had acted in a purely fatherly capacity when he drew her into his arms and let her snuggle her head against his shoulder. But damned if the custodian hadn't walked into the room at that moment, only to retreat hastily with muttered apologies. The die had been cast. There was nothing that could set a brush fire on campus as quickly as gossip.

Juan had laughed rather shakily. "Well, that does it! What is it they say, Pamelita? An item? You and I are about to become an item. Old Hughie, I understand, is the best storyteller in New England."

They left the building shortly after that, with Juan insisting on driving her home. But the fates were not quite through with them yet. Juan skidded on a patch of icy road and they wound up in a ditch, unconscious.

Fortunately, their injuries had not been too serious. Still, they had both spent several days in the hospital. Afterward, Grace Basilio insisted that Pamela move in with Juan and herself until she was fully recovered . . . emotionally, as well as physically.

"Also," Grace had said, actually laughing about it, "this'll be one way to stop the gossip. Either that, or Juan will be accused of orchestrating a ménage à trois!"

Shortly thereafter, Grace rented a U-Haul and drove over to the apartment Pamela had been sharing with Glenn Babcock. There, with the help of some college students, she'd moved out every last possession of Pamela's and stored them in their basement until Pamela could decide where she wanted to live.

At that point, Pamela began literally to worship Grace Basilio. Later, this worship had evolved into love and respect mixed with sincere affection.

Pamela was suddenly aware that Miguel Rivero was patiently waiting for her to continue with what she'd been telling him about Juan and Grace. "Anyway, I've been invited to stay with the Basilios as long as I wish. But good friends though they are, I don't want to impose, so I'll probably try to find a place of my own once I get acclimated."

"Of course."

"The language will be a problem," she admitted. "My Spanish is . . . limited. I just finished a crash course, but I'm afraid all it did was make me tongue-tied."

Miguel smiled. "You will learn Spanish quickly. You have a musical voice, so I suspect you also have a musical ear. That's a great asset in learning languages."

"Then *you* must have a very musical ear," she countered. "Your English is flawless."

He shook his head. "By no means, Miss Merrill. I have lapses, especially when I get excited. But I've had a lot of practice with English. I went to college in the States, both undergraduate and graduate school. Six years in all. Unlike you, I stopped short of going for a doctorate. But I did get my master's. In agronomy."

"Agronomy?"

"Specifically, that branch of agriculture that deals with crop production and soil management," Miguel Rivero told her. "I inherited a large banana plantation from my father," he continued levelly. "It was his father's before him. So, my home in Arucas is surrounded by hundreds of acres of banana trees. As you may already know, that's not likely to be true much longer. Because of the drought, it is almost a certainty that within a few years the banana trees will disappear from the islands.

Pamela was honestly shocked. "I didn't realize it was that bad," she said.

"It is very bad," Miguel replied gravely. "I've tried to extend the life of my plantation. But I think we are being shown on Grand Canary that although in many instances man can create either his own salvation or destruction, he is powerless against the basic forces of nature."

He reached for his vermouth. "There will be plenty of time for you to learn about our water problems when you get to the Canaries," he said. "Meanwhile, on behalf of the people of Gran Canaria, especially myself, may I bid you welcome?"

He raised his glass in a toast, and the gesture was every bit as charming as his accent. Only a woman of stone could completely resist a man like him.

Pamela was not a woman of stone. She had to remind herself that she was traveling to Grand Canary to escape romantic involvement, not to become involved anew.

Chapter Two

Pamela's first impression of Grand Canary Island was a kaleidoscopic blend of rich colors, sights, and sounds.

The scenery was spectacular. Viewed from the plane, the island appeared to rise out of the sea, its volcanic origin plainly evident from the many prominent cone-shaped mountains. Once these mountains had smoldered with hidden fire. Now, for centuries, almost all had been dormant.

The airport was, like most airports, an anonymous study in concrete, glass and chrome. But outside the terminal, the air was soft and warm, quite a contrast to windy, snowy Boston. The cloudless sky was as blue as flowering chicory, while sunlight sparkled on a myriad of lush tropical plantings.

Pamela, reveling in this beauty, felt as if she'd been transported to paradise. Soon, though, she was jolted by the rollicking bus ride up the coast from the airport to

Las Palmas. The modern highway that ran parallel to the coast vibrated with incessant traffic, and everyone seemed to be in an enormous hurry. Pamela, expecting the Spanish tempo to be far more laid-back, was immersed in culture shock.

The highway passed factories, clustered residential high-rises, warehouses, docks, and commercial areas. Here and there, interspersed among the industrial clutter, were fields that sloped from the level of the road, thickly planted and a rich green. Pamela realized that she was viewing her first banana trees. Miguel had told her that growers would attempt to cultivate any and all arable land, even in the most unlikely places.

She wished Miguel Rivero was at her side now to enlighten her about all the unfamiliar things she was seeing. She would have appreciated his knowledge... as well as his company. As it was, they'd parted at the airport, and the parting—for Pamela—had been an unexpected letdown.

They'd sat next to each other on the flight from Boston to New York, and had experienced another long wait at Kennedy. By then, their schedules were hopelessly mixed up, and it was hours before they were able to board a late-night Iberia jet for Madrid.

Miguel arranged for them to sit together once more on the trip across the Atlantic. After dinner, they donned headphones and tried watching the in-flight movie, but quickly agreed the film was less than mediocre.

Pamela then attempted to turn her attention to the fashion magazine she'd bought at the airport, but she found herself unable to concentrate. She was intensely conscious of the man next to her, who also was reading, and evidently more interested in his book than she was in her magazine. Every so often, she glanced at him surreptitiously, realizing more and more how much she liked his looks, his manners, everything about him. She couldn't remember when a man had intrigued her as much as Miguel Rivero did. She conceded wryly that he was the exact opposite of Charles.

During the long hours they'd spent together at Kennedy, Miguel had been a delightful companion. He'd made light of their travel difficulties, spicing the situation with a keen humor that went a long way toward helping Pamela forget her problems.

On their arrival in New York, Pamela had wondered if Charles might still be waiting, even though her flight was four hours late. Knowing him as she did, she doubted he would have stayed around. He would expect her to phone him immediately, and would probably feel she should delay her trip by at least another day so they could resolve the sticky issues between them.

She'd been right about Charles. He was nowhere in sight. She gave thought to phoning him, but decided it would be an exercise in futility. Her mind was on her interrupted trip and the necessity of straightening out her flight schedule; she wasn't ready to cope with a man who was going to insist upon addressing issues she didn't want to address.

Having made the decision not to contact Charles from Kennedy, but to phone or write him from Las Palmas, Pamela had let Miguel Rivero take over.

Gazing out the bus window, Pamela remembered how, on the plane last night, he had looked up from the book he'd been so immersed in and had favored her with a lazy and unexpectedly sweet smile.

"So," he observed, "like myself, you evidently find it difficult to sleep on airplanes."

"Impossible," she confessed.

Miguel stretched, and Pamela was again struck by his near-perfect physique. He'd told her earlier that he was thirty-six. The quiet strength about him made Pamela suspect he must be quite diligent about keeping his body in top physical shape.

"I've been wondering about something," he said.

"What?" she asked absently.

"What made you decide to take on the study of water as your lifework?"

She smiled. "Hydrology is not actually the study of water. Technically speaking, it's the science that deals with the distribution and circulation of water on land, in the soil, and in the atmosphere."

"I stand corrected," Miguel murmured, but there was a mischievous gleam in his dark eyes.

"Well," Pamela went on, "since you come from the Canaries I'm sure you're more aware than most people that rainfall does not occur uniformly throughout the world."

"I'm very aware of it," he admitted ruefully.

"Rainfall, and everything involving rainfall, follows an unending sequence we call the hydrologic cycle. Some regions are normally wet, some are normally dry, even though there are usually significant variations from year to year almost everywhere."

She cast a sideways glance at Miguel, wondering what his reaction would be to her outpouring of scientific information. She discovered he was listening to her intently. The humor had faded from his dark eyes and his expression was almost too serious. Evidently, water was as important to his life as it was to hers, although for entirely different reasons.

Abruptly, he said, "Please go on."

"Well, my own interest is primarily in applied hydrology," Pamela continued. "That's to say the planning and operation of programs designed to forecast the varying phases of the hydrologic cycle. It includes flood control, water supplies for irrigation, and structures such as dams that will control stream flow..."

She stopped in midsentence. "If I keep on," she said, "I will certainly bore you."

Miguel's midnight gaze melted her. His voice was a caress. "I doubt very much, Pamela, if you could ever bore me," he assured her softly.

The stewardess appeared just then to offer hors d'oeuvres and drinks. Although these past two days had completely upset their personal time schedules, Miguel observed whimsically that they had probably reached the cocktail hour.

Their conversation never got back to anything serious. After touching down at Madrid's Barajas Airport, Miguel shepherded Pamela through customs, then led the way from the international terminal to the national one, removing language barriers en route. Despite her crash course, the swift-flowing Spanish Pamela was hearing on all sides was completely incomprehensible.

The flight from Madrid to Las Palmas was uneventful, and neither she nor Miguel spoke very much while in the air. This was natural enough; they were both extremely tired. Also, she noted, her companion appeared to become more and more preoccupied as they neared the Canaries.

At the airport outside of Las Palmas, Miguel called the Basilios' number for Pamela, then handed her the receiver. He waited until it was decided that Juan would meet her at a downtown hotel, where the airport bus would let her off. Only then did he take his leave, courteously but swiftly.

Pamela was left with the unsettling impression that Miguel definitely had other things on his mind, and was probably glad to get away. It appeared that once he was back on his own soil, the intriguing Spaniard had become totally immersed in his own affairs. She really couldn't blame him for that; anyone involved in the cultivation of bananas in the Canary Islands certainly had more than his share of problems.

On the other hand, she wondered if he was meeting someone, either outside the airport or in town. A woman, perhaps, whom he didn't want to see him in the company of another woman, even someone he'd just met casually.

Certainly, there must be at least one woman in Miguel Rivero's life. He was not only extremely attractive and sophisticated, but—to judge from the way he dressed—wealthy as well.

How little she knew about him! For all the talking they'd done in the past day, very few facts of a personal nature had been revealed. Miguel was adroit at keeping things on a pleasant but general level, and now Pamela wished she'd been more inquisitive. As it was, she knew only that Miguel had gone to college in the States, lived in a town called Arucas outside of Las Palmas, ran a banana plantation he'd inherited from his father and that his widowed sister kept house for him.

Her attention was diverted from these thoughts by a building complex strung along the waterfront. Her Spanish was adequate enough to translate the large sign proclaiming this the desalinization plant that provided potable water for the residents of Las Palmas. The process removed the salt from seawater, making it usable and even drinkable, but not very tasty.

She knew that, like desalinization plants in other locales—Aruca, in the Caribbean, was another she had studied—this operation must have been constructed at enormous cost. That was one of the problems.

As the bus continued on toward Las Palmas, signs in Spanish made Pamela keenly aware that she'd ventured into foreign territory. And this was not Spain. She was careening along a highway on an island that was far closer to Africa than to Europe, one of a group of seven islands of whose existence she would have barely known, had it not been for the friendship long ago established between the Basilios and herself.

The bus veered off the coastal highway, and suddenly they were driving through the midst of the city, a city whose charm immediately offset the impression Pamela had got from the high rises on its outskirts.

They drove along wide boulevards with narrow parks as dividers. The parks were mostly lawn with gardens of lush, tropical flowers. Palm trees bordered the sidewalks, and Pamela noted that the trunks of many of them had been entwined with strips of bright material or plastic. She saw two men, dressed like clowns, ambling happily along a side street, and a little boy and a little girl were in cowboy and ballerina costumes. Then she remembered Miguel saying that she was arriving at carnival time—the most exciting time of the year in Las Palmas.

The bus turned onto the first of a series of narrow side streets, colorful streets crowded with people and clogged with traffic. Honking horns added to the cacophony of city sounds. The pastel buildings, pressed together, were stained with dirt. The ground floor of practically every one had been converted into small shops that vied with one another in displaying endless merchandise. Pamela saw store windows devoted entirely to dolls, others to lace, some to exotic costumes, probably meant for the carnival, others to perfumes, watches and cameras. Las Palmas was a duty free port, renowned for its excellent "buys."

The excitement and bustle of this seaport city was irrepressibly contagious and completely unlike anything Pamela had expected. She smiled ruefully. She had done her homework concerning the water situation, but had neglected just about everything else. Here on the scene, she would have to learn as she went along.

The bus driver obligingly called out the name of the hotel where Pamela was to meet Juan Basilio. Although the hotel was on waterfront property, its main entrance was on a side street that was too narrow for the bus to turn into. Pamela was one of a number of passengers who were let out on the nearest corner.

Wide stone steps flanked the entrance to the hotel and, clutching her suitcase in one hand and her carry-on bag in the other, Pamela mounted them. Adjusting her eyes as she entered the dim lobby, she walked into a surprisingly opulent mirror-and-marble setting. But she scarcely had time to appraise her surroundings before she was enveloped by a strong pair of arms.

"Pamelita!" Juan Basilio shouted, causing people strolling through the lobby to turn and beam indulgently. Even the very proper looking uniformed clerks behind the marble reception counter smiled slightly. *"Bienvenido a Gran Canaria!"*

Juan released Pamela as he spoke, and gathered up her luggage. "Come," he urged. "My car is parked in a No Parking zone."

Juan had appropriated a parking place that caused the traffic along the narrow street to crawl around his car with a caution that Pamela already suspected was rare for Las Palmas. A couple of drivers yelled complaints as Juan slid behind the wheel of his small European sedan. But the complaints were voiced good-naturedly, and Juan was equally boisterous as he shouted back in Spanish.

"If you could have given me a more definite time of arrival, Grace and I would have met you at the airport," Juan chided her, pulling out into traffic and hitting his horn almost immediately. "As it was, one or the other of us stayed by the phone constantly. It seems like forever since you were supposed to leave Boston."

"Tell me about it!" Pamela retorted. "I feel as if I've been airborne all my life."

Juan laughed, then said easily, "No matter. You have arrived." He added, "We don't live far from here, but I thought it would be easier for you to find this hotel. Our house is at the end of a small cul-de-sac, and not so easy to find, even though it is centrally located and just a five-minute walk to the beach."

"You sound like a real estate agent!" Pamela accused him impishly.

Juan grinned. He was a big man, not tall, but broad shouldered. He wasn't considered handsome; his features were too rugged. But Pamela could well understand why Grace had found him devastatingly attractive. Juan had tremendous charm and personality.

"Grace wouldn't allow me to sell this house," he told her. "When we found it, she said to me, 'This is our forever place, Juanito. Wherever we may go, this is the home we will come back to.'" He smiled. "I could not believe my good luck," he confessed. "I was uncertain about how she would respond to Gran Canaria. We had been here only briefly a couple of times, primarily to visit my sister."

"What if Grace hadn't liked it here, Juan?"

"Then we would have compromised," Juan replied without hesitation. "Perhaps we would have stayed here long enough for me to write my book, or at least a first draft. Then we would have gone to Grace's kind of place for a while." He shrugged, a gesture that somehow reminded Pamela of Miguel. "That is life, Pamelita. A series of compromises. Those who refuse to compromise only thwart their own growth."

As Juan said this, he turned down the narrowest street she'd seen so far. It ended in a small loop, where Juan jerked the car to a halt. "My private parking place," he announced triumphantly.

The gray stone house was three stories high. It was narrow, and had tall windows ornamented with black iron grillwork. A heavy wooden door was flush with the sidewalk, and with an air of proprietorship that Pamela found both endearing and amusing, Juan produced a large key from his coat pocket, turned it in the ornate metal lock and pushed the door open.

"Es su casa," he told her, his sincerity bringing a tear to Pamela's eyes. She recognized this Spanish statement, more of a custom than a statement, really.

As she stepped through the doorway, her excitement mounted. A small square patio, filled with flowers and exotic plants and surrounding a small fountain, replaced the conventional foyer of a formal American home. From the patio, a spiral wrought iron staircase led to the second floor. Then Grace appeared at the top of the stairs, looking every bit the Spanish hostess and lady of the house in her colorfully embroidered caftan.

She and Pamela met at the base of the stairs and hugged each other exuberantly. It was only when they paused for breath that Pamela, looking around, managed to say shakily, "This is exquisite."

"Wait till you see the rest of it," Grace promised. "It's small, like a dollhouse, but I love every inch of it, and so will you."

Pamela was immediately taken on a tour of the Basilio residence. On the second floor—called the first floor, following the Spanish custom—were a formal drawing room, an equally formal dining room, and what Grace called "the spillover room, where we really live." This was a combination living room, library, and family room.

"The kitchen and sleeping quarters for the servants, so-called, are on the ground floor, back of the patio," Grace said. "Would you believe it, we have a man and his wife—they pretty much run this ménage—and there is also a girl who comes in to help clean." She grinned. "It makes me feel like a plutocrat. In fact, I'm getting so lazy you won't believe it!"

Pamela, knowing that Grace Basilio was the last person in the world who would let herself become lazy, shook her head. "Whatever you're doing, it agrees with you," she said honestly.

This was true. Grace was in her late thirties and although her hair already had turned silver, it made her all the more striking, and actually lent a youthfulness to her pretty heart-shaped face. Whereas Juan tended to be portly, Grace was naturally thin. Wearing little makeup over her smooth pale skin, she looked vibrant, healthy...and very happy.

They continued the house tour, pausing briefly in Juan's private study just off the drawing room.

"This is forbidden territory to all of us when Juan is writing," Grace said, her deep-set blue eyes aglow. She cast a fond glance at her husband. "He is a veritable demon when he is working," she added, but Pamela knew that this, too, was the furthest thing from the truth. There would never be a time in his life when Juan wouldn't welcome an interruption by Grace.

The sleeping quarters were on the next floor. The Basilios had a comfortable suite for themselves that included a solarium, and there was a single guest room, beautifully furnished in tones of rose and cream, with a pink-tiled adjoining bathroom.

Pamela glanced wistfully at the big, pink bathtub with ornate, gold-plated fittings. "Do you suppose I could get in that and just soak and soak and soak?" she asked. "Or does the water shortage make this tub an obsolete antique?"

"There's no shortage of water in the city, thanks to the desalinization plant. You can soak as long and as often as you desire," Grace assured her. "You must be suffering from jet lag, darling. So have a nice bath, then take a good siesta. Come downstairs when you're ready. We'll have a predinner drink and some hors d'oeuvres. We seldom eat before nine o'clock, which is early according to Spanish custom. But during those years in the States I'm afraid Juan became hopelessly Americanized."

"Hunger pangs know no nationality," Juan interjected. "Anyway, by the traditional Spanish dining hour of ten or so, I am in agony."

The Basilios left Pamela, insisting that if she needed anything she had only to push the buzzer next to the door. Their housekeeper, Octavia, or their maid, Rosa, would answer her summons and see that she had whatever she wanted. "And remember, don't drink the water

from the tap, unless you're dying of thirst," Grace
warned her. "We have bottled water in the fridge that
tastes a thousand times better."

Pamela quickly decided she didn't need a thing. Grace
had thoughtfully provided a bottle of almond scented
bubble bath that transformed her bath into a foaming,
fragrant delight. Pamela lingered in the tub until she realized that in another minute she'd fall asleep. Then she
wrapped herself in an enormous, thick, rose-colored terry
towel and curled up on the bed, pulling a cream satin
quilt over her. Seldom in her life had she felt so luxuri-
ous, so transported toward peace.

Sleep came swiftly, blissful and dreamless. When she
finally awakened, Pamela saw that someone must have
come into her room while she slept. The draperies had
been drawn across the tall windows, shutting out the last
rays of evening sunlight. She lay in bed, quietly savoring
the tranquility of the moment until there was not a crack
of light left at the windows. Only then did she get up and
leisurely put on a moss-green silk dress.

Arriving downstairs in the family room, she found the
Basilios occupying adjacent armchairs. Grace was reading a novel and Juan was scanning a magazine.

"Ah," Juan commented, getting to his feet. "You look
much more rested, and therefore more beautiful than
ever."

Grace agreed. "That dress is smashing. It does all sorts
of things for both your figure and your coloring." She
added, teasingly, "Darling, why didn't you tell us Miguel Rivero was your companion all the way from Boston?"

This was the last thing Pamela had expected to hear.
She stared at Grace, flabbergasted, until Juan Basilio
laughed aloud.

"No, my wife has not been gazing in her crystal ball," he reported. "The fact is that Miguel called while you were asleep. He wanted to be sure that you had met me as scheduled." Juan added, "I think he was feeling guilty because he hadn't personally escorted you to the hotel."

"Really?" Pamela murmured skeptically.

Juan chuckled. "You must have made quite an impression on him, Pamelita."

"He was very kind," Pamela responded, as she attempted to regain her composure. "I asked him if he knew you," she added, implying that this might have had something to do with Miguel Rivero's kindness to her. "He said he did...that it was a small world. I gather that your sister and his are quite close."

Juan nodded. "Yes, Carmen and Dolores are old friends. They have shared the best and the worst of life's experiences, so there is quite a bond between them. They live a short distance from each other in Arucas. Like the Riveros, my sister Carmen's husband was involved in the growing and exporting of bananas. After his death, Carmen sold the acreage she had inherited to Miguel. But she decided to remain in her home in Arucas. She'd established her life there, her two daughters grew up there. Both are now married. One lives in Madrid, the other in Barcelona. They visit the Canaries very seldom. So, I imagine that Carmen must be lonely at times, though she hides it well and keeps busy. Dolores, on the other hand, is a more...melancholy widow, shall we say?"

"Dolores," Grace interposed with an acidity that was unlike her, "has never learned what it means to face reality. The same thing, I suspect, could be said of Carmen, to a point. Both women have been so protected all their lives by the men in their families that sometimes I doubt they know what it means to stand on their own feet. But occasionally they prove me wrong. They can both be matriarchs, in the truest sense of the word."

"Spanish women are sometimes rather cloistered, even today," Juan agreed. "I admit Dolores and Carmen have been protected. For that matter, they still are protected, especially by Miguel. He treats Carmen as if she, too, were an older sister."

"I don't envy Miguel," Grace observed. "Carmen is easy to get along with, but I'd guess Dolores de Avero can be a trial at times. Then he also has Rafael on his hands, of course."

"Rafael?" Pamela queried.

"Miguel's son," Juan explained.

Pamela felt her spirits plummet.

"Rafael is fifteen," Juan went on, not noticing the change in Pamela's expression.

"And a good candidate for the year's leading juvenile delinquent!" Grace interrupted.

"Grace, Grace," Juan protested, "the boy is not that bad. He lives in a house with a melancholy widow and a father who already has his hands full."

"Dolores constantly spoils Rafael," Grace stated firmly. "Certainly, that doesn't make Miguel's already difficult life any easier."

Just what was that supposed to mean? Pamela yearned to ask, but the words stuck in her throat. She was grateful for the arrival of a young girl in a black and white maid's uniform whom Grace introduced as Rosa. Rosa had brought with her a pitcher of sangria and a plateful of tempting appetizers.

Juan spoke to her in rapid Spanish, then turned to Pamela to explain. "I told Rosa I was about to starve to death, and she was just in time to save me."

Pamela forced herself to smile, but it was an effort to control her facial muscles since she didn't feel like smiling at all.

She knew that Grace was watching her closely, and Grace was very astute. Under ordinary circumstances, she would readily have confided her interest in Miguel Rivero. Grace was a real romantic, and this was a confidence they could have mutually enjoyed.

But common sense told Pamela she should hold back. Miguel, charming as he was, not only had a teenage son who was evidently a problem, but—to judge from what Grace had said—a number of other difficulties to cope with as well.

Most important of all, though, was the question that was flashing through Pamela's mind like an inextinguishable red light: What about Rafael Rivero's mother? Where was she?

Chapter Three

On her first night in Las Palmas, Pamela discovered that Spanish dining was not something to be hurried. Even though the Basilios dined early by most local standards, it was quite late by the time they left the table.

Octavia had outdone herself in preparing a delicious meal—"wrinkled potatoes," served with a spicy sauce, fish sautéed in olive oil with a hint of garlic, delicious smoked pork and, for dessert, custard flamed with aromatic rum.

Octavia and her husband, Roberto, served the meal together, and Pamela was effusive in her compliments, which were translated by Juan. Neither Octavia nor Roberto spoke much English, but their delight at Pamela's pleasure was obvious. They smiled at her broadly and, after they left the room, Juan said, "You have won their undying approval. They are good people. Like most

Canarians, they are true friends when they like someone."

"And when they don't..." Grace warned, with a laugh.

They adjourned to the family room, where Juan suggested a glass of Madeira as a nightcap. That was all Pamela needed to make her so sleepy that, despite every effort to remain alert, she began to yawn.

"Bedtime for you," Grace stated promptly. "You're still suffering from jet lag."

Pamela wasn't sure whether or not it was jet lag that was bothering her, but once she was in bed she found herself wide-awake, regardless of her fatigue.

The night air was scented with jasmine from Grace's garden on the small patio. Pamela inhaled the lovely aroma, and suddenly tears filled her eyes. She brushed them away impatiently. Her problem, she diagnosed, was Miguel Rivero. She was being ridiculous about him; he'd neither said nor done anything to lead her to believe there would be any continuation of their companionship after they'd landed outside Las Palmas.

Now she could understand why he'd left her at the airport as he had. Maybe later he'd felt a little guilty about this, as Juan Basilio had inferred, but probably not. There was no reason why he should have had any later qualms. He'd known that Juan was going to meet her in town, so there hadn't been the need to deliver her personally into Juan's hands. His call to the house had no doubt been made out of courtesy, nothing more.

Pamela rationalized all of this, but there was still an achy lump in her throat that refused to budge. Pamela tended to be wary, where men were concerned. But Miguel had pierced her armor, damn it!

She'd had three serious relationships in her life—the latest being with Charles—and the first two, at least, had done nothing to build her confidence in men.

There had been the disastrous episode with Glenn Babcock while she was still in college, from which Juan and Grace had literally rescued her. Without Grace, Pamela knew very well she might have gone back to Glenn, and *that* would have been a terrible mistake. Glenn, she realized in retrospect, was an inherently selfish person, and a chauvinist in the bargain.

Later, while beginning the work on her doctorate, she'd met Jack Trent, a career Air Force officer. Because he traveled frequently, their romance was somewhat sporadic, which for a while actually made things interesting. Pamela had fallen in love with Jack, an attractive, marvelously coordinated person who shared her interest in skiing and windsurfing. Their rendezvous had been action-packed, and eventually it came as a shock to Pamela to realize they had never really talked very much about anything.

After an affair lasting about a year, interrupted by the demands of her studies and Jack's military obligations, Jack told her he felt the point had come in his life when he wanted a serious commitment. He wanted a wife and a family. He wanted, before too much longer, to buy a home where he could retire when the time came. Meanwhile, his wife could "hold the fort," as he put it, and bring up the kids, while he went off on one mission after another.

Pamela discovered that it had never occurred to Jack that she would not be willing to give up her career for him. Thinking of this as she lay in bed in Las Palmas, inhaling the sweet scent of jasmine, she remembered how completely Jack's attitude had turned her off. Looking back, she supposed she might have reacted differently had she truly loved him. Still, anyone who really loved her would never be so blithe about asking her to give up her life's work.

Terminating the relationship had been painful; it had taken Pamela some time to get over him. She'd temporarily abandoned her doctoral thesis, and had gotten a job with an independent firm in Washington working on government contracts in her field.

She'd met Charles during a reception at the British Embassy that she attended with a man she'd been dating casually. Charles was a New York lawyer who frequently was called to Washington for special consultation. He came from a wealthy family, had attended all the right schools, and Pamela never doubted that he had a brilliant future ahead of him.

She'd been surprised—shocked, really—at the intensity with which he'd fallen in love with her, for Charles was a rather austere and sophisticated person. Very self-assured, he was not easily rattled, but for reasons Pamela still couldn't fully fathom, something about her had certainly "rattled" him. He'd been pursuing her ever since day one, and was by no means satisfied with the kind of relationship she was willing to share. Like Jack Trent, Charles wanted marriage. Unlike Jack, however, he could appreciate Pamela's interest in her career.

Charles had encouraged her to return to work on her doctorate. But when she announced she was going to Las Palmas because the Canary Islands were such a perfect research site, his liberal attitude faded. He didn't relish having her "on the other side of the world" for several months, he stated frankly. At the very least, he wanted a formal engagement before she left.

Pamela had not wanted to become engaged, formally or otherwise. Although she responded to Charles physically, she didn't feel really close to him. Their personalities and life-styles didn't mesh easily, a real problem if they were ever to have a deep and enduring relationship. She viewed this Canary Island interlude as a testing period. If their feelings for each other couldn't transcend this physical separation, she and Charles certainly shouldn't attempt to handle the demands of marriage.

Despite her convictions, she'd agreed to meet him in New York and talk things over. Then fate thwarted *that* and, instead, lured her toward temptation by dangling Miguel Rivero before her eyes.

Pamela blinked, as if she saw a vision of her handsome, transatlantic companion. She tried to convince herself that it was just as well their brief encounter had ended at the airport. There was a chance, of course, that she would see him again. Juan and Grace had already spoken of driving up to Arucas to visit Juan's sister.

If she did see Miguel again, she'd be ready for him. She would be pleasant and casual, nothing more. Eventually she'd be able to view her meeting with Miguel Rivero as a fantasy for her memory book. Later, back home in Boston on gray, dreary days, she could safely recall him.

Visions of winter days in the city made Pamela think of snow. She drifted off to sleep, imagining herself walking across the Boston Common with Miguel as large flakes from the first snowfall of the season drifted lazily around them.

Pamela didn't remember dreaming that night. For this she was grateful; unquestionably, her dreams would have been of Miguel. When she awakened in the morning, though, she still didn't feel rested. She was about to wash up in the pretty pink bathroom, when there was a knock at the door.

Expecting Grace, Pamela called out, "Come in." But the door opened to reveal Octavia, whose broad brown face was wreathed in a smile.

"Flores para la señorita," Octavia announced, holding out a magnificent arrangement of yellow roses in an elaborate crystal vase.

"These can't be for me!" Pamela protested.

Octavia stared at her blankly, so Pamela attempted a little Spanish. *"No para mí,"* she told the housekeeper. *"Para la Señora Grace."*

Octavia shook her head. "Yes, for you, *señorita*," she insisted, in heavily accented English. "Is a card," she added, pointing to a small white envelope taped to the side of the vase.

It couldn't be. It couldn't be! Pamela tried telling herself that the flowers couldn't be from Miguel, even though logic pointed out that she knew exactly five people on Grand Canary Island. Octavia, Roberto, Grace, Juan . . . and Miguel Rivero.

It wasn't until she opened the envelope and saw Miguel's signature that she admitted to herself how disappointed she would have been if the flowers had come from the Basilios as a welcome gift.

"I am delighted that I am to see you again so soon," was written in a strong, slanting script.

What was that supposed to mean?

The answer came a moment later when Grace stopped by. She announced that Juan had gone out, but she hoped Pamela would join her in the family room for *café con leche*, and some rolls and fruit.

"We usually have a continental breakfast in the morning," Grace said, "because lunch and dinner are really like two dinners."

Grace had obviously already seen the flowers. "Gorgeous, aren't they?" she commented. "And that vase looks like a family heirloom. You must rate with Miguel Rivero, Miss Merrill. I would never have thought him so quixotic."

"He's just being friendly to a foreigner," Pamela said quickly.

"Friendly?" Grace cast a skeptical glance in her guest's direction. "Miguel isn't in the diplomatic corps, darling."

Pamela hesitated. "His card mentions seeing me again."

Grace nodded. "Tonight," she said breezily. "Juan invited him to dinner when he called yesterday. Didn't we tell you?"

"No, you didn't," Pamela retorted shortly.

Her tone and expression seemed to perplex Grace. "You don't mind our having invited him over, do you?"

"Good heavens, it's your house," Pamela reminded her hostess.

"Stop hedging, Pam." Only Grace and, occasionally, Charles called her Pam. "It's too late to renege on the invitation, but I'm curious about why you wouldn't want to see him again."

"It isn't that I don't want to see him again..." Pamela began, then found herself at a loss to complete the sentence.

"Miguel maintains an apartment here in Las Palmas," Grace said. "His personal hideaway, I suppose you could call it. He'll probably stay here for a couple of days before he goes back to Arucas. It isn't that far—a short drive, actually. But unless Miguel stays in town, we rarely see him. Even when we go up to Arucas to visit Carmen, and she has Dolores for dinner, Miguel usually can't make it. He has a lot of responsibility on his shoulders. All the family enterprises to look after..."

"Banana plantations," Pamela interposed.

"Yes," Grace agreed. "Miguel owns extensive banana plantations. Cousins are also involved in the business, but Miguel is in command, there's no doubt of that. Juan once suggested to him that he should delegate some of the responsibilities. But evidently Miguel's one of those people who thinks the only way to get anything done right is to do it himself. He's something of a workaholic."

Miguel Rivero had not appeared to Pamela like a man who lived and breathed work. He'd seemed relaxed, and had kept *her* far more so than she otherwise would have been. He'd begun to be preoccupied, and somewhat distant, only towards the end of their trip.

"I suppose that when he's away from the Canaries, it's like being on a vacation," she mused, as she recalled that he'd never mentioned exactly why he'd been in the States.

Grace shook her head. "I don't think Miguel has taken an honest vacation in years," she said. "His trips invariably concern business. I suppose he does get some respite from both Dolores and Rafael when he goes away, but..."

"Is Rafael really that bad, Grace?"

It was a difficult question to pose; Pamela was actually afraid of opening up the subject of Rafael. Talking about the boy might lead to a discussion about the woman who was—or had been—Rafael's mother. Pamela found herself in the uncomfortable position of wanting, yet not wanting to know.

"Rafael is a brat," Grace stated flatly. "I don't suppose you can blame him entirely. But to be honest with you, I can't see much of Miguel in him, apart from a certain physical resemblance. As I mentioned last night, Dolores certainly hasn't helped the situation. She's tried to make Rafael the son she never had, and all she's succeeded in doing is spoiling him dreadfully."

Grace shrugged. "There are some things one can't do anything about," she observed philosophically. "Darling, if I don't have some coffee pretty soon my mind is going to stop functioning completely. Just throw on a robe, and let's go downstairs, okay?"

Pamela slipped into a lilac-colored lounger and followed her hostess down to the family room. Octavia soon appeared with a tray laden with coffee, a pitcher of warm milk, a heaping assortment of fresh rolls, plus butter, a variety of jams, and several kinds of fresh fruit.

Surveying the tray, Pamela said, "And you call this a light breakfast?"

"This is what the people here usually eat," Grace told her. "If you have bacon and eggs and all that sort of thing, it's called an English breakfast."

"This is more than I ever eat," Pamela said, watching Grace pour equal amounts of coffee and foaming milk into thick white cups. Pamela picked up a banana about half the size of the ones she purchased in Boston. "These look like minibananas."

"A Canary variety," Grace told her. "They're very popular in the European markets, and quite delicious."

"Everything I've had here has been delicious," Pamela answered, buttering a roll. "I won't be able to get into my clothes if I keep eating like this. I'm not like you, Grace. I can't eat to my heart's content without gaining an ounce."

"Well, you have other talents," Grace answered enigmatically. "But I think you could do quite a bit of eating without worrying a bit about your weight."

They relaxed over the informal breakfast, drifting into a conversation about people they'd known back in the States. Grace had heard from some of these friends, Pamela from others, so together, they brought themselves up to date.

"Are you in the mood for shopping or sightseeing today?" Grace asked. "Or would you rather be lazy?"

Pamela laughed. "I'm for being lazy," she admitted. "Juan said you're near the beach. I'd be up for taking a walk, but that's about as much as I want to commit myself to, today."

"We can stroll down the *paseo* before *comida*," Grace decided. "Let's say in an hour or so."

It was closer to two hours before they actually left the house, for Grace, Pamela was amused to discover, had adapted well to the relatively casual Spanish attitude toward time.

The broad promenade that ran along the beachfront was only a few minutes' walk from the Basilios' house. It was flanked by hotels, restaurants, and shops of all description on one side, while on the other, steps led to the wide stretch of copper-colored sand.

"That's the Playa de las Canteras," Grace said, then translated, "Las Canteras beach. It's one of the most popular beaches on the island. As you might guess, there are beaches all around Grand Canary...and this is a large island. You'll explore a lot while you're here—the variety of landscapes seems limitless."

People were sunbathing on the beach, lying out on brightly colored lounge chairs, mostly blue or green.

"You can rent a chair for just a few pesetas, and keep it all day if you like," Grace reported.

Pamela was visually feasting on the beautiful scenery. The beach was a long crescent nestled within the protective confines of a shallow bay. She compared it to the North Atlantic off the coast of Massachusetts. There, the water was usually a deep blue. Here, even though it was the same ocean, the water was a very pale turquoise.

Off to her left, she recognized the distinctive cone-shaped mountains she had seen from the jet. The vista could be mistaken for a most unusual paradise.

"Lovely, isn't it," Grace said quietly.

"It really is."

"You'll find magnificent scenery almost everywhere on Grand Canary," Grace promised. "If Juan has his way, I think you're going to see every last mile before you leave here." She added, impishly, "On the other hand, Miguel Rivero would make a great guide."

"Look, Grace," Pamela protested swiftly, "don't go getting ideas. I barely know Miguel Rivero. We happened to be on the same plane, that's all."

"You're going to be here for at least four months," Grace reminded her. "I'd say that's plenty of time to get to know him better."

Now was the perfect time to pose some questions about Miguel.

Pamela very nearly delved into the subject of his marriage and son, but it was a bright, beautiful day, and one she didn't want to cloud. As it happened, she was genuinely diverted by the sight of two little girls dressed in white satin ballet costumes with black ruffs around their necks, their faces painted like miniature Pierrots.

"Look at them!" she exclaimed.

"Dressed for carnival." Grace nodded. "You're going to see a lot of adorable children in carnival garb. Starting this weekend, there'll be parades and processions every night. The tempo will mount right up to Shrove Tuesday."

They continued to walk along slowly. "I almost wish I'd put on my bathing suit so I could go for a swim," Pamela said.

"Well, the water's still on the cool side," Grace told her. "Too cool for me anyway, though Juan gets in almost every day. For someone used to the ocean off Cape Cod, though, this will probably seem like a warm bath."

Pamela laughed. "Tomorrow, then," she decided.

Back home, Juan joined them for *comida*. As Grace had mentioned, this was more like dinner than lunch. Afterward, to Pamela's surprise, she was more than willing to espouse the Spanish custom of afternoon siesta, though ordinarily she never slept in the daytime.

She slept soundly and realized, on awakening, that she had no idea what time Miguel Rivero would be coming for dinner.

Octavia had placed the vase of yellow roses in the middle of the narrow table opposite the bed. Pamela sniffed the flowers, reveling in their perfume. She loved their color, and knew that for the rest of her life, yellow roses would remind her of Miguel Rivero.

The vase, as Grace had noted, was exquisite. Definitely heirloom quality. It made Pamela feel rather uneasy to think this might be something that belonged to Miguel's family.

Should she return the vase to him at some point? She had no idea of Spanish etiquette in such matters, and didn't want to make a mistake.

Pamela indulged in another bubble bath, then dressed for dinner in a soft gray chiffon dress. The shade brought out the gray in her eyes and, to augment it, she wore a single strand of freshwater pearls with matching earrings.

As she added touches of makeup and arranged her hair, she realized she was taking special pains with her appearance tonight.

And why not? she thought recklessly. Miguel Rivero had accepted Juan's dinner invitation, after all, and had sent her flowers as well. Despite his formal farewell at the airport, this did indicate that he must want to see her again.

She drew a long breath. Regardless of potential problems, regardless of anything or anyone else, she most certainly wanted to see him again! There was no denying it.

When Pamela wandered downstairs, the first floor was silent and empty, so she continued down the curving stairway onto the small patio. It was a delightful oasis, with the early evening sunlight striking the bubbling water of the fountain.

Some of the flowers and plants were familiar to Pamela, but most were not. She reminded herself to ask Grace about them, then heard a clatter of pots and pans and detected a delightfully spicy aroma wafting through the air.

It was peaceful and beautiful here. Blissful. Pamela closed her eyes, reveling in the mood of the moment.

"What a lovely sight!" A male voice startled her.

Pamela looked up to see Miguel Rivero standing in the kitchen doorway.

As he crossed the patio, she was again conscious of his easy, graceful stride. Her eyes filled with the sight of him as he came nearer. Deep inside her, desire twisted suddenly, surprisingly.

Miguel looked even more handsome than she remembered, wearing a cream-colored suit that set off his dark complexion. The only touch of color to his attire was a vivid crimson necktie.

He grinned in a way that was most disarming, and said, "I was early, so I've been in the kitchen talking with Octavia and Roberto. Octavia comes from Arucas. In fact, one of her sisters and several of her cousins work for me."

Pamela felt her pulse being held in check. Then, suddenly, it was released, and began beating much too hard and fast. "Is that right?" she managed.

Before she could rally, Miguel took her hand in his. Glancing down intently, he said, "I believe there's a song that speaks of *manitos blancos*—little white hands. You have beautiful hands, Pamela. Small and white . . . yet strong."

His eyes met hers, and Pamela tried telling herself that she couldn't drown in the middle of a patio.

"I am very, very glad to have this chance to see you again," Miguel said slowly, deliberately. "It was most unsatisfactory leaving you at the airport like I did, but you seemed to have your course all set. Even so . . ."

He frowned, and Pamela knew he wasn't going to finish whatever he'd been about to say.

Instead, he continued, "When I called here, you were sleeping. Juan said you were exhausted."

"The effects of the trip . . ."

"Yes. I know," Miguel agreed. "I wasn't functioning too well myself. Anyway, I planned to call you back, and then Juan was kind enough to ask me to dinner. . . ."

He broke off, shaking his head in self-reproach. "I'm rambling. It's your turn to say something."

"I want to thank you for the flowers," Pamela told him. "They're beautiful. And the vase is a treasure piece. Grace thinks it's a family heirloom."

"So it is," Miguel admitted. "For that reason I want you to have it, as a remembrance of that chaotic flight we shared, and as a memory of the beginning of our friendship."

Friendship? Yes, she wanted to be Miguel Rivero's friend, just as she wanted him to be her friend. But Pamela instinctively knew that there was no way she and Miguel would ever be able to keep things on a platonic level, if that's what "friendship" meant. The chemistry between them was too potent, laden with a sexuality that she hoped wouldn't be as obvious to others as it was to her. Otherwise Grace would be casting knowing glances in her direction long before the evening was over.

She'd shivered all the way to her toes when Miguel held her hand, and knew that part of his "rambling," as he put it, was due to the fact that he was physically affected by her. Their awareness of each other was heating up...leading to an explosion.

With relief, Pamela heard Grace's voice at the top of the stairs.

"Well, people," Grace suggested lightly, "why don't you come on up?"

A moment later, Miguel was bending over Grace's hand. He was the epitome of courtesy as he said gravely, *"Encantada, señora."* When he looked up, his dark eyes met Pamela's. Their knowing twinkle told her he'd been reading her mind.

Chapter Four

It was easy to forget his problems when he was with her, easy to forget everything except her. Miguel had discovered that on the flight across the Atlantic. Now, as he sat across from Pamela at the Basilios' dining table and watched the enchanting effect the flickering candlelight had on this lovely young American's expressive face, the same thought struck him anew.

How had he ever managed to leave her at the airport? A smile tugged at the corner of his mouth as he silently answered his own question. As luck would have it, Juan Basilio was an old friend. Otherwise he would not have been so casual in parting from her. She had made too much of an impression to let her go so easily.

On the other hand, Miguel reminded himself, his smile fading, he could not afford to become involved with her. He could not afford to become seriously involved with anyone, for a number of reasons. For one thing, he thought, his lips twisting in a bitter smile, he was not free. He had nothing to offer a woman in the way of companionship, especially a woman like Pamela.

The candlelight flickered across his face, creating an interesting blend of highlights and shadows. Pamela found his face fascinating; it was very difficult not to stare at him. Her glances were surreptitious; she was well aware that he was watching her closely. She felt as if he was analyzing her, but it was a pleasant feeling. She knew, instinctively, that the analysis was favorable.

Then his eyes literally darkened, while his mouth twisted with pain. Abruptly, he fixed his gaze on his plate, as if the dessert Roberto had just placed before him was the most important thing in the world.

It was fortunate that Juan Basilio was such an outgoing person, and thoroughly enjoyed being a host. He was telling an entertaining story about an experience he'd had while teaching in the States, and was concentrating entirely upon his own performance.

Juan was an excellent raconteur, and Pamela usually loved his stories. But the change in Miguel's expression was so intense that it distracted her, and she totally lost the gist of what Juan was saying.

Juan came to the end, and both Miguel and Pamela smiled appreciatively and chuckled slightly, as if they'd rehearsed their reactions and were performing on cue. Juan was satisfied, but Pamela saw the expression that passed swiftly over Grace's face, and knew they hadn't fooled their hostess. She was equally sure that Grace had noted Miguel's momentary grimace.

They adjourned to the drawing room for coffee, served in fragile, floral-patterned demitasse cups. Pamela wished that Grace had opted for the "spillover room" instead, which would have been a far less formal setting.

Nonetheless, it wasn't the setting that was causing problems, but rather a sudden tension emanating from Miguel. He was charming—she couldn't imagine him being other than charming—but his smile and casual conversation during the next hour were automatic.

Finally, Miguel rose to leave. He kissed Grace on the cheek and thanked her for dinner, but his midnight eyes were on Pamela.

She was shocked at the hunger she saw in them. The attraction between them was undeniable, but this was something else. It wasn't merely a question of desire, here was a different kind of need.

Pamela had been told many times how unusually perceptive she was. Sometimes she considered this awareness a virtue, other times more of a vice. There were moments when she wished she could ignore her insight, times she wished she could be far more casual in her relationships. Now she could feel Miguel reaching out to her. His need for both communion and communication was as apparent to her as if he'd verbalized it.

He needs to talk, she found herself thinking. *He needs to unload and share some of his burdens.*

Juan Basilio's question broke into her thoughts. "Will you be going back to Arucas soon, Miguel?"

Miguel shook his head, wresting his eyes away from Pamela with what appeared to be a visible effort. Pamela was sure that this time, Grace had noticed.

"I have business here in Las Palmas that will keep me in town for perhaps a week," he said. "I could commute," he added, "but there are a number of matters that would be better settled on the spot, as quickly as possible. Once I'm back in Arucas again, there will be so many other things to contend with.

"My business here will take up only part of my time, actually." Suddenly he grinned, as if he'd made the decision to cast caution to the wind. "So," he said, turning to face Pamela, "if you would accept my services as a guide, I would be delighted to introduce you to Las Palmas."

"Excellent!" Juan approved, before Pamela could answer for herself. "I am going to be tied up finishing a very dull article for which I have an impossible deadline. Grace is serving as my editor on this project, and I was afraid that until we are finished, Pamela would find this place boring. But now..."

Pamela smiled wryly. Juan was being a shade too hearty in his approval, to the point of embarrassment. Then she met Miguel's eyes and saw the laughter lurking in their depths. She felt as if she were watching fireflies flickering on a summer night as they studded the darkness with a tiny display of pyrotechnics. She also found herself sharing Miguel's secret laughter, sharing his delight that they were going to spend some time together.

It was noon the next day when he telephoned, and an hour later when he came by the Basilios' house to pick Pamela up. He'd said to dress casually and, above all else, to wear comfortable footwear.

He had on fawn-colored slacks and a dark-brown shirt, open at the throat. Casual enough, yet there was an elegance about the way he wore even these ordinary clothes.

Pamela had chosen a white sundress patterned with vivid green leaves, and flat green sandals. She'd twisted her hair into a makeshift chignon and, as they left the house through the flower-filled patio, Miguel impetuously plucked a white gardenia and tucked it behind her ear. "The perfect final touch," he told her.

They strolled the short distance to the Paseo de las Canteras, the broad promenade paved in shades of beige and rust. The spectacle of the wide beach, the turquoise water and the harbor edged with conical mountains struck Pamela anew. Dark clouds hovered over the most distant mountains, their shadows slanting towards the sea.

"Looks like it's going to rain," she said.

Miguel shook his head. "I wish," he admitted. "But clouds like those generally turn out to be a tease. More often than not they dissipate before there is any precipitation. Would that you could wave a wand, beautiful hydrologist, and make them burst into cascades of showers!"

He spoke lightly, but Pamela knew that rain was a subject very close to his heart; the future of his inheritance depended upon a solution to Grand Canary's water problem. More than ever, the thought of her own studies here on Grand Canary excited her. Not that she could hope to find an answer to the problem, but she could at least learn a great deal more about this island's particular situation.

They stopped at the seaside edge of the *paseo* simply to take in the magnificent scenery, but then Miguel grew more practical.

"Have you had any lunch yet?" he asked.

"No, I haven't," Pamela answered. "Grace and Juan were about to have their *comida*, but frankly I knew that if I ate even a fraction of Octavia's cooking I wouldn't be able to move for hours."

"Good," Miguel approved. "I'm not about to suggest a full-scale *comida*, but I do hope you are a little hungry. These sidewalk cafés are wonderful...so, if you'll just follow me..."

Miguel was leading Pamela to a row of umbrella-shaded tables lined up along the edge of the beach. A waiter in black slacks and a crisp white shirt appeared as soon as they were seated, and Miguel conversed with him in rapid Spanish that Pamela couldn't even begin to follow. Smiling apologetically, he said, "I hope you don't mind. I ordered for both of us."

"Not in the least," she assured him.

A pitcher of fresh sangria was delivered first. Miguel filled their glasses, then drank a silent toast to her.

As she sipped her drink, she gazed down a long stretch of the *paseo*. Today there were even more people dressed in carnival costume than there had been yesterday, costumes of incredible variety and, by and large, homemade. After a moment, she said reflectively, "You know, I can really feel it."

"Feel what?" Miguel asked curiously.

"The carnival atmosphere. It's actually in the air, wouldn't you say? A festival feeling, a sort of unabashed celebration..."

He didn't answer her immediately, but during this small silent interval, his eyes never left her face. Finally, he said thoughtfully, "You are very sensitive to impressions, I can see that. I've always felt the carnival in the air. Tantalizing and stimulating, like a new wine. But I can't say that everyone has shared my...what should I call them? My vibes?"

"Yes, you could call them that."

"You are a very special person, Pamelita," Miguel whispered, his tone husky.

Only Juan had ever called her Pamelita before, yet how different this affectionate diminutive sounded, coming from Miguel's lips. Each syllable was a caress, as if he had touched her physically, as well as emotionally.

Pamela became acutely conscious of how much she wanted to encounter all that was tangible and masculine and strong about Miguel. She wanted this so much that she swayed toward him slightly, forgetting they were in the midst of a busy seaport city; they might as well have been alone on a desert isle.

Then the waiter reappeared, and the spell was broken. Probably a good thing, Pamela thought wryly. This magical feeling was very new, and she felt herself on the verge of giving in to its power completely. Never before had she been a true believer in magic. But now...

Miguel had ordered a dish that was typical of the island fare. Succulent fresh fillets of white fish were sautéed in oil and a little garlic, seasoned with a touch of herbs, and served with crusty bread and slices of ripe red tomato.

"Simple, wholesome and delicious," Miguel commented.

Pamela had never in her life eaten anything that tasted better.

They lingered over the repast—small by Spanish standards—enjoying the food, the scenery, and each other. Nothing was hurried, nothing was pressured. Although the waiter appeared immediately when Miguel beckoned for their check, they could have lingered until dark without being made to feel that they were usurping space, as was so often the case at cafés in the States.

If this was indicative of the Spanish tempo of life, Pamela liked it. She liked strolling by Miguel's side along the *paseo*. She followed him down a narrow side street where palms were planted along the curbs with little space to spare, many of them growing so tall that their fronds brushed the balconies of the upper floor apartments over the storefronts.

After they'd walked a few blocks, Pamela glimpsed some greenery ahead, studded with all sorts of improbable colors.

Following her gaze, Miguel said, "The Parque de Santa Catalina, all decked out for fiesta. I think you will like this, Pamelita. There is a bazaar with merchandise from all over the world, especially from northern Africa. You should prepare yourself to haggle the prices. It is certainly not wise to accept the initial amount suggested. Come, we shall have coffee first. Then perhaps you would like to shop around?"

As they neared the park, Pamela saw that the colors in the trees were actually giant cutouts of different kinds of fruit. Enormous oranges, apples, bananas and pineapples hung from the branches. The trees along the curb were festooned with ribbons and plastic garlands in rainbow shades, like those she'd noticed on the bus ride from the airport. The park was thronged with people dressed in masquerade, including the vendors.

They had coffee in a glass-enclosed café-restaurant in the center of the park. Nearby, Pamela saw clusters of men gathered around low tables, all of them deeply occupied.

"They are playing dominoes and chess," Miguel explained. "And, as you might suspect, it is a very serious pastime. You should get a closer look at some of the sets they use. The dominoes are often decorated with varying colors, and are really beautiful."

When they finished their coffee, they stood and watched the players, but Pamela could get only an over-the-shoulder glimpse of the game pieces Miguel had mentioned. The rectangles were dotted with deep shades of sapphire blue and turquoise as pure as the offshore waters of the Atlantic.

As they wandered around the bazaar, Pamela was offered "bargains" in everything from Moroccan caftans and huge ottomans tooled with gold leather to all sorts of handbags and jewelry and miscellaneous trivia. Miguel laughed when one vendor insisted that he should buy her a fringed harem costume, detailing in excited Spanish how much it would become her. Pamela couldn't understand him, but his gestures were graphic enough to bring on a fever. She was sure her cheeks must be as red as the huge apple cutouts that swung from the tree branches high over her head.

She lingered at several jewelry stalls, fingering some of the lovely pins, earrings, rings and necklaces that were being offered at extremely reasonable prices, reminding herself that the American dollar went quite a long way when converted to Spanish pesetas.

"Don't look quite so delighted, *querida*," Miguel whispered in her ear. "Nor so ready to buy. You really can do better on most of these things."

He was right, Pamela realized, although she'd never been much of a bargainer.

One piece caught her fancy—a floral-patterned pin fashioned in a soft shade of coral and pale, gray-greenish jade.

"Almost the color of your eyes," Miguel observed softly, touching the jade. "Do you like this?"

Pamela smiled. "I was about to buy it without quibbling," she confessed.

"Impossible!" he said sternly. He spoke in rapid Spanish to the very attractive young woman who was managing the stall. Shortly thereafter the pin was placed in a small, intricately embroidered silk pouch. Then the pouch was passed to Miguel, who put it in his shirt pocket.

It was not until they were standing in front of a shop window filled with perfumes that Miguel said, "Stop looking so miffed. It is for you, you know."

Pamela hadn't known, and was slightly annoyed at his high-handedness. She assumed that he'd bought the pin at a lower price, but would later let her pay for it. It hadn't occurred to her that he intended it as a gift.

He laughed at the expression on her face. "Pamelita, if it will assuage your puritan conscience, I paid the young lady the price she was demanding. Otherwise, I do not think I could have lived with your displeasure. Also..." He lowered his voice, as he tended to do during moments fraught with emotion. "I wish very much for this to be a small *recuerdo* of this afternoon. I have found it a very perfect afternoon. You have...you have been a tonic to me, Pamela. So, if you will please just take it...."

There was a touching humility to Miguel's voice as he continued, "You do me a favor simply by being with me. More of a favor than you can realize, more than I can express to you at this moment. Later, perhaps..."

He smiled ruefully. "Let us not get into later."

Curiosity raced through Pamela's veins side by side with all the other intangible emotions that this man aroused in her.

He fastened the coral and jade pin to the fabric of her green sundress. "It is a delightful match," he said, obviously pleased. "The green suits you, but then..."

He was about to say more, Pamela sensed, but bit off his words abruptly. To her chagrin, he glanced at his heavy gold wristwatch. "We should start back. The Basilios will be expecting you to join them for drinks, I am sure. Next time, we will lay our plans more carefully."

There would be a next time. That was the consolation Pamela felt when Miguel bade her goodbye as soon as Roberto opened the door of Grace's little patio. She slowly ascended the spiral iron staircase to the first floor, feeling strangely bereft. It occurred to her that, thus far, Miguel had not even kissed her. Yet she already felt a closeness to him that she'd never truly experienced in other, far more intimate relationships.

That reminded her of Charles. Tonight, she had to call him and try to explain the flight delay, and gently begin to pave the way for the inevitable. She wasn't deluding herself into thinking that the future held anything for her as far as a relationship with Miguel Rivero was concerned. She reminded herself—much as it hurt—that Miguel had a teenage son, which meant that at some point he'd had, and still might have a wife.

Nevertheless, there was no way she could continue to encourage Charles when she'd not only forgotten him, but had met someone else who'd made an unprecedented impact on her.

She tried to tell herself that if she were never to see Miguel again, she had reason to be grateful to him. Without trying to teach her anything at all, he'd taught her that it was possible for two people, even two people with such different backgrounds, to achieve a rare understanding in an astonishingly short space of time.

She tried telling herself that this, in itself, could be enough. And she failed.

Miguel didn't call the next day, so the hours seemed endless. In the afternoon, Grace broke away from editing Juan's book and went with Pamela to the beach. They rented chairs and lounged in the sun, but the water was too cool even for someone who, as Grace said again, laughingly, was used to the torturously cold waters off New England.

Pamela yearned to ask Grace all sorts of questions about Miguel, but suppressed them. It was not that her curiosity was dimmed. She just wanted to hear the answers to her questions about Miguel from Miguel himself.

He called late the next morning just as she and Grace were about to head out on a shopping spree.

Grace answered the phone, and there was a pleased smile on her face as she turned to Pamela. "For you. It's Miguel."

Pamela drew a long, steady breath, trying to tell herself that it was ridiculous to be affected like this. "Hello?" She was pleased to think that she sounded reasonably well controlled.

"Yesterday," Miguel said without preamble, "was a horror story. I had to drive to Arucas unexpectedly—just one more family crisis that didn't amount to anything—but it took up my entire day and it was simpler to stay over. I nearly called you last night, but I thought I might be interrupting something...."

There was a ragged edge to his voice as he paused, then went on, "Now I'm tied up here in business affairs for the next few hours, but I thought you might enjoy it if we had dinner at one of my favorite restaurants in the old section of town tonight. Then maybe we could drive to the southern end of the island for a fling at the casino. Would that be possible, Pamelita, or have the Basilios made other plans?"

One look at Grace convinced Pamela that whatever other plans the Basilios might have made for her would be scrapped without question once she relayed Miguel's invitation.

Grace said quickly, "There's nothing on the agenda that can't be rearranged."

Once she hung up the phone, after agreeing to an eight o'clock date, Pamela was tempted once again to ply Grace with questions about the entire Rivero clan. But caution held her tongue.

She chose a chic black dress, then decided that her two favorite pieces of jewelry would be the perfect complement. One was an emerald pendant, suspended on a thin gold chain, that had belonged to her grandmother. The letters GBM were inscribed on the back of the gold setting in tiny letters. Geraldine Balch Merrill. The other was an emerald ring, also an antique gold setting, a twenty-first birthday gift from her mother. She wore the ring on her left hand simply because it was too snug for her right; she was sure that Miguel noticed this when he held open the door of his sleek, silver-gray Mercedes.

The restaurant where he took her was a small place on a side street in the old section of Las Palmas, a short distance from the magnificent cathedral, bathed in floodlights in honor of carnival time. Off the beaten track, the restaurant was not a spot likely to be frequented by tourists; Pamela was sure she was the only American in the place.

The smiling headwaiter knew Miguel and, without being asked, brought a carafe of wine, which, Miguel explained, was *vino herreño*, a strictly local product.

"I think you'll enjoy it," he said. "There's never enough of a crop for export, or perhaps we are just natural wine drinkers on this island, and manage to imbibe all that comes from the vineyards ourselves."

A variety of appetizers were brought to the table soon after the first glass of wine had been poured. As he helped Pamela to a serving of a special kind of smoked ham, Miguel said, "I have asked for a little of everything, Pamelita. I want you to have a sampling of our food."

She was again treated to the small, salted potatoes, known locally as "wrinkled potatoes." Course after course arrived—*churros de pescado*, *pata de cerdo*, and a delicious chicken. Finally there was a cheese from one of the mountain districts, which had a distinctive but excellent flavor.

Again, time was not a factor. She and Miguel lingered over more wine, and then a strong, sugared coffee and small, delectable pastries. When they were ushered to the door by both the headwaiter and their own waiter, Pamela felt as if a red carpet had been laid down just for them, stretching all the way to the curb. As she settled herself into the front seat of Miguel's car, she said appreciatively, "That was really terrific, Miguel. It was one of the most memorable dinners I've ever had."

Miguel nearly bit his tongue in the effort not to answer Pamela too quickly. It was a dinner he, too, would never forget. He, who had been so jaundiced for so long about women, could not believe how much he wanted to be a part not only of this lovely American's present, but of her future.

As he drove across the city and then headed south along the coast highway, Miguel suddenly felt weary, almost old beyond his years. It was too much. Sometimes it was all too much, and a hopelessness descended upon him that would have crushed a weaker man. Usually he could deal with his depressions; he could never afford to allow himself to become steeped in depression for very long, no matter how valid his despair.

Still, he had never faced anything like this. He'd known Pamela Merrill for a ridiculously short time. She was from another country, another culture. Yet he could already imagine how bleak his life would be if she left. He, who had experienced so much bleakness for so long, winced at the thought of days, months and years without her.

Yesterday, forced back to Arucas because of the problems his sister Dolores insisted she was having with his son, he'd gone for a walk by himself during that hazy blue hour before nightfall. He'd skirted the edge of his plantation, looking back at the imposing house that had been in his family for so many decades. He'd tried to picture Pamela living among these surroundings, dealing with his sister and his son, and God knows what else.

Standing alone in the banana fields, he'd watched the day fade to night's total blackness, and had tried to forget about Pamela. It could never be.

How could he ever suggest to Pamela that they might make a life together in Arucas—or anywhere else—when he didn't know whether or not he was married to another woman?

Chapter Five

Miguel was a fast driver, but very skillful. She glanced at him occasionally. Although he seemed to be concentrating on the highway, where traffic streamed incessantly, his mind was not fully on the road—or on her.

The highway was reduced to two lanes now, hilly and pitch-dark except for the glare of the oncoming traffic. Miguel downshifted as they neared a rock-sided rise, then said mysteriously, "Watch ahead."

He negotiated a sharp turn and, without warning, an astonishing panorama of twinkling white lights stretched before Pamela like a fairyland.

She turned to see Miguel smiling at her. "Spectacular, isn't it?" he asked.

"It's fantastic!" Pamela agreed enthusiastically. "Absolutely enchanting!"

"Playa del Ingles," Miguel interjected, "which translates as the English Beach. It is a favorite haunt of people from the British Isles, and from Germany and Scandinavia. This town, San Agustin, and the next, Maspalomas, all run together. Not so long ago, it was a quiet and deserted stretch of sand dunes and palm trees. Now, it is all big hotels, restaurants and discos—a tourist's paradise."

He shrugged. "I liked it better the way it was, but that's my hang-up... and probably rather typical of any native. More often than not, we do not see change as progress. One cannot negate the fact that these changes represent financial progress. But otherwise..."

After a moment, he added, "I thought of taking you to one of the popular nightclubs, but frankly their floor shows are not nearly so good as some in the States. The flamenco isn't really flamenco, for example. To me, there is a tinseled quality about the whole scene, though I've experienced my share of nightlife here and even enjoyed it. Those lights you see all over the hills, incidentally, are individual bungalows, one on top of the next. They are like thousands of beehives clustered together, but the tourists think they are vacation paradises."

Miguel shook his head impatiently. "Excuse me if I sound cynical. I'm really not that bad. Anyway, the Casino Gran Canaria is a typical European gambling club. Have you ever been to one?"

"No, I haven't. This is my first trip to Europe, although we seem closer to Africa."

"Very true," Miguel agreed. "Ah *Dios!*" he exclaimed suddenly, lapsing into Spanish. "I should have remembered to tell you to bring your passport. Foreigners must have passports in order to be admitted to the casino."

"Worry not," Pamela said lightly. "I'm rather fond of that particular document, and take it wherever I go." She patted her slim handbag. "Safe and sound," she assured him.

"Very good."

It was after midnight when they reached the casino, which was located on the lower level of a large hotel in Playa San Agustin. "One may gamble here until three in the morning," Miguel said, as they strolled across the parking lot. "But I will accede to your wishes and leave whenever you want."

Once, on a trip to Nevada during college spring break, Pamela had tried her luck at slot machines. The more sophisticated roulette and blackjack were unfamiliar to her. Now, as they entered the bustling casino, she was furnished with a flyer printed in Spanish, English and German explaining how to play blackjack, known locally as *veintiuno*. But, she was hesitant to plunge into betting and, for the most part, was content to watch Miguel.

After an hour, he confessed ruefully that this was not his night. Bestowing a dazzling smile upon Pamela as he escorted her from the playing table, he said, "I cannot concentrate on anything else when you are near."

"Come on," Pamela teased him, trying to camouflage an emotional rush. "I really don't think my presence was affecting the cards you were drawing."

"Perhaps not, but the way I was playing, yes," Miguel insisted. Amusement lit his jet-black eyes as he gazed down at her.

Driving back to Las Palmas, Miguel appeared considerably more relaxed than he had earlier. He talked about a variety of things, even touching lightly on his business.

"We have quite a few acres in sugarcane," he confided, "and that may be the way to go in the future. Also, I am a partner in a distillery with two of my cousins." He smiled wryly. "For better or worse. In addition to the several different types of rum we produce, we make a banana liqueur. In fact, it happens to be our most popular product."

They passed the cathedral, still floodlighted and breathcatching in its beauty, as they arrived back in Las Palmas. Then Miguel turned off the highway and drove into a quieter residential section of the city.

Miguel pulled up in front of a small apartment house and brought the car to a stop. The light from a nearby street lamp slanted through the windshield, and for a moment it seemed to Pamela as if he were dressed for carnival, with half of his face illuminated, the other half dark as midnight. It was as if she were seeing his character divided. She'd felt a surprisingly deep rapport with Miguel, but suddenly he was a stranger.

It struck her that she really didn't know Miguel Rivero at all. She'd based her reaction to him entirely upon emotional, primal feelings. There wasn't any logic in thinking that this man was closer to her in spirit than anyone she'd ever known before. No logic at all . . .

"Pamelita," he said softly, his voice deep velvet.

The Spanish pronunciation of her name did treacherous things to her. Logic? Of what value was the word when it could so easily be cast aside?

"Look," he said. "I want you to know this and believe me . . . because it is true. I have never before asked a woman to come up to my apartment, here in Las Palmas."

Pamela could not find the words to respond.

"I am asking you now because I need, so much, to be alone with you," Miguel said huskily. "Yes, I want to make love to you. But that is not all I want, Pamelita. I want to *know* you, and I want you to know me."

To her surprise, he suddenly said something in Spanish, then laughed. "Right now," he confessed, "I am afraid my English is about to desert me."

Pamela still could not speak, though her mind was racing. She'd seen a new side of Miguel tonight, and wasn't too sure she liked it.

For one, he was quite a gambler. She'd flinched at the amounts he'd wagered on the blackjack table and roulette wheel—bet and lost, for the most part, without any visible sign of regret. He'd thrown away quite a sum, and it didn't help that she'd always had an inherent uneasiness concerning waste of any kind.

Still, she had to smile, remembering that Miguel had paid the vendor in the Parque de Santa Catalina her full price because he didn't want to offend Pamela's puritan conscience. Well, maybe she did have a puritan conscience. She came from a long line of New Englanders and was eligible for every American patriot organization from the Society of Mayflower Descendants to the Daughters of the American Revolution.

This innately cautious Pamela had noticed that Miguel had done his share of drinking at the casino, downing several hefty highballs as he'd gambled. Yet on the return drive to Las Palmas, he'd seemed more in control of himself than he had on the way over. His full attention had been on the highway—just as well since the traffic had been fast paced and heavy, even in the small hours of the morning.

Now he was inviting her up to his apartment, indicating that what happened thereafter was pretty much up to her, though that wasn't exactly the way he'd put it. Could she truly believe that this was the first time he'd ever invited a woman to his private quarters in Las Palmas?

It was difficult to think that Miguel hadn't played host here to any number of women. He was so blatantly attractive that Pamela couldn't imagine a woman not being more than eager to accept any invitation he might proffer.

Like myself! she admitted, facing up to the not so puritanical notion that she wanted him every bit as much as he wanted her.

She still hadn't said a word when Miguel abruptly turned the key in the ignition.

Impetuously, Pamela reached out to deter him. He didn't exactly shake her off, but turned to face her, still bathed in shadows. "There is no need to explain," he said stiffly. "It is very late, and you must be tired. I'll take you home."

"Please," she began anxiously. "Please, you're misreading me. I...I want to go with you."

For a moment, she thought Miguel was going to brush away her statement. With the diesel motor running, Pamela thought she heard her own heart pumping against a new set of odds.

"Oh, God!" The despair in Miguel's voice struck her as nothing else could have at that moment, tearing away any last remnants of doubt. He turned toward her beseechingly. "I have to be honest with you. We shouldn't do this. I..."

Instinct prompted her to press a slim finger against his lips. A moment later, he reached for that finger, for her hand, turned it over and kissed her palm. His lips felt as if they'd been set afire; her palm was branded by his imprint.

"*Querida*," he said shakily. "I do not know what it is you are doing to me."

Temporarily, Miguel seemed to lose his fluent English. His words were more heavily accented than Pamela had ever heard them before, and if the desire that flamed between them needed underlining, this was all it took to pencil in the final stroke.

He shut off the motor, and a moment later was opening the car door for her. She saw him take a large key from his coat pocket, and say, "This is a small place, only six apartments in all, two to a floor. After midnight, the front entrance is locked."

He was turning the key as he spoke, but when he swung the massive wooden door open, they stepped not into a vestibule, as Pamela expected, but into a courtyard that overflowed with potted palms and exotic plants. At the far side was a lacy iron staircase leading to the upper floor.

Miguel started up it saying, "There is an elevator, but it's as slow as a mule cart. Anyway, my flat is only one floor up."

The corridor outside his apartment was dim, the silence acute. In the stillness, Pamela suddenly had second thoughts, passion abating as she watched Miguel unlock his front door with yet another key, push it open, then switch on an inside light before he invited her to cross the threshold.

Tentatively she entered the square foyer from which three steps led down into a spacious living room. The walls were stark white, offset by dark wood corner posts and beams. The furniture was all made of carved wood, and typical of the Spanish style. There were long, low couches and comfortable armchairs, the upholstery a rich terra-cotta color with bright orange and yellow cushions, lamps and decorative pottery.

Looking around, Pamela said, "Someone has quite an eye."

Miguel laughed. "Thank you for the implied compliment," he said, "but I followed my own instincts here. Let us say that I've never had the chance to express my taste fully in the family homestead in Arucas. So, here I chose things that I would like to live with."

He moved to a corner cabinet that Pamela saw served as a bar, and took out two thin-stemmed glasses. These he filled with an amber liquid, then crossed the room to hand her one.

"Spanish brandy," he said.

I can use it, Pamela found herself thinking, she, who ordinarily drank very little.

She sat down on the nearest couch, as did Miguel. But he was on the far side of the plush center cushion; the separation seemed vast. Suddenly, resolutely, he set his glass of brandy down on the exquisite coffee table in front of them. And, when he turned to face her, Pamela saw that the light had vanished from his eyes. They were dull now...no merriment, no fireflies. Nothing but a quiet agony.

"We can't, can we?" he asked simply.

She didn't know what to say, so she said nothing.

"You know I have a son?" he asked, the question taking her by surprise.

She hesitated only briefly, then nodded awkwardly.

"Juan told you?"

"No," Pamela answered, then amended, "Yes." Then she changed that to, "I don't know, I don't remember. It came up in casual conversation. Grace, or maybe it was Juan, mentioned something about your living with your sister and your son. I think that was it."

She was stumbling badly, thoroughly conscious that Miguel was aware of this. He probably thought she was hedging, but that was really all she knew.

He asked, wanting to verify his suspicions, "What else did the Basilios tell you about me?"

"Nothing!" Pamela blurted. "Seriously, I mean that," she went on, seeing the doubt etched across his face. "They didn't discuss you...or your affairs. If anything, I could say only that it's obvious both Juan and Grace think very highly of you...."

"Please," he interrupted. "Please, no platitudes. Not from you. How long have you known that I have a son?"

"Since my first day at the Basilios. You called to be sure I'd arrived at the hotel..."

"Yes," he interrupted angrily. "I called because I was thoroughly annoyed at myself for having let you take the bus into Las Palmas. And do you know why I did that, Pamelita?"

She shook her head.

"Because I knew I should let you go, that I should not even attempt to see you again. But I could not live with my own resolution, so I called Juan. When he invited me to dinner the next night I almost tripped over my own tongue, I was so quick about accepting his invitation.

"And since...since, I have wanted to be with you every moment. *Every moment*, you understand, not merely every waking moment. I have yearned to have you next to me, longed to have you share my bed at night. I have tried, tried like hell, to hold back, tried not to call you again, tried to let you go. I have told myself that once I go back to Arucas and become swamped in my work, once you start your research and become equally involved in your own affairs, we will soon forget about each other. And then this...this thing that has blazed between us...will simmer down. But I don't believe that. Do you?''

Pamela moistened her lips. "No," she whispered.

Miguel's lips twisted mirthlessly, barely suppressing wretched bitterness.

"Thank you," he said simply. "Thank you for being honest, Pamela. God knows I have had very little honesty from women in my life."

Her question was automatic. "Who was she, Miguel? Or should I say, who is she?''

"She was my wife," Miguel responded, his words thin slivers of ice. "Or, perhaps, she is my wife—I do not truly know, Pamelita. She left me when Rafael was five, and ran off with my business partner, who also happened to be my best friend. When there was no word from them after a month, I hired detectives to trace them. For the next few years, reports came back to me from all over the world. Finally, there were fewer and fewer reports...but every now and then word still comes that they have been found, and I start out on yet another wild-goose chase.

"The latest chase took me to Boston. I made one final call from the airport before I left, as you will remember. Again, the trail came to nothing.

"At one point," he continued heavily, "it was believed that Anita and her lover had drowned in a boating accident off Malaga. Another time, there was evidence that they had been killed in the crash of a small plane in the Pyrenees. But when the victims in each case were finally identified, it was not them.

"After nearly ten years had passed, my advisers strongly recommended that I take legal steps to have both Anita and my ex-partner declared dead. Otherwise, my business affairs, to say nothing of my personal assets, were in danger of becoming hopelessly tied up. My partner's family agreed with this, and finally it was done, just last year.

"So...in the eyes of the law I am free," Miguel finished. "But in my eyes, I can never be free—as long as there is the chance that Anita may suddenly reappear."

Pamela set her glass of brandy down on the coffee table next to his. Both were untouched, and for a moment, she thought that Miguel was going to reach for his, but he didn't.

He rose instead, his face set. "Now, I think I'd better take you home."

There was a terrible resignation to Miguel's voice, and Pamela ached for him. True, he was legally free. Yet he obviously felt morally chained to Rafael's mother, despite her desertion. The emotional burden must be staggering, and the love he had once felt for this woman deeper than the depths of the sea.

She felt completely numb as she preceded Miguel through the door of his apartment, nearly stumbling in her own emotional weariness as she made her way down the steps and into the courtyard. She fancied she caught the scent of a gardenia, and suddenly her eyes filled with tears.

Miguel, reaching around her to open the outer door, stopped short. He said something in Spanish, something so fervent that Pamela felt each syllable being wrenched from him. Then, without warning, he pulled her savagely away from the door and drew her into his arms.

Pamela felt her bones melt like pliant plastic, bending like hay in the wind. It was as well that he held her against his chest, because she couldn't guarantee that her own legs would support her.

He gently cupped her chin with one hand, and gazed down into her eyes. "Please, Pamelita . . . whatever else you do, don't come to mistaken conclusions." Though his English was again fluent, Pamela was conscious of the Spanish accent that surfaced when he was troubled. "You are different to me than anyone else I have ever known," he whispered urgently, stressing each word with a sincerity that told her how much he wanted her to believe him. "You are unique to me. It is such a short time since we have known each other, and yet my feelings for you are so very strong. . . ."

Still cupping her chin, he bent closer, his beloved face seeming to swim before her until she shut her eyes and let herself feel without seeing. Let herself savor the fire of his mouth as his lips meshed with hers, his kiss claiming her heart . . . asking, demanding, willing her to give back something of herself.

She yielded to him, her body molding itself against his masculine contours while their lips clung together, their tongues probing, searching, blazing a trail for a future that Pamela knew was as inescapable as the sunrise that would cast a golden glow over the island in just a few more hours.

Time didn't stop—it became suspended. For a while there was no yesterday, no tomorrow. Then Miguel released her very gently. "Everything in me cries out to pick you up and carry you back upstairs, Pamelita." He sighed deeply and added, "But I am not going to, because tonight it would be wrong. We do not need to make peace with each other. It is I who must make peace with myself. Perhaps you, too, need to make peace with yourself. Do you understand what I am trying to say? When we do come together, there must not be any clouds, Pamelita. No shadow on our sun."

Pamela listened to him, her breathing ragged, her heart pounding furiously. She wanted him more than ever, yet she knew he was right. They needed to wait until the moment was right for making love. But during the silent drive back to the Basilios, she was wondering if there would ever be a time without a shadow on their sun.

Chapter Six

The carnival reached a crescendo on the Monday before Lent. That night, a parade that reminded Pamela of Mardi Gras in New Orleans formed in the Parque de Santa Catalina and wended its way through streets lined with cheering onlookers. Thousands of revelers joined the official marching groups, their costumes a colorful counterpart to the elaborate floats.

Pamela watched the spectacle with Juan and Grace from a balcony in their friends' office complex. The Calderons had invited several other people to their balcony party, and this turned into a small fiesta of its own. Part of Pamela enjoyed herself immensely, but another part of her was as lonely as if she was in exile.

She knew Miguel had been invited to the party because Grace told her so. Even though he was a good friend of the Calderons, Pamela suspected that Grace had spoken with Maria, just to insure his invitation.

They arrived at the party around eleven, but from the moment she walked in the door, Pamela was on edge, waiting for Miguel. It was not until two in the morning that she accepted the fact he was not going to come.

She'd seen him twice since the night in his apartment. Once, he'd invited the Basilios and her to join him for dinner, and had taken them to a rooftop restaurant in a fashionable hotel overlooking the Playa de las Canteras. The cuisine had been more French than Spanish, the service impeccable. Nevertheless, the evening had been something of a letdown for Pamela. She'd enjoyed their date in the old quarter much more.

Saturday, Miguel had called and asked her out for a drink with him prior to the evening *comida*, saying he had a business engagement later that he couldn't get out of. He'd met her at the Basilios and as they had strolled over to the *paseo* Miguel had been pleasant and scrupulously polite, but distant. Distant . . . and different.

Pamela couldn't analyze the difference in him precisely enough to come to terms with it. She thought she'd begun to know this man. Now the fact loomed that aside from their mutually fiery physical attraction, they still didn't know each other very well at all.

She found it difficult to talk to him. And he, for his part, kept their dialogue mainly on subjects related to the carnival and other local customs—things that ordinarily would have fascinated her, but now went in one ear and out the other.

They had vermouth aperitifs at a sidewalk café, and watched the lavender twilight fade into dusk. Lights began to twinkle all around the harbor, while the conical mountains became vanishing silhouettes.

"Let's walk for a little while, and then I'll take you home," Miguel said abruptly.

The *paseo* was crowded on this last Saturday evening of carnival. Vendors had set up carts along the seawall, selling everything from food and drinks to jewelry and souvenirs. Pamela stopped at one of the jewelry stands and bought a few trinkets to give as small presents once she was back in the States. She managed the transaction in pesetas without appealing to Miguel for help, and felt a small, childish sense of pride.

Miguel caught her mood. He drew her away from the jewelry stand and held out something that glinted in the darkness. "Another small *recuerdo* for you. Symbolic of the carnival season . . . but also of life."

He'd bought her a brass pin with the two carnival masks, one representing joy, the other tragedy. Miguel didn't attempt to fasten the pin to her dress, but as he handed it to her, the poignancy in his expression was as eloquent as that of the masks. She sensed that Miguel's gift was saying a lot of things to her that he couldn't express.

On Sunday, the church bells chimed as the Basilios headed off to the late-morning mass. Pamela, restless, got out the city map Juan had given her to find a route to the Parque de Santa Catalina just a few blocks away. But when she arrived at the park, she found the stalls were shuttered and the adjoining shops closed. Obviously, business wasn't conducted in Las Palmas on Sunday, even at the height of carnival.

Then came Monday, and the festival tempo picked up again. Celebration was in the air almost to the exclusion of everything else.

"Tomorrow it will begin to be different," Juan told her. "Tomorrow you will find that most of the revelers change into black costumes. Some are very elaborate, too...all satin and velvet. Then, late in the evening, there is another parade. This one ends at midnight at a square in the middle of the old town. There a sardine is buried, symbolizing the end of the festivities and the beginning of Lent."

"A sardine?" Pamela echoed.

Juan shrugged. "Yes, and don't ask me what it means because I don't know. It's an old custom and, like many old customs, the *raison d'être* has been forgotten."

"Do you and Grace dress in black and follow the parade?" Pamela teased, knowing Juan well enough to guess that this was probably the last thing in the world he would do.

"Heaven forbid!" he exclaimed in mock horror. "In case you haven't noticed, I hate to get caught up in crowds. It gives me claustrophobia. During carnival, I stay home more than I do at any other time of the year!"

For all of this, Pamela was curious about the Shrove Tuesday parade, which, Juan said, was in effect a kind of funeral procession putting a finish to levity and starting the solemn, introspective forty-day Lenten period. She wondered if Miguel ever watched the burial of the sardine, and decided to ask him when she saw him at the Calderons on Monday night. Except that she didn't see him at the Calderons, because he didn't come.

On Tuesday, Pamela unexpectedly succumbed to a tropical virus that attacked her digestive system with a vengeance, leaving her totally drained. For two days she kept to her room, unable to hold down even water. On the third day, she made the short trek to the small solarium off the master bedroom, and let Grace install her in a lounge chair and ply her with Coca-Cola which, Grace insisted, was still one of the best things in the world to settle stomachs.

Pamela sipped very slowly, having no desire to let disaster overtake her again. She'd been so sick, she'd barely thought of Miguel. Not coherently, anyway. But now, as her strength slowly returned, so did the thousand questions. Had he called at all, while she'd been so out of it?

Pamela didn't want to ask Grace; she was beginning to feel rather cautious about Miguel. After his failure to appear at the Calderons, common sense told her to soft pedal her interest in him, even to Grace.

Fortunately, Grace volunteered the information.

"Miguel has called several times," she said, calmly stretching out on the lounge chair adjacent to Pamela's. She sipped an iced tea, then added, "He was very concerned about you, especially since he had to go back to Arucas this morning."

"He's left Las Palmas?" Pamela blurted, her agitation underscoring her sense of helplessness.

Grace, stirring her iced tea, looked up swiftly. "It isn't the end of the world, darling," she said sympathetically. "Arucas is only a few kilometers up in the hills."

"Arucas might as well be on the moon," Pamela rejoined.

"Come on, Pam," Grace protested mildly. "I don't think Miguel's interest in you could be any plainer. And I'd have to be blind not to see that you're attracted to him. He's not going to leave it at that, believe me."

There was a knock on the door, and Rosa entered the room carrying a florist's box filled with fragrant yellow roses.

"*Perdón, Señorita Pamela,*" the girl said. "*Flores, para usted.*"

Again, there was a card. Again, Pamela looked down at Miguel's strong, slanted writing. The words blurred, but not so much that she couldn't read them.

"Please get better quickly," he'd written. "I will be in touch as soon as I am able."

It was a strangely unsatisfactory message, perhaps because it conveyed no affection. He'd called her Pamelita. Had, at moments, called her *querida*. Either of these words would have lent a different tone to his card. As it was...

Grace spoke in Spanish to Rosa, then turned back to Pamela. "I told her to put the flowers in the crystal vase Miguel gave you, then put them in your room. All right?"

Pamela nodded. "That's fine."

Grace watched Rosa retreat. "Pam, you needn't look so *bereft*. If Miguel didn't care for you he wouldn't be sending you roses."

That wasn't the problem, Pamela realized suddenly, Miguel cared for her, just as she cared for him. But there were too many obstacles. There was a wife who might or might not be dead. And a headstrong son who was evidently determined to cause his father considerable grief. Finally, there was his banana plantation, a business upon which the family fortune depended, and which was almost certainly destined to fail.

Pamela didn't want to discuss these things with Grace, so she merely said, "I'm edgy because I still feel so weak, that's all. Give me another day and I'll be bright as a new peseta." She forced herself to smile.

So saying, Pamela ate a little soup to please both Grace and Octavia, then went back to her room for a long siesta. There, with time to think, she knew there was no way she was going to brighten up again...not for a long time to come.

There'd been other traumatic times in Pamela's life. First, her dismal love affair with Glenn Babcock. Then, her parents' deaths within a year of each other when she was only in her early twenties. Then, the heartache following her breakup with Jack Trent and, more recently, her relationship with Charles.

She hadn't thought much about Charles since arriving in Las Palmas, but now Pamela began to consider him from a new angle. He was in love with her—deeply in love, she feared. Too much in love. Now that she was in love with Miguel Rivero, she felt a new empathy for Charles. A far deeper feeling, actually, than anything she'd felt for him before.

Too much in love. The phrase haunted her, chafed her emotions. Until she'd said that, she hadn't verbalized the overwhelming fact that she'd fallen hopelessly in love with a handsome Spanish stranger.

Facing up to the implications of her silent admission, Pamela hovered on the brink of chaos. Her only way back to relative security was to move, a step at a time, away from the tug of her heartstrings, toward a more logical approach.

It wasn't easy. In fact, the first step was as high as a mountain. But that evening, having requested a dinner tray in her room with perhaps soup and a little toast, Pamela got out her writing paper and wrote Charles a long letter.

She thought of calling him, wondering if maybe it was cowardly to put what she had to say on paper, rather than saying it to him directly. But in the long run, this way was better for both of them. She could make him understand her position better if she could state it without interruption.

She didn't mention Miguel because there wasn't any point in doing so. Charles's ego would only be damaged all the more severely if he thought another man had preempted him.

Anyway, that wasn't really the case. Charles and herself would never have achieved a real and lasting relationship. Still, Pamela had to admit that this realization had come to her largely thanks to Miguel. Largely because she'd learned what it meant to be stirred by someone, truly fired by him, in tune with and transported by him to a realm beyond imagination.

She finished her letter to Charles, read it, and was dissatisfied. So she set it aside, deciding to rework it in the morning. This she did, twice, before she finally got down exactly what she wanted to say. Then, before she could change her mind, she rang for Roberto and managed to communicate with him sufficiently so he understood that she wanted him to mail the letter to the States for her as soon as possible.

By the following day, Pamela was feeling much stronger. In the morning, she and Grace took a walk along the *paseo*, but now the carnival atmosphere was gone. There were no more enchanting children in costumes, no more adults losing themselves to their fantasies by dressing outrageously and hiding behind masks, no more balloons, no vendors selling trinkets and souvenirs.

It was a beautiful day, though. People strolled along the *paseo*, sun worshippers stretched out on the blue and green lounges that studded the *playa*'s copper sands, while dark clouds brushed distant mountains.

It was the sight of clouds that reminded Pamela that she was here in the Canaries for a purpose, a purpose she hadn't even begun to address.

That afternoon, she knuckled down to work. Juan had amassed a wealth of material for her, all printed in English so, borrowing a card table from Grace, Pamela set up a corner of her bedroom as a study. As usual, work was the best of all therapies. When the time came to join Juan and Grace in the spillover room for cocktails, Pamela was already beginning to have a grasp, however sketchy, of the Canary Islands' water problems.

Once, she learned, Grand Canary had been well forested, mostly with pines. The species retained water, needing only about thirty percent of the water derived from the annual rainfall. The balance of the water that they retained was gradually returned to the soil.

Unfortunately, from the time of Columbus—who had visited the Canaries on several occasions—until the early years of the twentieth century, these pines had been cut down and used in construction. One of several theories was that the decimation of the forests had gradually caused what would become a perpetual drought.

This drought, persisting throughout most of the present century, represented a problem of a critical magnitude. It especially threatened the banana harvest, the island's major crop, for bananas require not only warm temperatures and protection from wind, but also a great deal of water.

The obvious solution would be to construct additional desalinization plants. But these plants were so enormously expensive that the economics automatically formed a vicious circle. No water meant no crops, at least not bananas. No crops meant no money to build the plants that would provide the water to irrigate the crops....

Pamela was still brooding about this as she joined the Basilios and accepted a glass of dry Spanish sherry.

"You are so pensive, little one," he complained, looking across at her. Pamela caught the warning glance

Grace shot him, though it evidently escaped Juan. Anyway, there was no need to warn him. Just now, at least, her depression was not because of Miguel Rivero.

"I've begun doing my homework," she said. "And though I know my study is strictly academic, I can't help but wish that I could do something, or invent something that might be a step toward solving the problem."

"Don't we all," Juan agreed grimly. "Is the material I've gathered for you satisfactory...for a beginning?"

"More than satisfactory. It's a tremendous help."

"Pamelita..." Juan began, then stopped.

Pamela's heart twisted painfully at this Spanish version of her name. "Look," he continued gently. "This is a nearly century-old problem we are dealing with here on Grand Canary. No one is expecting you to achieve a miracle with your thesis."

"I know that, Juan. It just seems so dreadful to me, that's all."

"Well," Juan observed, "it certainly proves nature's mastery over man."

Miguel, Pamela recalled, had said something of the same thing.

"Actually," Juan said contemplatively, "it occurs to me that you should do considerable traveling while you are in this part of the world. Each island in the Canaries is very different, you know. You really must see Lanzarote and Tenerife and Fuertaventura, and the smaller ones, if you can. They are all easily reached by hydrofoil or plane. Even more important, you must become familiar with the rest of Gran Canaria, not just Las Palmas. I feel it most important for you to visit Arucas, and the areas around Guia and Galdar, where there is so much banana cultivation. Only then can you really understand the geography.

"All of the Canaries, you see, are of volcanic origin," Juan went on. "The last major eruption took place around the time Columbus came here late in the fifteenth century, although there are still fires burning in craters on Lanzarote the most volcanic of all the islands, and very different topographically.

"As for Gran Canaria, the island is divided into north and south regions which, again, are very different geographically. Plus there is the relatively fertile central area where it is always green. In the south, it is sunny for at least three hundred and fifty days of the year. You are always guaranteed a sunny day at Maspalomas Beach, for example. In the north, it is often cloudy, although it seldom rains.

"Also, there are three distinct elevations. At about a thousand feet the tropical fruits are grown, including bananas. In the middle altitudes, around three thousand feet or so, you will find apples and pears. Above three thousand, there are chestnuts and walnuts. Quite a diversity."

"I would say so," Pamela agreed, forming visual images as Juan went along.

"But," her host concluded, "definitely this is something you must see for yourself." He turned to Grace. "It would be difficult for me to get away until this article is finished. Since you've finished the major part of your job why don't you and Pamela take a trip up to Arucas for a few days and visit Carmen?"

Pamela kept her immediate protest to herself, but only by making a very strong effort. She was spared from saying anything when Grace told her husband, "I've been intending to tell you this, Juan, but Carmen called late this afternoon, and she's driving down tomorrow. She wants to meet Pamela and do a little city shopping."

Juan swore softly under his breath, limiting himself to his native Spanish. Then he said impatiently, "Why didn't you make some excuse, Grace? This is not the time for a visit from Carmen. You know she never lets me work in peace."

"Carmen will forever be the older sister and Juan the baby brother," Grace told Pamela. "Think about it, though, Juan. I couldn't put Carmen off without blatantly hurting her feelings. She knows we have a houseguest. Undoubtedly she thinks that if you have enough time to entertain a guest you must have a bit left over for her."

"But I have not *entertained* Pamela!" Juan pointed out explosively. "She is like a member of our family."

"Carmen is also a member of our family," Grace reminded him succinctly.

Carmen de Moreno arrived the next afternoon in time to have tea and pastries with Grace and Pamela in the spillover room. Juan did not join them, locking himself up in his study. Earlier, Grace had confided, "He's been looking around for a Do Not Disturb sign, printed in Spanish, of course. Fortunately, we don't have one, or Carmen would really be insulted."

Carmen was short and plump, and possessed a strong facial resemblance to Juan, except that she managed to look quite pretty. She had lovely green eyes, and her hair was a lustrous jet black. Could there be a bit of artifice involved there? Pamela wondered whimsically; Carmen was in her late forties.

Her English was limited, but she made a great effort to communicate in deference to Pamela, only switching to Spanish with Grace when she literally ran out of vocabulary. During these short exchanges, Pamela envied the fluency of Grace's Spanish.

For the next two days, Grace and Carmen spent a good part of their time shopping, the focusing entirely upon Carmen, who wanted to replace a number of items in her wardrobe. While Carmen was trying on a dress, Grace confided to Pamela that Carmen had gone through the usual lengthy Spanish mourning period after her husband's death almost seven years before, and had worn nothing but black for a long time. Recently, she had begun to throw off the widow's weeds, which Grace and Juan were glad to see. "I doubt that Dolores, Miguel's sister, will ever dispense with black," Grace said. "But then Dolores tends to be morbid by nature."

When Carmen and Grace were speaking Spanish together, Pamela strained her ears, striving to hear that familiar name, Miguel. Or Dolores, or even Rafael. But as far as she could ascertain, the Rivero family was never even mentioned, let alone discussed.

Carmen stayed through the weekend, but on Monday morning, as they were sipping *café con leche* and munching croissants, she announced that she'd be driving back to Arucas that afternoon.

Juan, unexpectedly, had joined the women for their continental breakfast. He paused in the act of spreading rich guava jam on his croissant. "Have you spoken to Pamela, Carmen?" His sister looked puzzled, so he repeated the question in Spanish.

At once, Carmen said, in English, "No, I thought you would invite Pamela for me."

Pamela felt a sudden premonition of impending disaster. It took very little psychic talent to suspect that Juan had discussed Pamela's returning to Arucas with Carmen for a visit. To judge from the glow on her face, Carmen was decidedly enthusiastic about the idea.

Confirming this, Carmen said bravely, "I would love that you come home with me, Pamela. Then for yourself you can see the bananas, and you can learn more about the ... what is it, Juan?"

"The water problem," Juan said patiently.

"Ah, yes." Carmen nodded. "The water *problema*."

Pamela mounted her resistance. "That's very kind of you," she said, speaking slowly enough so Carmen would be almost certain to understand her. "And I would be delighted to visit you before I return to the United States. But right now my need is to study more before I go out into the field."

"Into the field?" Carmen echoed, frowning.

Again, Juan translated, then explained his translation to Pamela. "I told her that you don't mean literally going out into the field," he said. "Regardless, it doesn't make sense, Pamelita—your not taking Carmen up on her invitation, that is. She has plenty of time on her hands, and she has lived in Arucas for years. Through her, you will have an entree to all sorts of people and places...."

Including Dolores de Avero? Pamela wondered, cringing at the thought of meeting Miguel's sister. To say nothing of confronting Miguel, himself, in his home environment, when she hadn't heard a word from him since he'd sent the yellow roses.

She hoped that Grace might recognize how much she didn't want to go to Arucas with Carmen, and might espouse her cause. But this didn't happen.

Finishing her coffee, Grace said, in a suspiciously languid way, "Darling, I agree with Juan, of course. Moreover, Carmen really wants to offer you her hospitality.

Look, simply throw a few things in a bag and go along with her. I'll drive up on the weekend, with or without Juan, and bring you back to Las Palmas."

Chapter Seven

Carmen drove her small French sedan with surprising competence. Surprising to Pamela, anyway. She hadn't expected Carmen to be the type who could cope with the intricacies of modern machinery. Outwardly, she was so much the middle-aged, seemingly complacent Spanish *doña*.

They sped along the coastal highway, heading south. Then Carmen suddenly made a sharp right turn onto another road. Soon they were ascending so rapidly that within a few minutes they were high above the city, looking down upon an incredible vista of Las Palmas with the clear, tourmaline sea stretching like a silken carpet to the distant horizon.

It was only twenty kilometers from Las Palmas to Arucas—about twelve miles, Pamela calculated—but the road did not run straight as the crow flies, so it was the better part of half an hour before they reached the outskirts of Miguel's hometown.

While Carmen had been packing away the new clothes she'd bought, Pamela had snatched a few minutes to read up on Arucas. The city had a population of roughly thirty thousand people, and was in the very heart of the banana plantations. The book mentioned that the city lay at the base of a sixteen-hundred-foot hill of the same name, but now that she was seeing it for herself, Pamela decided that Arucas more correctly sprawled up its side. Many of the streets were very steeply inclined.

As she viewed the peak from the window of Carmen's car, Pamela realized that it was one of the extinct volcanos that were visible from Las Palmas. She'd gazed at this prominence with Miguel as they strolled along the *paseo*, and now wondered why he hadn't told her that it was next to where he lived.

But the mountain of Arucas was not nearly as impressive as the gigantic, multispired Gothic cathedral that dominated the center of the town.

"The Cathedral of San Juan," Carmen said, in her heavily accented English, and added proudly, "My church."

To Pamela there was nothing Spanish about the cathedral that dwarfed every other structure in town. There was a dusty little park in front of the entrance, the arid soil giving testimony to the fact that water was not readily available hereabouts.

Old men sat on stone benches that edged the paths crisscrossing the park, their eyes shut against the present as they dreamed of the past. They seemed oblivious to the small children who played as children do everywhere, oblivious to everything except themselves.

Carmen turned onto another ascending street just behind the cathedral, and they passed by a school playground. Older children, all wearing pale gray-green smocks, skipped and played happily during their recess period. Pamela wished she had a camera with her; the children made such a charming picture.

Even as she thought this, she watched a woman stop to smile indulgently at the children before continuing on her way across the square. This was a place where people took time out to pause and appreciate the moment.

Finally, Carmen pulled up to the curb in front of a highly polished pine door in the middle of a long, whitewashed wall. High to the side of the door, a bell was mounted on the wall.

Carmen pulled the rope with the imperiousness of proprietorship and in a moment, an elderly man garbed in black opened the door. He bowed low when he saw Carmen, murmuring soft words of greeting in melodious Spanish.

Carmen made introductions in Spanish. This, Pamela gathered, was Porfirio, Carmen's majordomo.

They stepped into a paved courtyard edged with flower beds. Aside from the colorful blooms, the area was barren.

The house itself was dazzling white and bathed in sunlight that emphasized its starkness. The main entrance was a large carved door of the same beautiful golden pine as the door to the street. Porfirio opened it with a flourish, bowed, and then stepped back to let the two women precede him.

Pamela moved into blissful darkness, her eyes adjusting slowly.

Carmen's house formed a square around a large inner courtyard. Each room opened onto a stone walk that followed the perimeter and was shaded by an overhead trellis. Bougainvillea, in vivid rose red and deep purple, covered most of the trellis, converting it into an exotic floral bower. There were also red geraniums, roses and calla lilies growing in profusion along the borders.

A maid, dressed in black, with a large white apron billowing from her ample waistline, appeared from the shadowy recesses at the far side of the patio. Her salt-and-pepper hair was pinned in a bun at the top of her head, and her face was broad and pleasant.

"Bienvenido, señorita," she beamed, addressing Pamela first.

"This is Conchita," Carmen explained. "She welcomes you to our house, Pamela. I phoned her from Las Palmas to say you were coming home with me, so she could make your room ready for you."

Carmen spoke carefully and, though her English was still heavily accented, Pamela began to suspect that Juan's sister was more fluent than she'd sounded in the Basilios' house. There, of course, both Juan and Grace had been available to translate for her. In any event, there was no doubt that she was more comfortable in her own idiom.

Pamela decided it was time to try a little Spanish. *"Gracias, Conchita,"* she told the maid, and saw Conchita's smile widen even farther.

The room to which she was shown was on the left side of the courtyard. It was quite spacious with a high ceiling. The furniture was all of dark wood, and was simply beautiful. The draperies, carpet and bedspread were in soft shades of green. Wide windows overlooked the courtyard, where birds sang and flowers bloomed. It was easy for Pamela to imagine that she'd stumbled into paradise.

"Una siesta, señorita?" Conchita asked.

Did she want to take a nap? To her surprise, Pamela found that she did. She wanted to relax for a while and let herself enjoy these lovely surroundings. For as long as possible, she told herself, she would try to stave off the knowledge that Miguel Rivero was somewhere very close by.

Pamela unpacked and slipped into a thin silk dressing gown. Then Conchita appeared with a tray on which stood a pitcher of cool orangeade and some delicious, fruit-filled cookies.

Pamela finished a glass of orangeade and two of the cookies, then stretched out and promptly fell asleep. It was a deep and dreamless sleep, and she felt greatly refreshed when she awakened. Glancing at her watch, she saw it was nearly seven, and was glad that the customary Spanish dinner hour was so late. Plenty of time to freshen up.

She wondered how she was supposed to dress. Conchita had pointed to a rope by the door and had indicated with vigorous gestures that Pamela was to pull this if she wanted anything. After a moment of thought, Pamela pulled down hard and Conchita soon appeared.

Smiling, Pamela walked over to the closet where she'd hung her clothes, and with her own kind of sign language conveyed to Conchita that she'd appreciate some advice.

Conchita took her time with the task, obviously relishing the lovely dresses. Finally, she selected an ivory dress, slim gold slippers, then indicated that these should be embellished with jewelry, perhaps a necklace.

Pamela thought she might be a bit too dressed up if she went along with Conchita's selection. On the other hand, the dress was cut very simply and, in lieu of the gold slippers, she could opt for cream-colored ones that weren't quite so flashy.

At the last minute, she decided to wear the gold slippers anyway, and added her grandmother's emerald pendant plus the emerald ring. She finished with a pair of dangling crystal and gold earrings that were especially becoming.

She emerged from her room to find Porfirio sitting on a bench a short distance away. When he stood, bowed and said politely, *"Señorita,"* Pamela realized he'd been waiting for her.

As he ushered her across the dimly lit courtyard, she heard voices. Evidently, she and Carmen would be having company for dinner; Pamela shrank from the thought of trying to communicate with Carmen's friends if they didn't speak English.

Porfirio stood back, bowed again, and bade her enter the door to which he was pointing. But when she did so, her knees suddenly turned to jelly; Miguel Rivero was standing not more than ten feet away. That familiar hunger clouded his dark eyes, and before she could even begin to rally, Miguel swiftly crossed the space between them and clasped her hands in his.

"This is so absolutely wonderful, Pamelita," he said, his soft velvet voice the most sensuous she'd ever heard. Just the sound of it sent a tremor running through her. Yet there was a false note that struck Pamela, though it was probably apparent only to her. At least, she hoped so. She wasn't especially eager to share her sudden conviction that Miguel didn't really want her in Arucas at all!

Carmen, resplendent in a royal-blue creation she'd bought in Las Palmas, embraced her houseguest lightly, before turning to a tall, slim woman who was watching this interchange with undisguised curiosity. "Come,"

Carmen said, gently urging Pamela toward this other woman. "You must meet Dolores."

Pamela had known few moments in her life when she wanted to turn around and run the other way. But there was no chance of retreat. She tried to smile as she and Carmen approached Dolores de Avero, but her effort fell short of success. Even so, it surpassed the perfunctory smile that crossed the other woman's patrician features.

She was dressed in black, unrelieved except for a string of pearls that made a graceful loop an inch below the high neckline of her beautifully cut, obviously expensive dress. Her hair was silver, fashioned in an elaborate chignon, and her eyes were as jet as Miguel's.

The resemblance between Miguel and his sister was unusually strong, their features strikingly similar. But Pamela could see no gentleness or humor in Dolores de Avero's face, and couldn't imagine Dolores's dark eyes ever having been lit by the mischievous glow that sometimes affected her brother's.

Dolores inclined her head slightly as the introductions were made, then said simply, *"Encantada."*

Pamela was at a complete loss. She wasn't accustomed to feeling so totally awkward in a social situation.

At her elbow, Miguel asked, "Sherry, Pamela?"

He proffered a glass of amber liquid, which Pamela accepted with a mumbled, "Thank you." Taking a nervous sip, she nearly gasped, discovering that he'd given her a glass of straight Scotch. Still, she was grateful to him for the jolt.

Miguel took hold of her elbow and, gently but firmly, led her away from the two older women toward an empty settee. Behind her, Pamela heard Carmen engaging Dolores in a fast-paced Spanish conversation, and then heard her chuckle.

"So, Carmen is on your side," Miguel observed. "A very good ally to have. Still, I wish we had arranged your introduction to my sister in a different manner. It might have been better if she entertained you first, in our house. But when Carmen called from Las Palmas with her invitation for dinner tonight, Dolores accepted for both of us."

"Or you wouldn't have come at all, is that it?" Pamela snapped back, her ire rising instantly.

She sat down stiffly on the edge of the settee, trying to keep a grip on her dignity, horrified to realize she might burst into tears if things went on this way.

"Why do you say that?" Miguel asked, taken aback.

They were beyond the earshot of Carmen and Dolores, but Pamela instinctively lowered her voice. "Because it's true!" A dull ache thickened her throat, and she found herself gasping for breath.

She never should have come to Arucas! She'd known it intuitively, but hadn't listened to the inner warning. The fact that Miguel had left Las Palmas while she was sick, had gone home and hadn't so much as called her since, should have been indication enough that however he felt about her, there were many other matters more important to him. And other people—to whom he was giving a greater priority, whether by desire or out of some self-imposed necessity.

She was startled when Miguel blurted, almost choking, "It is *not* true." There was downright anguish in his eyes as he continued in a low tone meant for her ears only, "Damn it, Pamela, don't make things any more difficult than they are already."

He sounded so American when he said that. But then she'd almost forgotten how good his English was. He had even less of an accent than Juan Basilio, except during those moments when emotion got the better of him. Seeing his dark eyes flaming with indignation, she realized he was emotional enough now, and more than angry.

"I have been trying..." he began, and then broke off.

"Trying to what?" Pamela queried, more calmly.

"It isn't that I have been trying to forget you," Miguel started again. "That... is something I will never be able to do."

The anger faded from his eyes as he looked down at her, and said softly, "*Querida*, try to be patient with me, will you? There is so much I must work out before I will really feel..."

The sentence was destined to remain unfinished; just then Porfirio announced dinner. Carmen led the way with Dolores on her elbow, followed by Miguel and Pamela, who walked along in silence.

Carmen's dining room was extremely formal, with heavy dark furniture and candles burning in tall, ornate silver holders. Framed oil paintings of ancestors, both Basilios and Morenos, were spaced at precise intervals around the walls.

Dinner began with a clear consommé in which avocado slices floated. Then came the main course—a succulent chicken dish accompanied by a savory rice mixture. *Flan* followed for dessert. After that the customary small cups of strong black coffee laced with sugar were served in the drawing room.

The conversation was at least eighty percent in Spanish, with Miguel responsible for most of the translating. Carmen tried to do her part, but Dolores spoke not one word in English.

Once or twice Pamela caught Miguel frowning at his sister. He seemed vexed with her, and Pamela began to suspect that maybe Dolores could speak at least some English after all, but wasn't about to, at least not tonight.

To Pamela's surprise, Carmen asked Miguel if he would play something on the ebony grand piano. Anyone who knew Miguel even slightly would have realized from his expression that this was the last thing he wanted to do. But his sister merely echoed something in sweet Spanish that undoubtedly meant she wished he'd play, so he rose reluctantly and went to the keyboard.

Only at the last minute did he call over his shoulder, "Come along, Pamelita, and keep me company."

Pamela was intensely aware of Dolores's eyes raking her as she crossed the room to stand next to the piano. She felt like an awkward fool standing there, but it helped when she saw an impish smile twist Miguel's face, and he began to play an old Beatles' song.

His was a natural talent, yet obviously schooled. Pamela's foot rapped to the beat as one tune merged easily into the next.

When he finished the medley, Dolores called out a request in Spanish.

He tossed back an incomprehensible answer, then said to Pamela, "She suggests something classical, but I'm not in the mood for anything classical tonight. Anyway, I'm out of practice."

"Judging from the way you play, you must have had a lot of lessons," Pamela commented. "You're really good."

Miguel shrugged. "In earlier years, I was better. There was a time when the family wanted to make a concert pianist out of me, but I rebelled, which was just as well. One day my father suffered a coronary, and the next day

I was called back to take over the family businesses. There was no one else to do the job, so..."

"Did you want to be a concert pianist?"

Miguel looked up and smiled. "No," he said frankly. "I was too restless, especially at that age, to practice as much as a concert career demands."

His fingers roved over the keyboard, then he began playing a soft melody that could be nothing other than a love song. He gazed up at Pamela, his eyes caressing her face, and said softly, "Have a little faith, will you please?" Then, before she could speak, he added, "To-morrow morning I have to go check out a few things at the distillery. It's just on the edge of town, so I thought perhaps you might enjoy coming with me and trying our famous liqueur. Then we could drive around a bit, and I can show you at least part of the plantation. Along the way, we might find the makings for lunch. Would you be agreeable to that, Pamelita? I spoke to Carmen earlier, and she has no specific plans for you. In fact, she re-minded me that you are here to study the effect of the drought. So...you can consider this a work project if you like."

The fireflies were once again dancing in Miguel's eyes, and his smile was enchanting. Pamela felt herself so drawn to him that it was difficult to remain poised.

"I appreciate the offer, Miguel," she said, slowly, "but I don't want to be a bother to you. I realize you have your hands full, and..."

He grinned unexpectedly. "You sound like a school-girl making a speech that the teacher's told her to mem-orize," he teased. "I admit it will be a terrible hardship to show you around, Pamelita, but for the sake of being courteous to a stranger in my country, I will gladly try to suffer through it."

His eyes were twinkling more than ever now, and Pamela had to laugh. She wished she had the nerve to shake him for teasing her like this. She wished even more that she could entwine her arms around him and join her mouth to his... savor, again, the deep potential for passion that flared in his kiss.

Instead, she asked demurely, "What time in the morning shall I be ready?"

"Ten?" he suggested. "Or is that too early for you?"

"Ten would be perfect." Just thinking about meeting him would be enough to keep her awake all night.

As it happened, it wasn't the thought of her impending rendezvous with Miguel that kept her from drifting off; it was the disturbing conversation she had with Carmen after Miguel and his sister left.

Closing the door behind her guests, Carmen said abruptly, striving for the right English words and obviously determined to find them, "I hope you will excuse Dolores. She was unforgivable tonight. Her English is a hundred times better than mine, but she refused to use it."

Carmen's mouth tightened as she mentally translated from Spanish into English, and then said vehemently, "I can only explain her actions with one word. Jealousy. She is—how shall I say it?—blind jealous of you, Pamelita!"

"How could she possibly be jealous of me?" Pamela stammered.

"Because of Miguel. She would like to think that she has the—ah, I wish my English was better—the complete control with Miguel. But if you ask me, a lot of the trouble between Miguel and Rafael has been her *culpa*. Her own fault, I should say. Dolores never had any children, so she has considered Rafael like her son, and has—

what is the word I want?—spoiled, she has spoiled him so much it is terrible. *Al mismo tiempo*," Carmen continued, then carefully translated, "At the same time, she complains to Miguel about Rafael. She makes trouble for both of them."

Carmen sighed. "Dolores is not a bad woman, Pamelita. You must understand that she is unhappy. What do you say? Frustrated?" She smiled suddenly. "I need to go around with the dictionary in my hand!"

Pamela returned the smile. She was becoming more and more fond of Carmen, and only wished she could feel an equal rapport toward Miguel's sister. But Dolores, definitely, had turned her off. As she must have turned Dolores off, she admitted ruefully, or certainly the older woman would have spoken English.

"You express yourself perfectly," Pamela insisted. "I hope that someday I'm able to speak Spanish even half as well as you do English."

"Thank you, Pamelita. You are very kind to say so."

"Still," Pamela added skeptically, "It's hard to imagine that a woman like Dolores could be jealous of me."

"You don't know her like I do!" Carmen replied.

"Perhaps if we could have communicated better..."

"But that was her fault, not yours," Carmen stated sternly. "I plan to speak to her..."

"Please don't. The two of you have been friends far too long to permit a stranger like myself to interfere with your relationship."

Carmen smiled softly. "You do not interfere, Pamelita," she said gently. "And certainly you are no longer a stranger. For myself, I am very pleased that you are the woman who interests Miguel so much. I have known Miguel since he was a small boy. I love him very much. So...this makes me happy."

With that, Carmen patted Pamela on the cheek and said good-night. "You have but to ring the bell, and Conchita will attend to anything you wish," she added, nodding graciously and then making her way toward her quarters.

Pamela, staggered by Carmen's statements about Miguel, felt dazed as she crossed the courtyard and entered her own room. Conchita had already been in to turn down the covers, and a lamp with a cream-colored shade glowed softly on the bedside table. Her nightgown was spread out on the bed. Conchita had even thought to provide her with a carafe of water and a glass on a small tray.

The setting was wonderfully relaxing. Moonlight slanted through the windows facing the patio, and the air was filled with the scents of sweet-smelling flowers, among them the gardenia aroma that would forever remind her of Miguel. Pamela would even have sworn that she heard the strains of a Spanish guitar, somewhere off in the distance.

If Miguel were only at her side, she thought wistfully, she would, for once, have attained perfection.

Chapter Eight

Miguel looked ten years younger than he had the previous night. He looked down at Pamela as if he had not a care in the world, his smile infectious. She felt herself brimming with excitement as she climbed in the passenger side of Miguel's "country car," as he called it—a bright-red, American Jeep.

"The first time I saw one of these," he said grinning, "I knew I had to have one."

"They don't sell Jeeps here, do they?" Pamela asked curiously.

"No, *querida*. I had it shipped from New Jersey! And, would you believe it, my friends would rather steal this than my Mercedes!"

Miguel pulled out into the narrow street, shifting gears furiously, and continued, "So, business first. Then, the rest of the day will be ours to do with as we please. I want you to see the distillery first, anyway, but there are a few matters I must go over with my cousin Ricardo. Ricardo Fonte," Miguel added. "He really runs the place for me."

"Fonte?" Pamela queried.

"My mother's name," he reminded her. "Rivero y Fonte. Ricardo is my cousin on the maternal side of my family."

Located on the outskirts of Arucas, the Rivero-Fonte distillery was only a short drive from Carmen's house. Miguel pulled up in front of a big concrete building and screeched to a halt, raising a wild cloud of dust.

Pamela, astonished to see a wealth of colored flowers against the tall white walls, commented, "The poinsettias grow like trees around here. When I think of the price just one plant brings back home at Christmas . . ."

"You see?" Miguel was teasing her again. "There are decided advantages to living in a tropical paradise. On the other hand," he continued, somewhat obliquely, "I would say that everything is relative." He walked around to Pamela's side of the car, and tugged open the door. "Come along," he urged. "I hope you'll find this interesting, but personally I can't wait to get back on the road."

Neither could Pamela. She wanted to be alone with Miguel, to share every precious, snatched moment of time. Because that's what it was. Miguel was snatching time away from business, very possibly urgent business, to be with her.

"When you were a child," she asked suddenly, "Did you ever play hooky from school? *Do* Spanish children play hooky from school?"

He was a step ahead of her, and turned to look at her quizzically. "Do I really seem so stolid to you?" he asked.

Pamela giggled, and shook her head. Stolid was the last adjective she would choose to describe Miguel Rivero.

"I was a serious student," he admitted. "More so during my teens than earlier. By then I was already feeling family pressure. I was the only son, you see. There were a number of male cousins on both sides of the family, but it was made clear to me that I must be the one to carry on."

"Didn't you want to run the business, Miguel?"

"No," he said. "I wanted to go to Spain, to play around a little, to study music in Madrid. Does that surprise you?"

"No," she said slowly, "although last night you mentioned that you never wanted to be a concert pianist. But when you played you had a certain touch, a certain feeling."

"You are imagining things, Pamelita," he chided. "I was playing ditties at Carmen's house. I play little else, these days," he confessed sheepishly. "I have no time for practicing, and so I merely relax and let my fingers play whatever comes to mind.

"But you asked if I ever played hooky. Yes, I played hooky. In fact, I did all the outrageous things normal boys do everywhere. Spanish kids are still kids, Pamelita. Don't let the culture gap become unnecessarily wide."

Behind them, Pamela heard the heavy throb of a motor, and turned to see a large tour bus swing into the distillery parking lot.

"Damn," Miguel muttered. "I welcome the tourists ordinarily, but right now I wanted to show you around in relative privacy. German, I think," he speculated, watching the first passengers emerge from the bus.

"I've heard a lot of German spoken in Las Palmas," Pamela commented. "And other languages that sounded like German, but were definitely something else."

"Probably Swedish or Norwegian, maybe some Danish. We get a lot of Scandinavian and German tourists in the Canaries at this time of year. A number of English, too, plus a lesser number of French and Italian, who have their own resorts on the Mediterranean. So, you Americans are a definite minority, but then you are not here as a tourist, are you?"

"Thus far, I've been behaving like one," Pamela admitted. "As I told Juan and Grace, and Carmen too, I've got to start doing some work."

"And so you shall, in a sense, this very afternoon," Miguel promised. "Now, let's get inside so we'll be a few steps ahead of that group. It will take them a little while to get organized, visit the rest rooms and so on, before they start their tour."

It was unexpectedly dark inside the distillery. The first room they entered was huge and their footsteps thudded on the stone floor. Large casks lined the high walls all the way around, and were also arranged in long rows down the center.

"You will see that the contents are recorded," Miguel explained, "along with the dates when the casks were filled. Come," he instructed, propelling her through a side door into another huge warehouse. "Here you see the vats in which the liquors are distilled. Those overhead pipes lead to funnels which, in turn, filter liquid into the storage casks you just saw. So, they are filled and labeled, and then they rest in peace until the moment is right for the contents to be bottled. And, hopefully, sold." He smiled impishly.

"One day you can come back if you like," he said, "and Ricardo will explain the process in more detail. For now, though, let us get ahead into the testing room so you can sample the products before we are inundated with those tourists."

"But it isn't even noon!" Pamela protested. "I can't drink at this hour of the morning."

"A mere sip here and there. I am not about to make a *borrachita* out of you, Pamelita. That is, I have no intention of getting you drunk. Certainly not until later, anyway," he teased.

The tasting room was a stone-floored chamber with a polished pine bar that stretched the full length of one wall. Already, several people were working behind the bar, setting out bottles and small plastic cups.

Miguel greeted his employees, but didn't make any introductions. Then he poured a shot of golden liquid into one of the cups. "Try it," he urged. "The banana liqueur."

The liqueur was smooth and delicious, the various rums Miguel offered considerably more fiery, but each was surprisingly distinctive. But after her fourth sip, she said, "Honestly, that's enough."

"As you wish." Miguel grinned. "Let us find Ricardo and then we can take off."

Ricardo Fonte's office was in the rear of the building and looked out on yet another courtyard around which bright flowers bloomed in profusion.

Ricardo was several inches shorter than Miguel, several pounds heavier, and several years younger. There wasn't much of a family resemblance, but dark-eyed, dark-haired Ricardo was decidedly attractive in his own way, and had a delightfully ebullient personality.

Unfortunately, from Pamela's point of view, his English was limited. When the time came to discuss business, Miguel asked her indulgence, then switched into Spanish.

Ricardo's desk was stacked high with papers. He brought forth several sheaves for Miguel's inspection, and spoke seriously. Miguel frowned a bit at the beginning of their dialogue, but seemed satisfied as they finished up.

The conference took far less time than Pamela had feared it might, and the sun was just about at its zenith as she and Miguel started out again, heading west.

"We will go over to Guia, just a few miles from here, and pick up some things for lunch," Miguel announced. "Along the way, take a close look at the houses, especially out in the country. You will see that the roofs are usually flat, and on every one of them there are cisterns to catch the rain. You see?" he said, pointing to a house off the side of the road. "That house has three cisterns on its roof. You never see less than two, and often as many as four or five. The people depend on them to collect water for many of the mundane chores you take for granted in the States... like washing clothes and bathing. See?" Miguel went on, pointing again. "There, on that rooftop, there are four cisterns."

"And there's a dog up there, too!" Pamela exclaimed.

"Probably the family pet. I think everyone on Grand Canary has at least one dog, and out here in the country you often see them up on the rooftops like that."

Pamela spotted another house with three round cisterns on the roof, plus two dogs who were stretched out asleep in the full rays of the noon sun.

"As you will see," Miguel continued, "there are really no flower or vegetable gardens. It would take too much water to raise a garden successfully. Very seldom is there a real yard around a house, even out here. In the towns, no matter how large or small, certain things are the same. The sidewalks are almost always narrow, and the houses front directly on the street. Occasionally, you may get a glimpse of a courtyard if the front door opens."

"I noticed the gorgeous pine doors and shutters on the houses in Arucas," Pamela told him.

"In the old houses, it's the original pine that you see," Miguel explained. "But now it's prohibited to cut down the trees for carpentry purposes. It has been so for many years, in the effort to conserve the pines we still have. As you have probably heard, cutting down the pines is considered, by some, to be responsible for our present water shortage.

"So, today," he said, "since customs and tastes change slowly here and people still want their pine doors and shutters, the pine is mostly imported from Central America."

They were approaching the outskirts of another small town, careening along the bumpy country road in total abandon.

"This is Guia," Miguel said. "Famous for its flower cheese—the kind of flower you sniff, not the flour bread is made from."

"Cheese... made from flowers?"

"Well, not exactly. It is made from a combination of goat's milk, sheep's milk and the flowers of wild artichokes. Stop wrinkling your nose, Pamelita! It is very good. It tastes rather like a tangy combination of feta and Muenster, with a pleasant, spongy texture. With some freshly baked bread and some of the local wine, you could not have a better *comida*!''

They stopped at a roadside shop that sold the products of the nearby vineyards. Another tour bus had already pulled up near the building. "We shall have to fight our way through a crowd of wine samplers," Miguel said wryly.

Inside, at a long counter, people were avidly tasting bread, cheese, and wine. Pamela heard snatches of English and German, and a couple of other languages she didn't recognize. She wondered how Miguel was going to get close enough to the counter to buy anything for their lunch.

After he'd surveyed the scene for a moment, he pulled her aside. "Just wait here, will you, Pamelita?"

He made his way to the far end of the room, walked around the counter, and became engaged in an animated conversation with a young man wearing a long white apron. In no time at all, he returned with a large paper bag, grinning widely. "See? Sometimes it pays to be a native."

They started out again and, after several more miles, Miguel turned onto a narrow, steep dirt road. They climbed to a point where the road leveled out, then he pulled off to the side and stopped. From this vantage point, Pamela could see Arucas mountain in the distance, the stark white buildings of the sprawling town, and the conspicuous spires of the Cathedral of San Juan. The sky was cloudless, the air soft and warm.

Beginning just below her and stretching all the way to the distant houses in Arucas, she saw what had to be tens of thousands of banana palms. There were acres and acres of them, appearing to take up every inch of available soil, growing thick and green. Where the hillsides were especially steep, the land had been terraced, accommodating even more.

"Is this your plantation?" Pamela asked, astonished.

"This part of it, yes," he nodded. "We own many acres, Pamelita. That is what makes our position so critical. You see the terraces over there?"

"Yes."

"In many places you will find bananas growing right down the sides of ravines," Miguel said. "Bananas require protection from the wind. They cannot be subjected to strong winds. So, wherever the contour of the land can be used to our advantage, this is done.

"We can deal with growing bananas down slopes and in ravines," he added. "And we can grow them in warm temperatures. But, the water..."

His smile was wry. "Would that you could come up with a miracle in the course of your research, *querida*," he told her.

If only she could! Pamela began pondering this, but her thoughts were cut short when Miguel said firmly, "No more business today! You have now officially begun your research by observing the local water storage system. For the rest of the day, let's just be frivolous, okay?"

Miguel, so fluent in English, gave a decidedly Spanish accent to the word "okay," and Pamela smiled. "Okay," she echoed, teasing him.

They spread a blanket on the ground, taking advantage of the scant shade provided by the Jeep. Miguel then produced a corkscrew, two stemmed, crystal glasses, and two pristine white linen napkins. Cutting the bread and cheese with his pocketknife, he handed Pamela chunks of both which she began to devour as rapidly as if she hadn't eaten for a week.

He was right. The cheese was excellent, as were the bread and wine. These simple foods, this gorgeous setting, Miguel close by her side, all created a very heady combination.

After a time, Miguel stretched out on the blanket and folded his arms behind his head. "I wish we could stop the clock, Pamelita. I wish we could forget about schedules and commitments and all the rest. My business...your thesis. I wish I could be here with you with nothing to intrude upon us until I have learned so much more about you than I know now."

His dark eyes studied her face and his hair glinted in the sunlight, thick, satin velvet.

He has the most beautiful hair I've ever seen, Pamela thought absently, *and he's probably the handsomest man I've ever seen, but there's so much more than that to Miguel. A depth that I can't even begin to appreciate. He's right—we both have so much to learn about each other. Will there ever be enough time for us? Will we ever...?*

Miguel frowned. "I have put a shadow on your face. I don't want that." He paused reflectively. "Perhaps that is my problem, Pamelita. Already, although we have known each other just a short time, I want only happiness for you. And happiness is the one thing in the world I cannot guarantee."

There was a shadow on his own face now. And, because she wanted to dispel it, because she wanted this moment to be free of intrusions, Pamela reached over impulsively and pressed a finger to his lips. "Shush," she cautioned. "Not today."

He captured her finger in his hand, and entwined his fingers with hers. "You are right," he murmured. "Not today."

He tugged, gently but insistently, and Pamela swayed toward him, let him pull her closer, let him take her into his arms. She felt his strength, his warmth, and caught his masculine scent.

Miguel got his wish. Time stopped.

The sun caressed the nape of her neck as she bent over him, her deep-gold hair falling around them like a shield obscuring their faces as their lips met. Sun-kissed, there was an exquisite sweetness to their mouths, like nectar stolen from the flowering bushes that bloomed along the roadside.

As their kiss deepened, Miguel's fingers trailed up and down Pamela's arms, stroking her softly. His touch was feather soft, so subtle, yet so suggestive, that he evoked a series of cascading repercussions deep within her. Suddenly she was fine-tuned, her senses sharpened, her stirred emotions as volatile as the lava that once boiled hot in the craters of Grand Canary's ancient volcanos.

Miguel took hold of the cotton jacket, and slowly drew away the fabric, sliding the sleeves down the length of her arms. The jacket discarded, he began to work on her slim shoulder straps, and then gently molded her body with his hands as he slid the shirred fabric of her dress down to her arched waist, then over the curve of her hips and across her firm thighs.

She began to protest, and murmured, more than a shade incoherently, "Miguel, someone could come along..."

He silenced her with a kiss, then said huskily, "No one, *cariña*, believe me. This is my land, and I know there is no one working in this entire area today. It is ours—the soil and the sun and the sky... and life, *vida de mi vida*. Life is so precious, so fleeting. Oh my God, Pamelita, do you have any idea how much I want you?"

She had a vivid idea. Miguel was totally aroused and, if Pamela had needed proof, this evidence in itself would have been enough. The chemistry that had been such a force between them almost from their first moment together was flaring out of control. Even if she could regain her senses, she wouldn't; she was possessed with an equal need for him.

Miguel moved away just enough to position her hands on the buttons of his fawn-colored sports shirt and, taking his cue, Pamela began to open his shirt, then buried her face in the nest of curling dark hair at his throat. She, who had never before been really out of control, knew that she was going to plunge over the edge. She couldn't hold herself back and Miguel, responding, helped her undress him, working his hands with hers, flesh touching flesh until they lay revealed to each other.

Then he began to make love to her, and their mounting passion became a part of nature itself. With the earth beneath them and the sky overhead, they felt as primal as the first man and woman. They shared each other, becoming more and more uninhibited, and when their moment of glorious culmination came with a transcending force that seemed to shake the ground beneath their bodies, it was a timeless phase of mutual triumph.

For a long while afterward, neither Pamela or Miguel tried to speak. They lay within the sanctuary of each other's arms, feeling and savoring...and loving. Yes, loving, Pamela thought, as Miguel brushed her temple with a tender kiss. What had happened between them on this enchanted afternoon was etched with love as pure and golden as the shimmering sunlight.

Later, Miguel poured the rest of the wine, and they sipped in silence. Then he packed up the remnants of their picnic lunch.

Pamela sensed the same reluctance in him that she was feeling herself, as they started back down the road to reality. Though Arucas was just a few kilometers away, it was in another world.

She felt her first uneasiness as they neared the town. "I must explain, Pamelita," Miguel began, "that my sister Dolores is a very religious woman. During Lent, she goes to church twice a day, and she seldom entertains at all before Easter. I say this because...well, because although I would like to invite you for dinner at my house, I'm afraid that I am going to meet with resistance."

"Because she took an instant dislike to me, isn't that what you mean?" Pamela blurted, her tongue tripping her before she had the chance to exercise any caution.

"I wouldn't say that Dolores dislikes you," Miguel said mildly, but unconvincingly, as far as Pamela was concerned. He glanced toward her, read her expression correctly, and added, "Look, I admit she's a difficult person. Dolores has...a persecution complex. She feels that God has given her several crosses to bear. Too heavy a load, in fact. Although she's not apt to tell her priest that. She'd rather suffer in silence."

"Everyone has crosses to bear," Pamela pointed out stiffly.

"But not as many as Dolores," Miguel said, unable to contain the cynicism in his tone. "She has her widowhood to maintain, which is really none of my business, though it's been over seven years since her husband died. But even if she could surmount that particular cross, she still has me, and Rafael."

"I take it your son doesn't get along with her," Pamela managed to say. It was still difficult for her to mention Miguel's son.

"No," Miguel said shortly. "No, he doesn't."

They were nearing Carmen's house, and he added hastily, "Look, I will call you. We can drive over to Las Palmas one evening and have dinner. Or..." He broke off. "I'll call you," he said again.

He pulled up in front of the wall that surrounded Carmen's house, and said apologetically, "Forgive me if I don't come in with you, but..."

She didn't want him to come in with her. Each fraction of a kilometer since they'd left their hillside oasis had been an anticlimax, and Pamela got out of the car as quickly as she could, even though she knew her obvious eagerness was hurting Miguel.

She rang the bell next to the beautiful golden pine door, and Porfirio admitted her, smiling warmly. "The *señora* is in kitchen," he managed, in heavily accented English. "Please to go to her."

Porfirio led the way to the kitchen, a large room with whitewashed walls on which an impressive number of shining copper pots were hung. Carmen was sitting at a big square table flanked with straight-backed wooden chairs. She was talking seriously with a slim, dark-haired boy who sat opposite her.

Pamela needed only one look to know that this was Rafael. *Miguel must have looked almost exactly like this when he was in his teens,* she thought instantly.

Rafael's jet hair was long and unruly—he obviously made no effort to discipline it—and needed a good washing. Nevertheless, it was Miguel's hair, just as Rafael's eyes were Miguel's eyes, midnight velvet as they swerved toward Pamela with curiosity at first, then, realizing who she was, with definite hostility.

She could feel his hostility. Dolores had been hostile in her own way, but her reaction had been conditioned by sophistication and civility. Rafael had no such camou-flage. He let his feelings blaze with white-hot heat.

Carmen seemed oblivious to this. "Ah, there you are, Pamelita," she said cheerfully. "You have not, I think, met Miguel's son? Here, Rafael, is the chance to prac-tice your English. Rafael already has three years of En-glish in school."

Pamela waited for Miguel's son to say something to her. Instead, he muttered something in fast-paced Span-ish to Carmen.

Carmen shook her head. "Rafael pretends that he can read some English, but cannot say anything," Carmen reported. "Foolish *muchacho*, come and speak! If I can try, so can you."

A derisive smile crossed Rafael's handsome face. "I am very pleased to meet you, *señorita*," he told Pamela, his manner of exaggerating each syllable purposely be-traying the platitude.

Carmen glared at Rafael impatiently, and Pamela was sure that she'd caught the vibes emanating from this hostile young version of Miguel. She tried to offset the impression the boy was making by saying quickly, "I'm very pleased to meet you, Rafael." *Take the bull by the horns,* she decided. "Your father has spoken a great deal about you," she informed him.

She flinched from the look of disdain on Rafael's face. "How remarkable," he drawled, and Pamela had the sudden conviction that his English was a lot better than he was letting on.

She wondered if Miguel ever spoke English with his son. Miguel was so fluent that he'd make an excellent teacher. But Pamela was not about to ask this, or any other awkward question. She was not about to ask any questions at all!

She let her eyes wander to the pitcher half-full of milk in front of Rafael, an empty glass, and a plate of cookies. As she watched, he reached for a cookie and took a bite, his dark eyes never leaving her face. His expression was now impossible to read, but Pamela felt as if she'd been put on a glass slide under a microscope.

"Rafael has brought a message from Dolores," Carmen said, a little too loudly. "Dolores wishes us to come for *comida* at the Rivero house on Sunday, after mass. I hope that will be agreeable to you, Pamelita."

Pamela sought desperately for an excuse, and could think of only one. "I really should be going back to Las Palmas before Sunday, Carmen," she said hastily.

Carmen looked aghast. "But you have not even begun your studies here!" she protested. "Also, we have an excellent *biblioteca*—a library, that is to say—and there you will find many things to help you, I am sure."

Pamela smiled ruefully. "I'm afraid all the information will be in Spanish," she said, "and although I would like very much to learn your language, I can't do it that quickly! In Las Palmas, when I come across something in Spanish, either Juan or Grace can translate for me."

"And so Miguel could translate for you here," Carmen stated promptly. "Perhaps Rafael, too, could be of assistance."

She spoke to Rafael in Spanish, but his response was obviously negative. Carmen frowned, then said, "Certainly you must not go by Sunday, Pamelita. A few more days, I beg you."

Pamela was touched by Carmen's sincerity, and felt color rushing to her cheeks. "I appreciate your hospitality more than I can say, Carmen. Of course I'll stay, if you really want me to."

Carmen nodded, temporarily satisfied. She spoke in Spanish again to Rafael, then said to Pamela, "I have told Rafael to tell Dolores that we will be pleased to accept her invitation. So, that is good."

Rafael finished his cookie, and left a few minutes later through a kitchen door that opened onto a back alley. But not before he listened in silence to a series of small speeches by Carmen, all of which sounded like admonitions.

When the door had thudded behind him, Carmen sighed. "He is my godchild, you know, and I love him very much. He is a wonderful boy, but he has in him this..."

Carmen shrugged eloquently. "Ah, *Dios*," she complained, "I must improve my English or you must learn Spanish! So many things I want to tell you, I cannot find the words to say. With Rafael...he is a good boy, but he is also bad, do you know what I mean?"

Pamela considered this, then shook her head. "Not really," she admitted.

Carmen tapped her temple, and then said, "He has within him hatred, because of many things. This is bad, like a poison, like illness. Dolores is not good with him, so I try to speak to him, but I do not think he hears me. As for Miguel..."

Pamela waited and finally Carmen said, "As for Miguel, I love him too. But I do not think he is much of a father."

Chapter Nine

As she dressed for *comida* early Sunday afternoon, Pamela was suffering a bad attack of the jitters. Fortunately, she'd brought relatively few clothes with her to Arucas, otherwise selecting what to wear would have been even more traumatic than it already was.

Dolores would undoubtedly drape herself in unrelieved black. On the other hand, Carmen, now that she'd decided to dispense with the trappings of widowhood, headed off for mass looking like a well-dressed parrot.

Although Pamela didn't want to fade into the woodwork in Miguel's house, she did want to be relatively inconspicuous. She chose a beige silk skirt with a matching overblouse, and added accessories of a similar tone. The effect was monochromatic, subdued, but attractively so. She wore her lovely emerald pendant again, suspended on its fine gold chain, and the emerald ring her mother had given her. The finishing touch came in the form of discreet gold earrings, fashioned in the shapes of small flowers.

Carmen returned home after mass, freshened her makeup and, without further ado, was ready to leave again. Pamela had no idea where Miguel's house was, but she suspected it might be reasonably close by. Carmen, however, drove swiftly to the outskirts of Arucas, flew past the distillery, and then took a road that started straight up Arucas mountain, but soon veered sharply to the right.

This road led to another, which led to yet another, this one dirt. It would have been a total maze had the area been thickly forested. As it was, Pamela could see for miles in most directions; soon the sea was visible, not nearly as far away as she would have guessed.

Miguel's house was on a high plateau. The land appeared to have been leveled to make room for it, but this was just another unusual contour of the Canary Islands.

Miguel's house? He owned not a house, but a veritable estate. Bananas were growing on both sides of the approach until it crested onto the plateau. With the appearance of a different crop, Carmen explained, "Tobacco. Miguel is—how do you say it?—he is experimenting."

Miguel's hacienda loomed in the middle of the planted fields. The high, whitewashed wall they were nearing was only one side of what appeared to be a large square or rectangle. In response to Carmen's beep, a solid gate swung open, revealing a wide cobblestoned courtyard with a long garage on the right. Ahead, there was an elaborate wrought iron gate in the center of a slightly lower wall. Through the grillwork, Pamela could see another courtyard where exotic tropical flowers flourished in abundance alongside various species of cactus and other bushes and plants she was not familiar with.

The house itself was beyond this courtyard, and centered by a magnificent golden pine door which, Pamela suspected, was fashioned from the original native wood. The manservant who had evidently been watching for their arrival, and had opened first the outer gate and then the inner one, went ahead to open the golden door. As she passed through, Pamela stepped into a scene of incredible beauty.

The central patio was exceptionally exquisite. The figure of a mermaid dominated a fountain that was tiled in shades of blues and greens and turquoise and aqua, each tile a work of art. But no water flowed from the fountain. Instead, more vivid flowers had been planted all around the statue's base. Obviously, the statue had been built before the island's water problem had become so acute.

The patio was tiled in varying earth tones, thus creating an unexpected affinity, as if earth and water were being tied together. Clusters of chairs and tables were grouped around the patio, and Pamela had the impression that the area was occupied during most of each day.

Transfixed by her surroundings, Pamela was brought back to reality by Carmen's greeting someone in Spanish. Then she saw Miguel emerging from the shadows, slowly approaching them.

Ordinarily, Miguel did not do things slowly and, as she watched him, it struck Pamela that he was not looking forward to this *comida*. In fact, she had a funny feeling that he dreaded it as much as she did. She wished that Dolores hadn't invited her.

Miguel was wearing slim black trousers, a crisp white shirt, a narrow black necktie, and a burgundy jacket. He looked terrific . . . but very, very Spanish and suddenly, very alien. Until that moment, Miguel had never seemed "foreign" to Pamela. Now he did, and she felt less than comfortable as he held out his hand and offered the traditional Spanish greeting, *"Es su casa."*

Pamela mumbled something in reply, and then spotted Dolores—tall and regal and clad from head to foot in black.

Dolores murmured more polite words, to which Carmen and Pamela murmured polite responses. Then Dolores led them to a table near the fountain, and a properly uniformed maid brought glasses of dry sherry on a beautiful old silver tray.

The conversation was principally in Spanish and, though she understood little of what was being said, Pamela sensed that tension was in the air. She wondered where Rafael was, and just then he appeared. He was wearing an outfit almost exactly like his father's, except that his jacket was very dark green. He bowed over the ladies' hands and said the right things, but there was a sardonic gleam in his eyes as he greeted Pamela, then dropped her hand as quickly as if her skin had scorched him.

Her situation was difficult at best, but especially so when Rafael's dislike was more than obvious, at least to her. Pamela wished she knew why he disliked her so much, but could think of no logical reason. No obvious one, anyway, unless he harbored anti-American feelings she knew nothing about—or unless someone had implanted ideas about her in his mind. That someone, Pamela thought ruefully, could only be Dolores.

It was easier to understand why she plainly wasn't Dolores's favorite person. Dolores had a definite position in this household, and Pamela had no doubt that she in-

GIVE YOUR HEART TO SILHOUETTE

FREE!

Mail this heart today!

AND WE'LL GIVE YOU
4 FREE BOOKS,
A FREE FOLDING UMBRELLA
AND A FREE MYSTERY GIFT!

SEE INSIDE!

❧ IT'S A ❧

SILHOUETTE HONEYMOON

A SWEETHEART

OF A FREE OFFER!

FOUR NEW SILHOUETTE SPECIAL EDITION NOVELS—FREE!

Take a "Silhouette Honeymoon" with four exciting romances—yours FREE from Silhouette Special Edition. Each of these hot-off-the-press novels brings you all the passion and tenderness of today's greatest love stories…your free passport to a bright new world of love and adventure! But wait…there's <u>even more</u> to this great offer!

SILHOUETTE FOLDING UMBRELLA— ABSOLUTELY FREE!

You'll love your Silhouette umbrella. Its bright color will cheer you up on even the gloomiest day. It's made of rugged nylon to last for years— and so compact (folds to 15") you can carry it in your purse or briefcase. Take it to work…shopping…vacations. This folding umbrella is yours free with this offer.

SPECIAL EXTRAS—FREE!

You'll get your free monthly newsletter, packed with news on your favorite writers, upcoming books, even recipes from your favorite authors.

MONEY-SAVING HOME DELIVERY!

Send for your Silhouette Special Edition novels and enjoy the <u>convenience</u> of previewing six new books every month, delivered right to your home. Each book is yours for only $1.95—55¢ less per book than what you pay in stores! Great savings plus total convenience add up to a sweetheart of a deal for y<u>ou</u>!

START YOUR SILHOUETTE HONEYMOON TODAY— JUST COMPLETE, DETACH & MAIL YOUR FREE OFFER CARD!

SILHOUETTE

SPECIAL EDITION®

FREE OFFER CARD

FREE FOLDING UMBRELLA

PLACE HEART STICKER HERE

FREE HOME DELIVERY!

4 FREE BOOKS

PLUS AN EXTRA BONUS MYSTERY GIFT!

☐ YES! Please send me my four SILHOUETTE SPECIAL EDITION novels, free, along with my free Folding Umbrella and Mystery Gift! Then send me six SILHOUETTE SPECIAL EDITION novels every month, as they come off the presses, and bill me just $1.95 per book (55¢ less than retail), with no extra charges for shipping and handling. If I am not completely satisfied, I may return a shipment and cancel at any time. The free books, Folding Umbrella and Mystery Gift remain mine to keep!

CHS027

NAME _____
(please print)

ADDRESS _____ APT. _____

CITY _____

STATE _____ ZIP _____

Terms and prices subject to change. Your enrollment is subject to acceptance by Silhouette Books.
SILHOUETTE SPECIAL EDITION is a registered trademark.

PRINTED IN U.S.A.

BUSINESS REPLY MAIL

FIRST CLASS PERMIT NO. 194 CLIFTON, N.J.

Postage will be paid by addressee

Silhouette Books
120 Brighton Road
P.O. Box 5084
Clifton, NJ 07015-9956

NO POSTAGE
NECESSARY
IF MAILED
IN THE
UNITED STATES

tended to defend it with everything at her command. Any woman in whom her brother appeared interested would certainly be suspect. Juan and Grace had both insisted that Miguel was interested in her, and Carmen had concurred in this, so what could be more normal than for her to have discussed the matter with Dolores, who supposedly was her best friend?

They were summoned to the midday meal, served in a magnificent, but very formal dining room. Portraits of ancestors, similar to those in Carmen's house, adorned the walls. Sneaking glances at them, Pamela tried to confirm a resemblance between Miguel and his haughty forebears. Miguel was just as aristocratic looking, and could probably look just as aloof. But there were laugh lines at the corner of his eyes and a manifest sense of humor that made him seem very different from these men.

Just now, though, there was nothing humorous in the least about Miguel Rivero y Fonte, at least not ostensibly. He presided at the head of his table with meticulous correctness, and was a considerate host, displaying impeccable manners. Pamela decided that he should give up banana growing, regardless of necessity, and go into the diplomatic corps. Certainly, he could do great things for Spain.

The *comida* finished not with *flan*, but with chocolate ice cream, and the sight and taste of the dessert evoked a sharp pang of nostalgia in Pamela. She hadn't consciously missed the States since leaving Kennedy Airport. But then she hadn't felt herself such a stranger in a strange land until today.

Homesickness, and a sense of personal uncertainty quite unlike anything she'd ever known, persisted as Pamela followed the others back out to the patio where coffee was served, black and sweet.

"Dolores would prefer coffee in the drawing room, but it's too much of a morgue, especially in the middle of the afternoon," Miguel managed to say softly into Pamela's ear, as he held her chair for her. She glanced up at him quickly and, to her astonishment, saw those telltale fireflies dancing in his dark eyes. His mouth twisted in a brief grin, then he said, again for her ears alone, "Hang in there."

Hang in there. Pamela nearly choked and, at that moment, happened to glance across the table, and met Rafael's eyes. Something stirred in those dark depths, so like his father's. Curiosity? Surprise? At least Rafael didn't appear hostile.

Coffee finished, Miguel suddenly asked, "Would you perhaps like to see the rest of the house?"

"Yes, very much," she answered quickly.

"Then if you will allow me..."

Pamela felt painfully self-conscious as Miguel led her onto the stone path that followed the patio's perimeter, from which doors opened into various rooms.

The drawing room was even more formal than the dining room. The furnishings were all exquisite antiques, and there wasn't a single objet d'art or painting that wasn't worth its weight in gold. Because of the incipient problems with the banana crop, Pamela had assumed that Miguel might not have much money to spare. This glimpse of his estate was rapidly changing her mind about that. From everything she could see, Miguel Rivero was a very wealthy man.

There was a library-study off one side of the drawing room, furnished with comfortable, upholstered chairs and a plush couch.

"Often, I sleep here," Miguel volunteered, "when I work late, which seems to be more and more frequently.

Sometimes I am too lazy to go upstairs to bed. My bedroom upstairs is very large. And...very lonely.''

He said this so deliberately that Pamela caught her breath. What was he trying to tell her? Was he trying to tell her anything? Except, perhaps, that since his wife had left him he'd been a lonely man.

Anita. Now and then Pamela had visions of this mysterious Spanish woman whose whereabouts, indeed whose fate was unknown...and who also had caused Miguel untold anguish. More than ten years had passed since she'd run off with Miguel's partner and best friend. Ten years in which Rafael had grown from a small boy, suddenly deprived of his mother's love, to a boy at the edge of manhood who was apparently crippled by resentment.

Pamela wondered if Anita had been beautiful, and was sure she must have been, probably in the classic Spanish style that Goya had painted so well. She visualized the perfect couple Miguel and Anita must have made and was stabbed by a shot of pure jealousy—quintessentially childish jealousy.

But...I love him, damn it, she thought then, nearly speaking the words aloud into the sudden stillness. "Love" had almost entered her vocabulary once before in connection with Miguel and herself. Now more than ever, she knew this love was true.

Miguel said softly, "I watch your face, and all I know is that I would give anything within my power to read your mind. So many expressions, *querida*...and yet you say so little. I find myself wishing you spoke Spanish because, when all is said and done, only in my own language could I possibly express to you everything I want to say, everything I want you to know. Oh my God, Pamelita, it is hell to know that you are here in Arucas . . . so near to me and yet so incredibly far away. A hundred times I have nearly picked up the phone to call you. At least a dozen times I actually walked out of my office, intending to simply go to Carmen's house, and find you, and take you in my arms and somehow, somehow, make it right between us. And yet, how can I?''

The agony in Miguel's voice twisted Pamela's heart. He had turned away from her, averting his face as he stared out the window of his study toward the patio, where Carmen and Dolores still sat sipping coffee. Rafael had vanished.

When Miguel spoke, the words seemed torn from him. ''Ever since the other afternoon I have been tormented beyond reason. I had no *right* to . . . to love you as I did, Pamelita. A legal right, yes. Legally, I am free, I told you that. But a moral right . . . no. Can you possibly know what I'm saying? Can you possibly understand that as long as there remains a chance in a million that Anita could suddenly walk into this house, I cannot be free. I . . .''

Pamela saw his mouth tighten painfully, saw him wince. She knew that in another second, she would not be able to resist enfolding him in her arms, despite everything he was saying. She yearned to express verbally the physical gift she'd shared with him on their hillside the other day, a commitment deeper than any she'd ever made before, or ever would again.

But he turned, forced a smile, and said, ''Come on, we must shake this mood. It's no good for either of us. Anyway, you must see the view we have from upstairs.''

The staircase, with its intricate wrought iron railing, curved gently upward from the ground floor. At the top, a balcony ran around three sides of the hacienda, overlooking the patio below.

"The servants' quarters are at the back," Miguel said. "Dolores has her apartment over there," he added, pointing, "where there are also two guest rooms. Rafael and I have our bedrooms on this side, with a sitting room in between."

He was leading her into his own bedchamber. It was the perfect word for this classical room, Pamela decided, with its heavy antique furniture, tall windows, and red velvet draperies tied back with thick gold cord.

The bed was an enormous four-poster, complete with canopy. "It looks like it must have belonged to a Spanish king," Pamela ventured.

"It was brought from Spain," Miguel conceded. "I believe my great-grandfather imported it, a long time ago, to be sure."

At the window, he drew back the draperies and said, "Take a look, Pamelita."

She gazed out upon a vista even lovelier than the one they'd had from their hillside the other day. She could see the ocean, the whitewashed houses of Arucas, and the spires of the massive Gothic cathedral. It was late afternoon, and the sunlight was casting a deep golden glow, burnishing everything it touched.

"It's so lovely," Pamela said softly. "So lovely." Then she felt Miguel behind her, felt his arms steal around her waist, felt his breath warm upon her cheek as he turned her around.

Instinctively, she flung her arms around his neck, and their lips came passionately together. When the kiss ended, Pamela was breathless. Then, lifting her face slightly, she peered over Miguel's shoulder, knowing she'd sensed a presence. She saw Rafael standing in the doorway, staring at them.

An instant later, it was as if she'd witnessed a mirage. Rafael disappeared so soundlessly that it was difficult to believe she'd actually seen him at all.

If she'd stiffened at that telltale instant, Miguel had evidently been sufficiently lost not to notice. He said huskily, "We had better go back downstairs, *querida*." Pamela could only nod.

Taking one last glimpse of the view from his window, she wondered if she should tell him about Rafael, but she held her tongue.

Carmen chatted volubly on the drive back, and there was no need for Pamela to say much in return. Carmen was mixing her Spanish and English, and some of what she was saying was unintelligible. But the fact came through, clearly enough, that Carmen was thoroughly annoyed with Dolores de Avero.

"She can be a very rude woman," Carmen stated firmly as Porfirio let them in the house, and then drove Carmen's car into the garage for the night. "I apologize for the way she behaved toward you, Pamelita."

"But there's no need for that," Pamela protested. "Dolores hasn't been rude to me. Cool, perhaps, but not rude."

"In my opinion, she has been miserable," Carmen insisted. "She does not even attempt to speak to you except for the tiniest sentence now and then. I think Miguel, he was also very annoyed at her." Carmen shrugged. "It is her loss, of course. If she keeps going like this, she will be a very lonely, very unhappy old lady."

Having made this prophecy, Carmen suggested they both have a glass of wine with some cheese and crackers. Pamela, so nervous she'd merely picked at the delicious meal at Miguel's house, agreed readily.

Carmen's house, though lovely, was not half as imposing as the Rivero residence. Pamela felt at home here, absolutely comfortable as she and Carmen sipped their wine. She wondered if she could ever feel half as comfortable in Miguel's house, with or without Dolores around. Not that she was likely to find out! Also, Carmen was a friend. It was doubtful that the day would ever come when she could hope to consider Dolores de Avero in the same light.

The next morning, Pamela resolved to get down to some business of her own and, while Carmen bustled around attending to a number of housekeeping details with Conchita and Porfirio, she sat out in the patio and started making notes about the various things she'd already seen and heard that related to her project.

She didn't expect to hear from Miguel for a while, if he followed his usual pattern. So it was a surprise when he telephoned late that afternoon.

"I have decided that before you suddenly make up your mind to return to Las Palmas, there are some things you must see," he announced. "So tomorrow I want you to go to Agaete with me."

"Agaete?" Pamela echoed.

"A small seaport directly across the island from Las Palmas," Miguel explained. "You'll definitely want to bring a bathing suit. The drive takes a couple of hours, so shall I pick you up about ten?"

"If Carmen has nothing planned..." Pamela hedged.

"Do you wish me to speak to her?"

"No, no," she said quickly. "If there's any conflict I'll call you back."

There wasn't any conflict, nor had she expected there would be. Nevertheless, Pamela gave every thought to inventing one. She was torn by the idea of again spending the better part of a day with Miguel. The chemistry between them was so volatile. But beyond the chemistry, her love for him deepened each time they were together; when the time came for them to part, it would be so incredibly hard, so emotionally awful that she dreaded even thinking about it.

Still, she couldn't say no to him.

Once again, they started forth on a perfect day, and as they drove across the northern end of the island, Pamela had to concede that Miguel was right. Speaking purely from a professional point of view, this was something she had to see.

The road snaked back and forth across the precipitous landscape, with treacherous hairpin turns. More than once, Miguel honked as he rounded a turn to find another car stopped, hugging the side of the road. There were very few guardrails to stop them from going over the edge, and the drops were often a long, long way down.

In this part of Gran Canaria, the evidence of many years of drought was terribly apparent.

"Look," Miguel said, as they approached a high vantage point. "Do you see those depressions scattered about down there, some of them round, some rectangular?"

"You mean those things that look like oversized swimming pools?" Pamela asked, pointing.

"They are water storage pools. If you got close enough to them, you would see that they are anything but full, and what water there is, is dull green and brackish. Not what you would call potable."

At another spot, Pamela gazed down into a ravine. "I don't see how anyone can grow bananas or anything else on terrain as steep as that."

"Each terrace is fortified with either stone or brick. Every inch of soil that can possibly be utilized is. And the bananas are protected."

"What about harvesting them?"

He grinned. "It helps to be half goat."

Houses, too, were often built on incredibly steep slopes. Most had the familiar flat roof topped with several cisterns. The rainwater was obviously used for clothes washing; clothes flapped in the breeze on several rooftops.

"How do those people get in and out of their houses?" Pamela asked. "There doesn't seem to be any access to or from this road."

"They travel on back roads, more like paths." Miguel pointed to a narrow, winding lane far below them. "See, it goes back over that stone bridge in the distance, and comes out...somewhere."

"It must be like doubling around Robin Hood's barn all the time," Pamela mused.

"I beg your pardon?" Miguel murmured politely.

"Do you mean to tell me I've finally used a slang phrase you don't recognize? It means going around in circles, actually. Or way out of one's way. Or..."

"Okay, okay," Miguel protested, smiling. "I get the point."

At another place, the road traversed an ancient stone bridge in front of an enormous dam.

"You will want to take a good look at this," Miguel advised. "It is, I think, the largest dam on Grand Canary, but as you will see, there is practically no water in the reservoir."

Peering down, Pamela saw that there was actually thick vegetation growing up the sides of the dam, dra-

matizing the enormity of the water problem as nothing
else had thus far.

"It's terrible," she muttered bitterly. "Really terrible."

"Yes, it is," Miguel agreed. "But we have had the
problem for a long time, Pamelita, and the people have
learned to live with it, to cope. Currently, there is a rainfall of only five or six inches a year," he went on. "Until
perhaps thirty or forty years ago, it was more like thirty-
five inches. So, the condition has been getting worse and
worse, obviously, which is why the future is so bleak for
banana export.

"However," Miguel added deliberately, "do you
know, my beautiful *señorita*, that when I am with you I
really don't give a damn about rainfall or bananas, or
much of anything else. I just want to be with you, Pamelita, and relax and forget that there are problems. On
another occasion, we can duplicate this ride mile by mile
and stop and take pictures along the way, and I will delve
into every aspect of Grand Canary's water shortage with
you. But for today, *querida* . . ."

"I think I get the message," Pamela told him, and
leaned back, letting herself bask in the mesmerizing glow
of his charm.

Along the hillsides, red geraniums and magnificent
bougainvillea vines bloomed, and cactus was everywhere. In the small towns, distances between streets and
ravines were too narrow to permit the more traditional
Spanish architecture, so most of the houses had balconies, lined with pots of flowers. Sometimes, there were
small patches outside the houses where roses and calla
lilies were growing. Generally speaking, though, the land
was extremely arid, and very barren.

"We are not going to stop in Agaete," Miguel said after a time, "but go on to Puerto de las Nieves, a little fishing village nearby. You did wear a bathing suit, as I suggested?"

"Yes. Right under my dress, *señor*."

"Stop giving me visions, Pamelita, or I'm apt to drive off the side of the road," Miguel protested.

Agaete was a pretty town, about the size of Arucas. And just beyond it, they came to Puerto de las Nieves. Pamela fell in love with the little fishing village at first sight, and was enchanted by the beach. The sand was black, edged with chunks of porous black rock.

"If you needed anything to convince you that the Canaries are volcanic, this should do it," Miguel told her.

For the next hour they sunned on the beach, using giant towels Miguel had brought along, and splashed together in the crystal-clear waters.

They were as giddy as two children on vacation as they capered in the water. "To anyone watching," Pamela yelled to Miguel, breathless, "we must look like a couple of porpoises."

They were walking back toward the spot where they'd left their towels and, gazing down at her, Miguel said, "You share my love for the water, and I am glad of that. Each time I find something for which we both have an affinity—aside from each other—it helps to balance the differences."

Pamela looked up at him, suddenly serious. "You feel that there are so many differences, Miguel?"

He nodded. "So many differences, Pamelita. But I was never one to refuse a challenge," he added, grinning.

After they had dried in the sun, they slipped on their clothes and wandered up the beach to a small restaurant that jutted out over the sand. They ate fresh fish, caught offshore just that morning, spread unsalted butter on chunks of thick, warm bread, and washed everything down with cool Spanish beer.

Sighing, Pamela said, "How much closer to heaven could anyone get?"

When Miguel didn't answer her immediately, she glanced up to see his dark eyes glistening with suspicious moisture. "I will never forget hearing you say that," he said huskily.

When she started to speak, he held up a cautioning finger, "Please," he urged, "don't say anything else, Pamelita. I want to preserve this moment . . ."

Tears filled Pamela's eyes. Swept by emotion, she acceded to Miguel's request and didn't say anything else. Not that she didn't want to, she just couldn't.

Chapter Ten

Dolores was waiting at Carmen's house when Pamela and Miguel got back to Arucas. She was pacing the length of the *sala*, while Carmen sat on the lovely old French sofa in the drawing room and watched her, plainly provoked.

When she saw Miguel and Pamela, Carmen rose quickly and cornered them while Dolores was still at the far end of the room.

"Your sister is insane," Carmen said tersely, speaking in English so that there would be no doubt about Pamela's understanding. "She came here about an hour ago raving that Rafael had disappeared. She is sure he has been kidnapped."

With this, Carmen's English deserted her, and she broke into agitated Spanish. Dolores was white and tight-lipped as she approached her brother.

She refrained from speaking until Carmen had come to the sputtering end of a sentence, though the effort this was costing her was obvious. Then she drew herself up to her full height and spoke in a voice so cold that it sent shivers coursing up and down Pamela's spine.

Miguel listened expressionlessly, his mouth drawn in a thin line. Then he spoke swiftly. To Pamela's surprise, he swung around to her and said, "Go find Porfirio and tell him to bring in some Scotch and a pitcher of ice water, will you, Pamelita? At this point, we all need a stiff drink before we decide what to do."

Pamela didn't pause to look for the bell rope by which she could summon Porfirio. Instead, she headed directly for the kitchen, glad to escape the scene in the *sala*. She found Porfirio and Conchita relaxing at the kitchen table, indulging in coffee and cake.

Porfirio quickly got to his feet, and Pamela carefully relayed Miguel's message using a mixture of words and sign language. As she finished speaking, she realized, with surprise, that she had spoken partly in Spanish. The language was beginning to rub off on her!

She returned to the drawing room to find Dolores positioned on the couch that Carmen had previously occupied. Carmen and Miguel were sitting in chairs at opposite ends of the couch. Miguel immediately got up, waved Pamela to take his seat, then took his place on the couch, moving as far away from his sister as he could get.

After a moment, Porfirio appeared with a full tray. Miguel asked him to set it on the coffee table in front of the couch. He did so then discreetly withdrew.

Miguel poured Scotch for all, lacing each glass with varying proportions of ice water. When Dolores protested as he handed her a drink, he said sharply, "Take it, you need it.'' He spoke in English, and Dolores didn't pretend that she didn't understand.

Noting this, Miguel said dryly, ''My sister has a complex about her linguistic abilities, Pamelita. She fears her English will seem very inadequate to you, and so she shies away from using it. In reality, Dolores does quite well with your language. Her late husband studied in the States, dealt with many English people in his business, and insisted that Dolores be able to keep up her end of the conversation when he invited these people to his house. So, I'm asking that from now on we converse in English, so you'll know what we're talking about. Slowly, for Carmen's sake... though I must congratulate you, Carmen. Already, since you have been practicing with Pamela, I have noticed a decided improvement.''

Carmen beamed, but Dolores literally glowered at her brother, then looked away, her head held high.

Ignoring this, Miguel continued, ''It seems that Dolores went to church this afternoon and, when she returned home, our man Ignacio, who has a position akin to Porfirio's, informed her that Rafael had not slept in his room last night, and apparently had been gone since some time last evening.

''Dolores seldom sees Rafael during the day. He is at school, and she does not arise until he has left the house. In the afternoon, once Rafael is home, Dolores is often engaged in church work, or is attending a service. Thus, they usually meet for dinner in the evening. When I can, I join them.''

Miguel drew a deep breath. ''Ignacio,'' he said, ''suggested that Rafael spent the night with a classmate, and hoped that his failure to return home would not be noticed. It was a foolish hope, of course. Ignacio's wife— her name is Maruca—normally makes up the bedrooms, and it was she who found Rafael's bed undisturbed, and reported this to Ignacio. He, in turn, told Dolores, who promptly became very upset, certain that Rafael was kidnapped by alleged enemies of mine. She rushed over here, thinking she would find me here—courting you," Miguel finished, the irony of the last two words sounding as heavy as if they'd been cast in lead.

He raised his eyebrows and grimaced, deliberately looking like an expert satirist.

Pamela had to fight the impulse to laugh; it would have been entirely the wrong response, given the circumstances. Instead, she asked evenly, "Do you think Rafael has been kidnapped, Miguel?"

"Of course not. I think Rafael spent the night somewhere, maybe with a certain male classmate of his, maybe with a girl. Who knows? Rafael, I admit, can be recalcitrant—excuse me, Carmen," he amended, bowing slightly in her direction. "What I mean to say is that Rafael is beginning to feel *muy macho*. He sometimes thinks he is far older and more experienced than he is, although this may not be the first time he has failed to sleep in his own bed, *hermana mia*," he finished, addressing this last remark to Dolores.

She began to speak in Spanish, but Miguel cut her off. "English, if you please," he remonstrated firmly.

"Very well," Dolores said icily. "For your information, I am certain this is definitely the first time Rafael has not occupied his own bed . . . unless I knew he would be elsewhere with friends."

Dolores's English was excellent, and now Pamela could understand Miguel's and Carmen's annoyance with her for having been so stubborn. But that, she was sure, had nothing to do with Dolores's alleged shyness about her ability with the language. She simply hadn't wanted to communicate with Pamela.

"So, you have ordered someone to make a bed check every morning?" Miguel asked archly.

"I beg your pardon?" his sister shot back, and Pamela decided Dolores honestly didn't understand her brother's use of the idiom, in this instance.

"I think you know what I'm implying, Dolores," Miguel said. "Have you always made certain that Rafael slept in his bed?"

"Maruca, or one of the others, would have reported to me," Dolores insisted.

"Maybe, maybe not." Miguel shrugged. "It doesn't matter, particularly. What does matter, I think, is that we *don't* call the police, as you evidently have been insisting to Carmen that we should. First I would like to know...does Rafael ever bring any friends home? When I'm not there, I mean?"

Dolores shook her head negatively.

"Can you think of the names of any friends? Anyone he has mentioned?"

"I know, through the church, that he attends school with the sons of several prominent local families," Dolores conceded. "The Zermeños, the Castillos, the Herreras, to name a few."

"Then I will call those people and ask if Rafael has been at their homes."

Dolores sat up very straight. "Please, no!" she said insistently. "You will create more scandal if you call those families than if you call the *policia*. They will know for certain, then, that Rafael is in trouble."

"And why is that?" Miguel asked sardonically.

"Because one should know where one's own child is," Dolores said succinctly.

Pamela was almost afraid to look at Miguel. When she did, she was certain that he was counting to ten in English, in Spanish, and perhaps in a few other languages as well. Finally he got to his feet and said, his voice tightly controlled, "Very well, Dolores. I will go out myself and visit a few places around town. And maybe I will ask a few questions along the way of people who are not particularly important in the social scheme. All right?"

Saying this, Miguel turned on his heel and left the room without a backward glance. After a few silent seconds, Carmen moved to the chair he had vacated, and said, "Give me your glass, Dolores."

"What?" Dolores asked blankly, staring after her brother.

"Your glass! You too, Pamelita. We can all do with another drink," Carmen decided.

Time passed, slowly, awkwardly, anxiously. Hours and hours, it felt like to Pamela. Porfirio appeared every now and then to ask if anyone wanted something to eat. A sandwich, or maybe some hot soup?

He spoke Spanish with such solicitude that even Pamela was able to understand almost every word.

Finally, Conchita came in with a tureen of soup, a basket of rolls, soup plates, spoons and napkins. She arranged everything on the coffee table, and politely withdrew after Carmen indicated she'd serve the food herself.

There was no doubt they needed something hot in their stomachs. The soup was perfect for the occasion, and delicious into the bargain. But Pamela had never had less of an appetite. She had no wish to get drunk on the Scotch, though, so she forced herself to eat.

Porfirio had just removed the soup plates when Miguel telephoned. Conchita took the call, and came into the room to relay Miguel's message.

She spoke swiftly, and Pamela couldn't follow what she said. But as soon as she left the room, Carmen said quickly, "It is all right, Pamelita. Miguel found Rafael in a local bar, where he should not be at all. It is a place where there have been drug problems, gambling, all sorts of things. Anyway, Miguel has taken Rafael home. He is there now, a bit *borracho*—drunk, that is—but otherwise unharmed."

Dolores roused herself from the reverie she'd dropped into—Scotch-induced to a point, Pamela imagined—and got up rather shakily. "I must get back," she said, in English.

Carmen spoke to her in Spanish, but Dolores refused to stay. A minute later she left, her back ramrod straight as she walked out the door, totally forgetting, whether by accident or design, to say good-night to Pamela in either English or Spanish.

Carmen saw Dolores off, then returned looking thoroughly disgruntled. "Why I am fond of that woman I do not understand!" she exclaimed. "Poor Miguel! He has had nothing but trouble. First that woman he had to marry..."

Had to marry? Pamela stared at Carmen, wondering if this was Carmen's faulty English or if Carmen meant exactly what she'd said. But Carmen, amazingly enough, was reaching for what was left of the Scotch and pouring herself one last drink. Her thoughts were already elsewhere, so the question would have to wait.

It was at some point during the sleepless night that followed that Pamela realized it was time to get back to Las Palmas.

She told Carmen this as they lingered over their breakfast *café con leche* and finished the last of some pastries Conchita had brought back from the little town of Moya, on a visit to her family there. Moya was famous throughout the island both for the quality of its pastries, and for the exquisite embroidery done by the local women, their techniques passed down from generation to generation.

Carmen vigorously protested Pamela's decision, then said discerningly, "You wish to do this because of last night, do you not? Because of Miguel's problem with Rafael, and the way Dolores behaves to you?"

"Partly, Carmen," Pamela admitted honestly. "But not entirely. I don't know how long I can stay here in the Canaries, and it really is necessary for me to get started on my thesis."

"And you have learned nothing here?" Carmen asked, arching her eyebrows in disbelief.

Pamela had learned a great deal here in Arucas, but a disproportionate amount had nothing to do with hydrology. Even so, the mute evidence of the dried-up reservoir, the near-empty water storage pools, the arid land, had all certainly illuminated her subject matter. These sights were mentally engraved in a way no words could portray.

Right now, though, she needed books. She needed facts, figures, history... and escape. Her studies had offered an escape route before, they would do so again, though she knew it wasn't going to be easy to put Miguel and his problems out of her mind.

Later that morning, Pamela was sitting out in Carmen's patio writing some postcards, when Miguel suddenly appeared. He strode briskly across the courtyard and stopped just short of her table, looming over her like the persistent thunderclouds that so often hovered over the nearby mountains.

"What is this I hear about your leaving?" he demanded.

"Miguel, I'm only going back to Las Palmas," Pamela protested. "You know I need to get on with my work there."

Miguel exhaled sharply, as if he'd been about to explode, then pulled out a chair and sat down next to her, his eyes scanning her face as if he hoped to ferret out hidden messages.

After a moment, he said, "I thought you were going back to the States...immediately! Carmen's translation got mixed up, I guess. Anyway, it really shook me up."

"Carmen told you I was going back to the States?"

"I think so," Miguel said. "She said you were leaving, something about your time running out..."

"She misunderstood me," Pamela said calmly. "You must know I wouldn't do anything like that without telling you myself."

Again, his dark eyes scanned her face. "How can I be sure of that? After last night, how could I blame you for anything you might do?"

Pamela tried to smile, but it was a sorry attempt. "I take it that's a rhetorical question?"

"I've never been entirely sure what a rhetorical question is," Miguel countered. "No, please," as she started to speak, "don't give me a lesson in English semantics just now. I couldn't concentrate, not until I get a grip on myself."

Pamela stared at him curiously. "Are you saying that I'm responsible for your losing your grip on yourself?"

Miguel shook his head slowly, his eyebrows arching devilishly. "Yes, *señorita*," he mocked, "indeed you are responsible. I cope with my business, my sister, my son...but I begin to think that you, *querida mía*, are the straw about to break this camel's back!''

Miguel suddenly got to his feet, and marched toward the far end of the patio, where the kitchen was located. ''Porfirio!'' he shouted. *''Ven aquí!''*

Porfirio appeared quickly, and Miguel addressed him in rapid Spanish. Then he returned, frowning again as he resumed his place at the table. ''I asked him for coffee, and told him to bring coffee for you, too, and some brandy.''

''I'll have coffee,'' Pamela agreed. ''But brandy, no. Not at this hour of the morning.''

''It is already noon,'' Miguel informed her. ''The sun is directly above us. When are you going back to Las Palmas?''

''Tomorrow,'' she said resolutely.

''Then I will drive you,'' he decided firmly. ''I have business in the city. We can leave tomorrow directly after *comida*.''

Carmen looked on dolefully the next morning as Pamela packed. Although Pamela had been assuring her over and over again that this was only a temporary parting, Carmen would not be consoled.

''You will not return here,'' she stated sadly. ''Because of Dolores. *Dios*, that woman!''

''Dolores has nothing to do with it,'' Pamela protested, even though this wasn't entirely true. She didn't relish the thought of coming back to Arucas because of Miguel's sister, but for Carmen's sake, she planned to make another visit before returning to the States. ''Anyway, until my next visit, you can come to Las Palmas. You're making it sound like a million miles away instead of just a few kilometers down the road!''

''Perhaps,'' Carmen conceded. ''Perhaps.''

Miguel appeared as they were about to have dessert, and accepted the offer of a piece of delicious fruit tart and a cup of coffee. Then they headed off, while Carmen stood at the curb, waving until they were out of sight.

Watching Carmen in his rearview mirror, Miguel said, "I think she has fallen in love with you, Pamelita. Does everyone fall in love with you, *querida*?"

"Maybe you can answer that question," Pamela answered impulsively, then wished she'd curbed her tongue.

"Dolores and Rafael, it's to them you are referring, isn't it?" He kept his eyes on the road. "Well, I don't know what to say. They both behaved abominably... as I have told them, believe me."

"You shouldn't have, Miguel," Pamela said quickly. "Anything you say about me will only make matters worse."

"Give me one good reason why I should spare their feelings," he challenged her. "I care for you, I care a great deal for you. Also, you have been a guest not only in my town, but in my own home. I find fault in both cases, damn it, and I am not about to whitewash it!" he finished heatedly.

After a moment of intense silence, he flashed her a dazzling smile. "Let's promise each other something, okay? Let's not talk about business or Dolores or Rafael. Let's just enjoy each other, the beautiful day, the scenery... all right?"

His charm was magnetic. How easily she was mesmerized by Miguel, to the point where she forgot about everyone and everything else!

She was relaxed now, but when they reached the coastal highway, she noticed that Miguel turned north, rather than south toward Las Palmas, and she looked at him questioningly.

"A detour," he said. "A deliberate detour, of course. You are not in any special hurry, are you?"

"No."

"Then there are a couple of things I want to show you. You remember those extinct volcanoes you can see from the *paseo*?"

"Yes."

"Well, Arucas is one of those mountains. Another is at Guia, where we stopped for the flower cheese and bread. Just outside the town there is a big, extinct volcano. See, up ahead there?"

Close up, the volcano looked enormous. "Is there a chance that one day it might erupt again?"

Miguel shrugged. "Volcanoes can be strange," he admitted. "They can appear to be totally extinct, then suddenly erupt. But I don't think there's much danger of that happening here on Grand Canary. Our volcanoes have been inactive for most of five centuries, so it seems unlikely to me that we wouldn't get a warning."

He slowed the car, and pulled off the road at a relatively level spot. "See," he said pointing. "Bananas grow all around the base and way up the sides. They would have been planted right to the top, except that bananas cannot grow above a thousand feet. Anyway, there are more than two million banana trees on that mountain alone. And when you think that there are at least twenty solid kilometers of banana plantations here . . ."

"Are some of these yours?"

"Some." He nodded. "Carmen's husband owned many acres of bananas, too. After he died, Carmen sold them to me. Some are in this area, but most are on the far side of Arucas. I am growing tobacco and sugar cane there now. Sugar for the rum. Gradually, I'm trying to convert to other crops.''

Miguel grinned ruefully. ''And I am the one who said we must not talk about business.''

''It's all very interesting,'' Pamela told him. ''All very new. One day I'd like to learn more about your banana plantation.''

''So you will,'' he promised, ''next time you come to Arucas.''

''There's something else I'd like to see, too,'' Pamela announced.

''Oh? And what might that be?''

''The canaries,'' she said. ''I thought I'd see canaries flying all over the place, but unless I've been missing something...''

Miguel laughed. ''Canaries are native to these islands, and there are plenty of them around, though most are not as golden as the ones you find in pet shops in the States. Still, you will see some. When it comes to names, though, the islands were not named for the birds. The birds were named for the islands.''

''What?''

''That's right.'' He nodded. ''Hundreds and hundreds of years ago, there were large dogs roaming in these islands. When the Romans touched here, about 30 B.C., they came upon these dogs and actually took a couple of them back to Rome with them. So the islands were named after the dogs. The word Canaries comes from the Latin *canis*.''

''Well!'' Pamela said, impressed.

''While we're into history,'' Miguel continued, pulling the car out onto the road, ''I want to take you over to Galdar, the next town. We have our own prehistory, did you know that?''

"Some think the islands are the visible remnants of the lost continent of Atlantis," Pamela remembered.

"Not without reason," Miguel said. "Thousands of years ago, people called the Guanches lived here. Around Guia and Galdar, there are mountain caves that go back to prehistoric times, caves in which the Guanches—who were allegedly tall and blond—lived. There," he said suddenly, again pulling the car over to the roadside. "You see the way the mountainside is hollowed out in spots?"

"All over the place, almost like Swiss cheese!"

"The Guanche caves. Now that you know what to look for, you will see them in many, many places here in the north. Often, farmers use them to shelter their cattle from the intense sun. Some of the larger ones have been modernized, actually wired with electricity so people can live in them comfortably."

"Seriously?"

"Seriously." Miguel pulled out into the road again. "From here, I am going to take you up into the mountains, *querida*, to a charming little inn I discovered by accident one day when I was driving around by myself, with no particular place to go." He hesitated, then added, with a wry laugh, "Oh, hell, I might as well make a complete confession. I have booked a room there for the night."

Pamela sat bolt upright, her eyes widening. *"What?"* she demanded, outraged. "Damn it, Miguel, you had no right to do anything like that without asking me. Anyway, it's out of the question. The Basilios are expecting me in Las Palmas in time for dinner..."

Miguel reached over and pressed a gentle finger against her lips. "On another occasion, you did that to me, remember?" he asked. "Please, Pamelita, before you become too angry with me, I must tell you that I called Juan after you did, and I explained to him there were...things I wanted to show you."

"You told Juan you were taking me up to some...some mountain inn for the night?"

Miguel chuckled. "Well, I didn't exactly put it that way. I was a little more diplomatic. But Juan agreed that they had no major plans for this evening, and said that he and Grace would be happy to see both of us toward dinnertime tomorrow, so..."

Pamela slumped back in her seat. Part of her was really angry with him. He'd been presumptuous to take matters in his own hands, to say the least.

However, the thought of spending the next twenty-four hours with Miguel in a remote inn high in the mountains on this beautiful, strangely mythic island was nothing short of overwhelming.

Miguel's voice sounded strained. "Please...do not ask me to turn back, because if you insist, I will of course do what you want. You should know that I will always attempt to do what you want, Pamelita. The last thing in the world I wish is to force you into anything. But...hear me out, will you?"

When she was silent, he continued huskily, "Once, someone very wise—my grandfather, as it happens—said to me, 'You can never be sure of the next moment. So, when something is really important, the moment must be seized.' I am translating this from the Spanish, *querida*, and it does not sound the same in English. But do you follow me?"

"Yes," Pamela said, her own voice husky. "Yes, I follow you."

"This moment, this small space of time, we are as certain of as we are of anything in life," Miguel said soberly. "But I was afraid that if I asked you to go to the inn with me, you would have said no. Am I not right?"

"Probably," Pamela conceded, thinking of Dolores, of Rafael, and of Miguel's moral loyalty to a woman who might be dead. A woman from whom he was legally free, yet who haunted him every day of his life.

Did he still love Anita?

No, he doesn't, because . . . he loves me! The silent words came to Pamela spontaneously. Overwhelmed, her eyes filled with tears.

Miguel looked away. "Again I have made you unhappy. It is not the first time I have made you unhappy, is it *querida*?" He slipped into Spanish, murmuring to himself, and Pamela would have given everything she possessed to know what he was saying. But then he switched back to English, and said exactly what she wanted to hear.

"I love you," he told her simply. "*Te quiero con toda mi vida, mi alma, mi corazón*. That means I love you with all my life, my soul and my heart. Please, Pamelita . . . will you come with me?"

Chapter Eleven

The inn was small and quaint and very Spanish, with a red tile roof and dazzling white walls. Window boxes lined its facade, overflowing with brilliant red geraniums and pink phlox. The path that curved up the hillside to the entrance was bordered with incredibly beautiful double hibiscus in shades ranging from pure peach to the deepest rose. There were still many pines and deciduous trees growing at this altitude, and the air was fragrant with their scent.

Paradise, Pamela thought, as she and Miguel mounted the steps to the entrance, holding hands. *I've stumbled into paradise.*

And it *was* paradise; time and worries seemed to float away. They spent languorous hours in their spacious room, looking out over valleys and mountains, exploring each other in every possible way. Their physical explorations were sensual beyond belief. Every nuance of touch, of feeling, of tenderness flowered as they came together in the essence of union first during the early evening, then throughout the night. When they awakened the next morning, they turned to each other at once, again bonded by mutual desire.

Between episodes of lovemaking, Miguel and Pamela talked. They talked while they wandered through the forested paths surrounding the inn, and when they shared a wonderful supper in the beautiful dining room. They talked wherever they were, but did not speak of Dolores or Rafael...or Anita. Or of the men who'd played a part in Pamela's life. By unspoken agreement, these controversial subjects were temporarily put on hold. Instead, they talked of all the little things, their likes and dislikes, their habits and hobbies, and came to know each other more intimately every minute.

During siesta the next day, knowing that there would be an interval, no telling how long or short, when they would not be together, they wooed each other with tenderness and a depth of understanding that transcended passion, and took them both into a new dimension. This was caring at its ultimate, Pamela discovered, as they lay in each other's arms, aware that they must get up, pack the few things they'd taken out of their suitcases, and drive back to Las Palmas, to an entirely different existence.

During the drive, they said very little to each other. Miguel seemed deeply preoccupied, and Pamela began to wonder if perhaps they'd been wrong not to discuss Dolores and Rafael, and Anita, too. No doubt doing so would have spoiled this precious time together, so she couldn't be sorry. Problems didn't disappear, and Miguel's problems certainly were not about to disappear.

This hiatus had been just that—an interval, an escape within an escape that she would never forget.

They reached the Basilios' in time to join Grace and Juan in the spillover room for drinks before dinner. Pamela had been away less than two weeks, but it seemed so much longer. She looked around somewhat dazedly, trying to get in touch with her surroundings.

Miguel was charming and pleasant, but—although the others probably didn't notice—there was something lacking in him that night. Pamela was only too aware that at least part of Miguel's mind was already elsewhere. She felt him slipping away as they sipped coffee and brandy in the drawing room later on. To try to reach him just now would be like clutching at an elusive cloud.

She walked down the spiral staircase with Miguel when it came time for him to leave. Suddenly, he was a stranger again as he bent and kissed her. His lips were cool, and the fleeting kiss left her feeling oddly bereft.

"I will call you," he said.

Pamela, who had involuntarily closed her eyes, opened them to hear the door thud behind him. He was gone—in the total sense of the word.

She got up the next morning with new resolve. She would drive herself crazy if she sat around brooding, waiting to hear from Miguel, wondering whether or not he was going to get in touch before he left the city and went back to Arucas. Action was the prescription any good psychologist would have given her, and action was the course she would follow.

Grace was helping Juan with more editing that morning, so Pamela went back to her room after breakfast. She had to unpack from her trip and then planned to get down to some serious research.

It was when she opened the small jewelry case she'd taken with her that she discovered her emerald pendant was missing.

At first, it didn't really occur to her that the pendant was *gone*. She assumed it had just tumbled out among her belongings, so she shook out all her clothes and then felt around the corners of the suitcase, exploring every last inch. But the pendant was definitely gone.

Pamela sat down on the edge of her bed, shocked by this discovery. She'd always known the pendant was valuable. Her mother had had it appraised once, and the jeweler had mentioned at the time that the emeralds were of very fine quality, flawless, in fact.

Her grandmother had died when Pamela was quite young, but she still remembered her vividly. She'd loved her, and every time she wore the pendant she felt that love anew.

The loss was entirely sentimental, as far as she was concerned. She didn't care about the pendant's monetary value. It was something that money could not replace. Angrily, she berated herself for being so careless. She must have dropped it somewhere.

Racking her memory, she distinctly recalled wearing it to Dolores's *comida*. Had she worn it since? She didn't think so. She tried to remember another occasion when she would have worn the pendant.

No matter how many times she mulled this over, she couldn't remember having worn it since *comida* with the Riveros.

Pamela leaned back on the bed and stared at the ceiling. If she'd worn the pendant to the Riveros, then once she got back to Carmen's house she must have taken it off, and left it on top of the dresser, intending to put it away the next morning. But all the other jewelry she'd worn that night was in the case.

There was a chance the pendant had fallen behind the dresser. But that was doubtful. The dresser had been covered with a heavily embroidered cloth. No smooth surfaces from which a pendant and chain could slip.

Shocking as it was, the pendant had most certainly been stolen. The culprit must have been a member of Carmen's household; no one else would have had access to it. Carmen had several servants who seemed to come and go sporadically. But her regulars were Porfirio and Conchita, and a young niece of Conchita's named Esperanza.

Esperanza had usually made Pamela's bed in the morning, and straightened her room and the adjoining bathroom. The girl didn't speak a word of English, but they'd initially communicated well in sign language, and by the time Pamela had left Arucas they were saying a few, very basic words in each other's language.

Pamela thought of Esperanza's lovely young face. The girl had shimmering chestnut hair, deep green eyes, and an exquisite complexion. She was tall, slender, a very graceful girl, and a very obliging one. She'd done everything she could for Pamela, and had made it plain she only wished she could do more. By the end of her stay, Pamela had felt a real affection for her, and decided to buy her a trinket and send it back to her with a note of thanks.

Well, it seemed as though Esperanza had managed to acquire her own trinket.

The whole idea made Pamela sick at heart. She knew that she should talk to Grace about it, and ask Grace to call Carmen in the unlikely event that maybe the pendant really had slid off the dresser, regardless of the embroidered runner. But she was strangely reluctant to talk about the theft, even to Grace.

She knew, only too well, how upset Carmen would be. Esperanza would certainly be dismissed peremptorily, with a black mark against her record. Not that she didn't deserve this, if she really was the culprit. But a nagging doubt lingered in Pamela's mind.

Juan had a luncheon engagement, so Grace ordered sandwiches and iced tea, in lieu of the traditional *comida*. Pamela was grateful for this. She couldn't have managed a hot and heavy meal today. Grace was somewhat preoccupied with her unfinished editing. That was to the good, too. Grace was very perceptive and, under ordinary circumstances, certainly would have noticed that there was something on her guest's mind.

Pamela forced herself to take some books out onto Grace's solarium after lunch, but the words blurred. She kept thinking about Esperanza, and wished she could talk this whole thing over with Miguel.

It occurred to her that she had no telephone number for him, either in Las Palmas or in Arucas. It would be easy enough to ask Juan or Grace for his number, but just now she hardly felt like seeking out either of them.

All day, she kept hoping that Octavia would come to say there was a telephone call for her. But no one came, and no one phoned.

Finally, late that evening, Miguel called, and told her that he'd been completely tied up and, unfortunately, had to get back to Arucas in the morning. Although he promised he would be in touch again very soon, the call was a terrible letdown. It certainly wasn't the moment to bring up the subject of the lost pendant.

Pamela woke up with a sore throat and fever the next morning, and for the next two days spent most of her time in bed. Grace wanted to call a doctor, but Pamela persuaded her not to. She was miserable, but she wasn't that sick. Most of it was due to an emotional low.

By the time she felt really strong again, though, a week had passed since her return from Arucas. Miguel had called twice after his return home, but both conversations were very stilted, as if he was afraid to say much about anything.

On the afternoon after her second phone conversation with Miguel, Pamela went for a walk by herself along the *paseo*.

Grace was again busy with Juan and was trying to allow Pamela time for research. But Pamela's mind still refused to focus on the material Juan had gathered.

Now she knew which of the conical mountains was Arucas, and could picture Miguel's house. With a twisting ache, Pamela turned away from the *paseo*, cutting along side streets, not paying attention to where she was going, just trying to escape the magnificent waterfront view.

Soon, she glimpsed the trees in the Parque de Santa Catalina, and decided to browse in the bazaar for a while and pick up a few more things to take back to the States. She bought some coral earrings, an ivory and jade pin, and two carved giraffes from nearby Africa. Then, as she was passing a stall that specialized in antique jewelry, the world seemed to stop.

There could never be two pendants so exactly alike, not anywhere. Nevertheless, she reached for the exquisite emerald pendant that was resting in a jeweler's box lined with cream satin, and turned it over.

G.B.M. Geraldine Balch Merrill. Her grandmother.

Now there was no doubt.

The man presiding over the booth asked her something in Spanish, snapping Pamela out of her dismal reverie. Her voice quavering, she told him she didn't speak Spanish, so he switched to heavily accented English.

He was dark and swarthy, and didn't look especially Spanish. Perhaps half Spanish, half Arab? Perhaps Moroccan? It didn't really matter. What did matter was that he looked like someone she would hate to meet alone on a dark night. But appearances could be deceptive; maybe this man was actually gentle as a lamb.

He was certain to demand an exorbitant price for the jewel. She knew that she should put the pendant back in the box and feign interest in something else, then, after a while, return to it and make a lower offer. But she couldn't do any of those things.

Pamela asked him how much he wanted, he told her, and the price was indeed exorbitant. Still, she paid it, then swiftly walked away feeling as if the prize she'd just redeemed was burning a hole in her handbag.

Back at the Basilios', she used the key Grace had given her, instead of ringing for Roberto as she usually did, and then went directly to her room. Fortunately, she didn't meet anyone en route. She couldn't have coped with anyone at that moment, not even Miguel.

She tried to piece together a coherent account of what must have happened. There seemed no doubt that Esperanza must have stolen the pendant and then given it to someone—a boyfriend, perhaps—who in turn had fenced it. Sold it, either to an intermediary or directly to the man, the *pirate*, damn him, who handled antique jewelry in the park bazaar.

Carmen, of course, would have to know. It was impossible for Carmen unknowingly to have an employee in her house who would do something like this. Carmen had a lot of valuable jewelry of her own. Probably, Esperanza would not be so quick to steal from her employer as she might from a houseguest, because the risk of discovery was much greater. Even so, Carmen obviously had to be warned.

But she didn't want Carmen to be warned secondhand. She didn't want to tell Grace or Juan, and then have them relay the information. She wanted to tell Carmen herself, but not over the telephone. It would be disastrous if Carmen misunderstood her. The wrong person might be accused, or the facts might be distorted. No, she needed to see Carmen face to face, in order to explain exactly what had happened.

That evening at dinner, when Grace announced that Carmen had called and was coming for a visit at the beginning of the week, probably on Tuesday, it seemed absolutely providential.

Pamela was finally able to concentrate on her work. She made rapid progress, but the long hours of intensive reading demanded fresh air and exercise, so she took strolls along the *paseo* after *comida*, when most people were enjoying their siestas.

She hadn't adjusted to the long and lazy afternoons, and a predinner rest of half an hour was more than enough to refresh her. The only problem with her walks was that the shops were all closed at that time but it didn't really matter.

The day before Carmen was due in Las Palmas, Pamela was rounding a corner onto the Paseo de las Canteras when she was shocked to see a familiar figure striding half a block in front of her.

For a confusing moment, she thought it was Miguel. The stance, the walk, the dark hair that shone in the afternoon sunlight were all the same. Then she realized that this man was of a slighter build, and younger than Miguel. And, as he suddenly turned a corner onto a side street, she saw his profile.

Rafael! Rafael, here in Las Palmas! Did that also mean that Miguel was in Las Palmas? Pamela frowned; this didn't seem right. There was a perfectly good chance that Miguel could be in Las Palmas and hadn't yet gotten in touch with her. She admitted as much, but doubted that Miguel would have brought Rafael with him since Rafael was supposed to be in school.

Carmen had confided to Pamela on at least one occasion, there in Arucas, that while Rafael was a bright boy, he was also lazy. Carmen had considered her choice of words for a moment, then amended, "No, he is not really *flojo*, lazy that is, but he is—how shall I say?—indifferent. He does not have the incentive," Carmen continued, translating laboriously from Spanish to English. "If he were...ah, what do I want to say?"

"Motivated?" Pamela suggested.

"Yes, that is it! If someone could just motivate Rafael, I think he would be more than bright. I think he would be brilliant." Carmen paused, plainly pleased at her choice of expression. "I think," she then continued carefully, "that Rafael feels that no one cares what he does. Do you know what I mean?"

"Yes, I think I do," Pamela decided.

Later, she reflected that Carmen was implying that Miguel, among other people, didn't give a damn whether or not his son did well, at least in school. And that was hard to believe.

She wished it were possible to talk freely with Miguel about Rafael. But the subject of Rafael was definitely a stumbling block between them. She was not about to create an obstacle course, without an excellent reason. They had too little time together.

Pamela walked more rapidly now, reached the corner where Rafael had turned, and peered down the narrow side street. Maybe it was true that Miguel wouldn't care whether or not Rafael had skipped school for one day. But somehow she doubted this. She couldn't believe Miguel would be that casual about Rafael's life, and certainly not about his education. She could understand how Miguel might feel extremely frustrated over his rapport with Rafael. And frustrated with the fact that Dolores was such a dominating force in the Rivero household. But that didn't mean that Miguel would relinquish his authority where Rafael was concerned. Seeing that he attended school certainly fell within the scope of authority.

Rafael was already a block down the side street. Pamela hesitated briefly, then started to follow. It was easy to keep him in sight because at this hour of the day, most people were having their siestas, so the streets were relatively empty. The only problem was that he might suddenly turn around and see her.

Rafael moved like a person with a single goal in mind. Did he have a girlfriend here in Las Palmas? A relationship serious enough to cause him to cut school and, somehow, get to the city? By hitchhiking, maybe? She couldn't recall seeing any hitchhikers, but then she hadn't driven around all that much.

Suddenly, abruptly, Rafael turned off the street, virtually disappearing between two buildings. Pamela almost ran the short distance to his vanishing point, and discovered an alley there, a narrow back alley, lined with buildings on both sides. There were trash cans everywhere, and the smell of garbage was strong. She was certainly looking at the less glamorous side of Las Palmas.

Had Rafael darted into someone's kitchen? He'd definitely disappeared through one of the doors along the alley.

Frustrated, Pamela turned and started back toward the *paseo*. After walking for a couple of blocks, she sat down at a sidewalk café and, when a waiter appeared, ordered a glass of wine, something she couldn't remember ever having done before by herself.

As she sipped her wine, Pamela pondered Rafael's behavior. It seemed mysterious and, in retrospect, there had been a furtiveness about the way he had moved steadily along, *stealthily* even, as if he had wanted to reach his objective and vanish from sight as quickly as possible.

Should she tell Grace and Juan about seeing Rafael? Or should she wait, and tell Carmen tomorrow? Maybe she should just keep her own counsel and not say anything at all.

As she slowly walked back to the Basilios', Pamela decided to remain silent for the moment. She could probe a bit by asking Carmen about Rafael. Carmen might know why Rafael was in Las Palmas, or at least that he wasn't in Arucas. Remembering the way Dolores had pushed the panic button when it was discovered that his bed hadn't been slept in the night before, Pamela couldn't imagine that Rafael's absence for any length of time would go unnoticed for very long these days.

The next morning, Pamela became increasingly restless as she tried to concentrate on her work, and failed. She couldn't get Rafael's strange behavior out of her mind.

Carmen wasn't due until late afternoon. So, directly after *comida*, Pamela followed what had become her habit, and started out for a walk. Usually, she had no particular goal, but today she did—the alley off the side street of the *paseo*!

She'd forgotten to write down the name of the street in her haste to follow Rafael, but she did remember the small newspaper and tobacco store on the corner. Finding the alley again was no problem. She paused at the entrance, reluctant to walk down the narrow, smelly stretch of pavement.

There was nothing else to do, though, if she was going to find out anything at all. Wrinkling her nose at the stench, Pamela started down the alley. Midway she made a discovery.

As she'd suspected, the backs of the buildings opened onto the alley. These rear entrances were all nondescript and dirty, with one exception. Pamela found herself looking up at a door painted bright yellow and adorned with an impressive bronze knocker. Though she couldn't prove it, a sixth sense told her that it was through this door that Rafael had disappeared.

She was tempted to knock. If she'd had a decent grasp of the Spanish language, she *would* have knocked. Then she could have made some excuse that was comprehensible. As it was, she knew she'd be at a loss for words.

She turned and went back to the side street, and then to the *paseo*, her footsteps lagging. The house with the yellow door was connected with Rafael in some way. But she had no idea whose house it was, or what might be inside. Again, she was reluctant to ask. It would be so easy to put Miguel on the spot with her inquiries. Too easy.

She wasn't trying to be unduly charitable to Rafael, but she had the feeling that Rafael deserved a break.

Nevertheless . . . it was a heavy responsibility to know that he'd been in Las Palmas, possibly frequenting that house on the back alley, the house with the bright-yellow door. And to keep the knowledge to herself....

Miguel, of course, was the person she should tell, but it was hard to know how and when.

It didn't help when Carmen arrived later in the day. Carmen was so delighted to see her that the reunion would have been perfect, had it not been for the problem with Esperanza and the shadow of Rafael looming on Pamela's personal horizon.

In honor of Carmen, drinks and *tapas*—the Spanish version of hors d'oeuvres—were served in the drawing room that evening. Pamela, tongue in cheek, managed to bring up the subject of the Riveros by asking after Dolores. Carmen looked at her quizzically, but nevertheless answered that Dolores was very well. During this Lenten season, just going to church twice every day was enough to keep her busy.

Pamela's throat went dry and she swallowed with difficulty before managing to pose the next question. "And Rafael?" she asked.

"Rafael has been doing well," Carmen stated. "Attending to his studies. And Miguel," Carmen went on, with an arch glance at Pamela—obviously she'd known all along this was whom Pamela had really wanted to hear about—"is busy as usual. He flies to Madrid tomorrow, for ten days or so."

"Madrid?" Pamela echoed, her heart sinking.

"Business matters," Carmen said. "Also..."

Carmen hesitated, and Pamela waited to hear what else she was about to say. But Carmen became totally preoccupied with selecting a tidbit from the tray Roberto held before her.

It was Juan who finally prompted, "What else were you about to say regarding Miguel, Carmen?"

Carmen answered him in Spanish and, for a moment, Juan seemed to be digesting her words. Then he said heavily, in English, "Another wild-goose chase."

He turned to Pamela. "You know, I suppose, about Miguel's wife?"

Pamela moistened her lips. "Yes, he told me."

"The business that takes Miguel to Madrid primarily concerns her," Juan reported. "God knows how many detectives Miguel has hired over the years since she ran off. Now, according to Carmen, there have been rumors that she has been seen in the south of Spain, in a small town not far from Gibraltar. Miguel has hired a firm in Madrid who have great expertise with that sort of thing, and they promised him they would gather some definite information about Anita, if not Anita herself. Rumor has it that her lover, Miguel's ex-business partner, has died, and now she is alone."

Pamela found herself fighting recurring waves of blackness, waves that were threatening to engulf her and strip her of consciousness. It would have been easier to give in and faint, but she fought, struggling through each wave like a swimmer battling high seas.

Juan was staring broodingly at his glass. Grace and Carmen were watching Juan, obviously waiting for him to speak.

He sighed heavily. "Poor Miguel," he said. "Since he was such a young man he has been going through this. Searching for Anita, never finding her. Following one slender thread after another, only to have the threads snap in his face like an old rubber band. This will be another such failure, believe me. I can't see how it could be otherwise."

Pamela listened to Juan, and tried silently to agree, wanted desperately to agree.

But suppose they did find Anita...suppose they found her...alive and well?

Chapter Twelve

Carmen stayed in Las Palmas for nearly a week, and during all that time Pamela kept her secrets to herself. But there wasn't a moment of the day—or much of the night—when she wasn't thinking of Miguel searching in Spain for his long-lost wife.

This was the Lenten season, and social life was at its lowest ebb in Las Palmas. Even so, Carmen remarked one afternoon with a slight smile that it was lively in comparison to Arucas.

"Sometimes," she said, "I begin to think that in Arucas we are too devout. I am not sure God would like such long, unhappy faces."

She was referring to Dolores, without coming right out and speaking her name. For the first time, it struck Pamela that Dolores must also be agonizing over Miguel's quest. Suppose he *did* find Anita? Suppose she agreed to come back to him, after all these years...and he was willing to take her back, as unlikely as that might seem now? Dolores would quickly be supplanted as chatelaine of the Rivero estate, her position instantly preempted.

Pamela tried to feel some sympathy for Dolores, but couldn't. Regardless of Spanish custom, Dolores should have long ago loosened her hold on both Miguel and Rafael, and set about making a life of her own.

And what of Rafael? Where else could he be except in Arucas, dutifully going to school as he was supposed to?

She thought of asking Juan if he knew anything about the house with the yellow door, but like everything else, she kept the subject locked inside herself.

Carmen went home, after extracting a promise that the Basilios and Pamela would join her for Easter in Arucas. Pamela went along with her invitation because it was the simplest thing to do. There'd be time enough later to invent an excuse not to go.

The days of Lent passed, and all at once Easter was upon them. Pamela had no time to think of a viable reason not to go to Arucas unless she made the sudden decision to leave Grand Canary entirely and return to the States. Later, she would do her doctoral thesis about some other arid spot in the world, where hydrology would really be her main concern.

Good Friday came, and then Lent was over. On Saturday afternoon, once Juan had finished some work that had to be air-expressed to the States, they started out for Arucas with him at the wheel of his small European sedan.

Juan was a very fast driver, and they reached Arucas in what seemed like no time at all, certainly less time than the drive had taken with Carmen. When she saw the familiar, cone-shaped mountain looming closer and closer, Pamela knew that within minutes they would be at Carmen's house, and she came close to panicking. It was all she could do to sit silently in the back seat as Juan braked to a stop alongside the curb in front of Carmen's house.

Pamela scanned her surroundings, hoping she might suddenly discover an escape route. Then the golden pine door in the white wall opened, and Miguel was standing there, not Porfirio. Pamela wished she could solve all her problems by literally dissolving right into the ground.

She sat where she was, watching as Juan and Miguel indulged in an emotional bear hug. Miguel turned to Grace and kissed her cheek and then his jet-black eyes anxiously searched the car. As he came forward there were fireflies dancing in them once again.

He opened the car door and reached out a long slender hand. "Come along, *querida*."

Pamela was dimly aware that Juan and Grace had paused in the doorway. She took Miguel's hand, knowing that her fingers were cold and clammy, and cautiously stepped out onto the sidewalk. Before she realized what he was about to do, Miguel pulled her into his arms and kissed her.

There was no doubt about the fervor of that kiss; Miguel's fire ignited Pamela with matching flames of passion. She could feel his warmth rush all the way to her toes, feel those sensuous stirrings deep inside. It was only because Juan and Grace were still looking on that she exercised enough self-control to pull away.

Miguel turned to Juan and Grace with a grin so infectious that it would have endeared him to a statue. "I couldn't wait until we were alone," he said impishly.

The Basilios were smiling broadly. Pamela, though, felt as if her knees had suddenly turned to rubber. She clutched Miguel's hand as they reached the inner courtyard.

Miguel bent and placed his mouth to her ear. "Are you okay?" he whispered.

How could he be so damned casual? The last time she'd had any direct word from him was before he'd taken off for Spain, having hired a team of detectives to embark on yet another search for his missing wife. No one had said anything about that since Carmen had returned to Arucas. Day had followed day, with Juan and Grace especially busy with Juan's work, and with Pamela doing her utmost to stay equally busy with her research. She hadn't asked any questions, but neither had any information been forthcoming, though each day she'd hoped . . .

Miguel repeated his question, this time more urgently. "Are you okay?"

Pamela turned to him, her eyes flashing. "No!" she said angrily, keeping her voice low.

There was no chance for either of them to say anything else, because Carmen appeared. Another ecstatic reunion followed, and Esperanza hurried out to take Pamela's things to her room. Esperanza seemed so delighted to see her that it was very hard, very painful, to imagine that this girl actually had stolen from her. She wondered how Esperanza would react when she saw the pendant again.

"You look so tired, Pamelita," Carmen said suddenly. "Juan, you have been allowing her to work too hard."

"I'm all right," Pamela protested awkwardly, aware that Miguel was eyeing her closely. "I have a lot of material to cover, that's all."

"So, Roma was not built in a day!" Carmen said loftily. "In any event, you will get some rest, now that you are here with me. Do you wish to take a short siesta? You can, you know."

"No, thank you," Pamela said hastily. "I'm fine, Carmen. Really I am."

Carmen still looked doubtful and, darting a quick glance at Miguel, Pamela saw that he looked even more doubtful.

Carmen interrupted the awkward moment. "Shall we go into the *sala*? I think we will be more comfortable there. Porfirio will bring drinks, and—how do you say?—something to nibble on."

They followed Carmen into her drawing room, smaller than its counterpart in the Rivero hacienda but, in Pamela's opinion, much more livable due to the fact that Carmen's personality was so much more ebullient than Dolores's.

Juan, Grace and Carmen grouped themselves around a small table at one end of the room. Pamela was about to follow them, but Miguel tugged at her arm insistently. "Let them catch up with each other in Spanish," he urged. "As for you...I don't care what language I catch up with you in, *querida*, but I do have to know why you are looking as you are. I would ask what I have done, but I know what I have done. I have paid very little attention to you since the day we parted in Las Palmas, but Carmen told me you know why that is. The principal reason, anyway...."

Miguel looked at Pamela; her expression was guarded, shutting him out. He swore silently at himself for thinking that it might be otherwise.

How could he convince her that his absence, his lack of attention, were not sins of omission? He, more than most people, knew only too well how damning neglect could be. How could he convince Pamela that he'd made that crazy pilgrimage to Madrid not for himself, but for *her*? He'd hoped so desperately that these latest rumors were true, and that the new detectives he'd hired would find Anita so that he could resolve the dilemma of his "marriage" finally and forever. So that he could be totally free for Pamela.

Why had he felt that this was something he should finish on his own? Why hadn't he called Pamela, or asked her to meet him at the airport before he'd left for Madrid? He could have stayed with the Basilios that night, or at his apartment. One day wouldn't have made much difference, and they could have discussed his plans, his hopes at greater length.

As it turned out, one day wouldn't have made any difference at all. The detectives hadn't found Anita. The trail led to its usual dead end, this time to someone who looked like Anita and who, ironically, bore the same first name. But the woman was ten years younger than Anita would be today, and close up the resemblance was not that strong. So another hope had died.

This time, Miguel's disappointment was compounded by an entirely new twist, a love he'd neither planned for nor could escape from. On the return flight, he'd suddenly realized that he no longer *had* to suffer. He knew now, in a moment of total revelation, that he could face the future without flinching—because of Pamela. She mattered more to him, more to his life than he'd ever believed a woman could.

While thinking about Pamela, about what she meant to him, he saw things in a new light, as if he'd suddenly been granted clairvoyance. He could see now how his sister Dolores, with her religious fanaticism, had instilled in him the concept that he was still married, at least in the eyes of God. Perhaps, because of his own guilt, that had been what he'd wanted to hear. But on the flight back to the Canaries, Miguel began to dispute Dolores's theories. He finally accepted the overwhelming truth that he *was* legally free...and at this particular time in his life, that was all that mattered. He *felt* free—free to open his heart to Pamela. He could only pray that she would be willing to open her heart to him.

When Carmen told him that the Basilios and Pamela were coming for Easter, Miguel made up his mind to wait until then to tell her all the things he wanted to say to her. He pledged to himself that he'd find the chance to be alone with her, to talk things out completely, even if he had to kidnap her.

Looking at Pamela now, so silent and tense, it struck Miguel that it was late in the day. Very late in the day, and the fault was entirely his. He had to face up to the fact that Pamela was an American woman, accustomed to dealing with men differently from most Spanish women, even in this relatively liberated age. American women were used to relationships built on a considerably more equal footing.

Although he was "Americanized" in many ways, Miguel decided wryly that he'd been behaving like a Spaniard. And this had been the worst possible time to hold to the macho notion that men must forever be strong and solve their own problems, and keep women from bothering their pretty heads over things they need not know.

Porfirio appeared with a variety of drinks.

Surveying the tray, Miguel asked Pamela, "What would you like, Pamelita? Scotch, brandy, or sherry?"

"Sherry, thank you," she responded.

Her fingers were trembling as she accepted the wineglass from Miguel. For a telling instant, he kept his fingers on the glass so that it wouldn't escape her grasp. "Drink up," he urged. "You are so pale it frightens me."

Esperanza arrived with a tray of bite-sized sandwiches and other *tapas*, but Pamela shook her head. She couldn't help avoiding the young maid's eyes, and told herself ironically that it should be the other way around.

"I thought you were over your illness," Miguel said tersely.

"What illness?"

"You had a sore throat and a fever," he reminded her. "Before I went to Madrid, remember? Grace said you insisted you didn't need a doctor. Now, I think that perhaps you should see someone after all, even at this late date..."

Pamela shook her head stubbornly. "There's nothing wrong with me, Miguel."

Physically, nothing was wrong. Her problems were emotional, caused entirely by this man at her side, by his son, and by Esperanza.... Now, more than ever, Pamela wished she knew what lay behind that bright-yellow door.

They had a relatively light dinner because, Carmen warned them, laughingly, they must save their appetites for Easter dinner. Miguel left shortly after they had had coffee in the courtyard. And, as soon as she gracefully could, Pamela said she was rather tired, and asked to be excused.

The others were still lingering on the patio as Pamela undressed. She could hear the soft murmur of their Spanish language, with its melodic flow, and only wished she could speak it herself. Perhaps someday...

Finally, before getting into bed, she took off her emerald ring and placed it in her jewelry case. She started to unfasten the pendant but then, perhaps because she'd "lost and found" it so recently and still felt strange about its theft, she decided to keep it on. She put the jewelry case in the top drawer of the dresser, and closed the drawer firmly. Then, she dropped her earrings on top of the dresser, because they were of no real value, hating to have to think about things like that.

Climbing into bed, Pamela chided herself for not once meeting Esperanza's eyes tonight, even though Esperanza had helped serve the dinner. She'd missed the chance to observe any reaction to the reappearance of the pendant.

There was a cool breeze wafting in the window, and a shaft of moonlight slanted across Pamela's bed. The romantic setting made her feel all the more lonely. She closed her eyes, but visions darted in and out of her mind like whirling tops, and it was a long while before she fell into a restless sleep.

Once, she fancied she heard the floor creak. But when she quickly opened her eyes and peered into the predawn light, there was no one there.

It wasn't until morning that she discovered someone actually had been in her room. Whether by caution, instinct, or premonition, Pamela got out of bed not long after sunrise and pattered over to the dresser. She opened the top drawer and took out her jewelry case. It was like a nightmare come true—the emerald ring was gone.

Pamela paced the bedroom floor for the next two hours. This was Easter Sunday, the most joyous day of the year in the Christian calendar. A symbol of spring's renaissance. Yet her overwhelming sense was one of depression.

She could no longer keep the thefts to herself. This was Carmen's house, and Carmen had to be informed.

Pamela slumped down in a small armchair, exhausted before the day had begun. *I can't tell her today.* To bring up the matter of the thefts would ruin Easter for everyone. She and the Basilios would not be returning to Las Palmas until after *comida* tomorrow. There would be time enough to make her unhappy revelation on Monday morning.

A weary Pamela climbed back into bed and fell asleep. She was awakened by a loud knock on the door, and when she called out, *"Sí?"*, Carmen came into the room, fully dressed.

Pamela glanced quickly at her bedside clock, and was shocked to see it was noon!

"So," Carmen observed, "we all knew you were very tired, but I have not known you to sleep so late as this."

Pamela propped herself up, still feeling bone weary. "Are you leaving for church?" she asked.

"I have just returned from church," Carmen informed her. "Dolores and Miguel are here with me. Rafael will come later. The special Easter feast will be at four this afternoon, so for now we will just have coffee. Will you join us, Pamelita? Miguel said you were going for a drive somewhere, but you can discuss that with him."

Carmen left, and Pamela fought the temptation to call her back. She wanted to say she was sick and couldn't join the others for coffee, Easter dinner, or anything else. Any excuse that would permit her to remain closeted in her room until tomorrow.

She'd been plagued with weird dreams during her morning sleep, and they still haunted her as she dressed, choosing a simple, pink linen sheath. Later, she would put on something more elaborate.

Reluctantly, she walked out onto the patio, where Dolores, Miguel, Carmen and the Basilios were already indulging in coffee and pastries.

Dolores was actually wearing white. It was a shock to see her in anything but widow's black, and her becoming Easter costume revealed her potential beauty.

Dolores greeted her with a slight smile and Juan teased her about sleeping so late, but Grace looked at her inquisitively. Grace was simply too perceptive.

So was Miguel. She saw questions in his eyes. He took the first opportunity to say, in a low voice, "Drink your coffee, will you, and then let's get out of here for a while. The others already know that you and I are going to drive up to the top of Montaña de Arucas—Arucas Mountain—so you can see the view."

"Really?" Pamela whispered sarcastically. "Suppose I don't want to drive up to the top of Arucas Mountain?"

"I really don't give a damn about that!" Miguel growled. "If I have to carry you, I'm getting you out of here. I have to talk to you."

Pamela met his gaze; he was deadly serious. Suddenly, he grinned. "You're not really going to make me use force, are you?"

"Perhaps," she snapped.

But she had no such intention. Despite her anxiety over the thefts, she had to admit that she wanted nothing so much in the world as to be alone with Miguel, even for a little while.

She politely refused a second cup of coffee, and a few minutes later they left Carmen's house.

Now that they were alone together, there was an initial constrained silence between them. Pamela tried to ease it by commenting on the beautiful Easter weather.

Miguel agreed that it was a perfect day. "And there will be a perfect view from the mountain top," he added. "But I'm sure you know that's not why I'm taking you there."

"Oh?"

He laughed. "Don't be coy, Pamelita. It does not become you. Anyway, I cannot get into any deep discussions with you until we get to the top. As you'll see, the road requires total concentration."

The ascent was extremely steep, and the road wound around in a series of hairpin turns. With only one lane wide, it was necessary to blow the horn at each major bend; small turnoffs were provided at regular intervals so that cars could pass, one waiting while the other inched by.

"Usually, the car coming down gets first choice, unless the driver going up is especially stubborn," Miguel said.

At the top, there was a paved parking lot and a large concession area including a restaurant surrounded by outdoor chairs and tables. Just now the whole place was nearly deserted.

"Everyone is still in church, or visiting families," Miguel explained.

They slowly walked on paved walkways the short distance to the summit. As Miguel had promised, the view was spectacular. She could see the extensive stretches of vivid-green banana plantations. The aridity of this particular part of the island, with its mixture of mountains and plateaus, could not be ignored. Clusters of white houses dotted the mountainsides, and the blue sea seemed near enough to touch. Then, far in the distance, she spied an enormous, snow-capped mountain that looked like Fujiyama.

"Teide," Miguel told her, following her gaze. "Thirteen thousand feet. It is the highest mountain in all of Spain. Over on Tenerife. You can get there by jetfoil in less than two hours from here. The volcano is extinct, of course, but it is impressive, is it not?"

"Very."

"So are you," Miguel said softly. "You have impressed me so deeply, Pamelita. *Dios,*" he sighed. "There is so much I want to say to you, so much I want to tell you. And there is no place where we can be alone today, except on this mountaintop. Crazy, isn't it? When as much as I want to talk to you, I want even more...to make love to you. How can I keep my hands off you, Pamelita?"

She didn't want him to—that was the problem! Pamela looked up at him, yearning in her eyes.

"You are so absolutely beautiful," Miguel said softly. "And I love you so much."

Time stopped, the world stopped as they stared at each other. And it was frustrating, tremendously frustrating, to accept that right now there was no place where they could be alone. No place where they could make love.

Miguel, his voice husky, asked, "Pamela...aren't you going to answer me?"

Her mind, her emotions were still whirling. "Answer you?"

"Dearest, dearest Pamelita. *Vida. Corazón.* Do you love me at all?"

She found her voice, but couldn't hold back the tears. "Dear God," she implored him, "how could you ever doubt that? I love you so much.... But..."

Ignoring the curious glances of occasional passersby, Miguel drew her into his arms. "Please," he said, "no buts, not just now. Let me try to tell you, first, why I've been so evasive about so many things. We could get a glass of wine, and sit out in the sun, okay?''

Pamela nodded mutely, and brushed the tears from her cheeks. With his arm around her shoulders Miguel led her back down the path toward the restaurant.

More and more people were now making their way to the top of the mountain, and the restaurant was beginning to do a brisk business. Although Miguel chose a table as far removed as possible from most of the action, he and Pamela could not achieve the total sense of privacy they both wanted and needed so badly.

There were many distractions. Young lovers, strolling arm in arm, beautiful children dressed in Easter finery, older people enjoying quiet times in the sun. The hum of Spanish and, inside the restaurant, festive music. Lent was over, this was the beginning of a new season, and there was joy everywhere.

Joy for Pamela, too, because Miguel had told her he loved her, because he was trying to explain his reluctance to tell her why he had gone to Madrid.

She sensed how difficult it was for him to talk about this freely, even now. It was a subject he'd kept locked tightly inside himself for years. She listened, without interposing any questions, following Miguel as he told her how he'd thought out his problems on the trip back to Gran Canaria. He told her why he'd convinced himself that he was free, regardless of whether Anita's fate was ever determined.

But that was exactly what he'd done, Pamela thought dully. He'd convinced himself, or tried to do so. He'd argued things over in his efforts to dissipate those lowering mental clouds, and he'd reached the conclusion that he desperately wanted to believe in. Had he really succeeded? she wondered. Or would the echoes of the past return?

And that wasn't all of it. The worst came when Miguel finished and then smiled across at her. "So now," he said, his voice tender, "there are no secrets between us, *querida*. And we must keep it that way."

Pamela felt a twinge of guilt, one that was only intensified when, instead of answering him, she drew his attention to a group of children doing an impromptu flamenco.

She knew only too well that she had several dark secrets . . . among them Rafael's unaccounted for presence in Las Palmas, and the theft of her jewelry. Thinking of both, Pamela had the sudden, horrible fear that they might be related.

She saw now that it had been easy to assume Esperanza was responsible for the theft. There was a strong chance she'd been premature in her assumption. Certainly Esperanza had given no indication of feeling any guilt. On the other hand, Rafael had.

Esperanza was a simple country girl from what Pamela had observed of her. The young maid had a pleasant, easy-going disposition, was deeply religious, and appeared to be totally content with her life here in Arucas.

Maybe she'd taken the jewelry. The possibility couldn't be dismissed . . . yet. But, painful though it was to face, Rafael was beginning to appear a much more likely suspect.

Chapter Thirteen

Miguel was in an effusive mood on the drive back to Carmen's house. He seemed totally at peace with himself, as happy as a man could be. Pamela, on the other hand, found it impossible to match his mood. She'd never felt less lighthearted, and wasn't a good enough actress to put across even a semblance of false gaiety.

She caught Miguel looking at her with increasing concern as they neared Carmen's familiar white wall. Finally, he said, "There is something bothering you. Why can't you tell me what it is?"

She shook her head. "There's nothing, really," she fibbed.

"Then you must be coming down with something again," Miguel countered. "Do you feel ill?"

"No," Pamela said quickly. "I've been rather tired since I had that sore throat in Las Palmas. But I'm fine, really I'm fine."

She was anything but fine, she thought wryly, as she changed into an exquisite, pale-peach lace dress. It had a drop waist and a handkerchief hem, and her emerald pendant complemented it perfectly. She twisted her hair into an elaborate chignon that set off her dangling gold and crystal earrings.

But no matter how great she looked, she dreaded walking across Carmen's patio and entering the *sala*, where everyone would be assembled by now.

Rafael would be there too. Pamela knew she must watch him very carefully. His first glimpse of the pendant around her neck would be all-important. If he'd had anything to do with the theft, he would almost certainly reveal *something*, at least for a fleeting second.

She hoped and prayed with all her heart that she was wrong, that Rafael would not only look innocent, but *be* innocent.

Pamela took a deep breath, then paused on the threshold of the *sala*, surveying the group already gathered there. Carmen had invited several of her close friends for the Easter dinner, and the conversation was flowing. People were laughing, with the solemnity of Lent gone for another year.

Miguel saw her, and stood up. He'd gone home and changed, and looked especially handsome in a dark-blue suit. He rushed toward her, love for her shining in his eyes. "Ah, there you are," he said. Simple words, but they carried a wealth of feeling.

He took her hand, and led her toward the other guests, and Pamela knew he was going to introduce her all around. She was determined to say, *"Mucho gusto"* to each person she met, but when she saw Rafael, the words faltered on her lips.

He looked very handsome today, wearing a suit like his father's, though a lighter shade of blue. He'd carefully combed his thick black hair, and his gray tie was knotted at just the right angle. One day, Pamela thought, he would be as attractive as Miguel. Right now, he was too thin and vulnerable.

She watched silently, then felt sick. There was no doubt about Rafael's reaction. The sight of the pendant visibly jolted him. His eyes became riveted to the lovely old piece of jewelry, and he actually paled.

Pamela was so distressed that she would have faltered over an English greeting, let alone a Spanish one. Her grip on Miguel's hand tightened involuntarily. How she wished she'd never discovered her pendant at the bazaar in the Parque de Santa Catalina! Things would be a thousand times better if she'd never found the thief.

Miguel, feeling her clench his hand, asked anxiously, "What is it, *querida*?"

"Nothing," she replied quickly.

Miguel gritted his teeth. "I am getting tired of this 'nothing' answer all the time," he said, not restraining his impatience. "Come, let me get you something to drink."

He led Pamela to a sideboard where he poured her a brandy. "I suggest you drink it down. You look like you just saw a ghost."

He watched her flinch as the brandy burned her throat, then said, his voice low, his tone savage, "This isn't the time or place to get into whatever it is that's bothering you. But, damn it, there is never a right time or place for us! *Dios*, Pamelita, don't try to tell me nothing is wrong. You have been acting very strangely since you came here yesterday. Something happened, please don't try to deny that to me. I love you, remember? I like to think I know you. Or am I wrong about that?"

Miguel was angry, and Pamela could not blame him for feeling as he did. It was true. Except for those stolen moments on the hillside, and one night at the beautiful mountain inn, they'd had very little private time all their own.

She remembered how he'd promised earlier that in the future there would be no secrets between them. He'd assumed she was making the same promise to him. She only wished she could.

But to be totally honest with him, she'd have to come out and say, "Miguel, I think your son is a thief." And she couldn't do that.

"All right," Miguel said tightly. "I can't make you talk to me if you don't want to. But I have the gut feeling you are holding back. And I don't appreciate that."

He added, abruptly, "Let us join the others."

Pamela was aware that they'd been drawing discreet, but curious glances from some of Carmen's guests. Then she saw Dolores; Dolores's face was stony, her lips set in the thinnest of lines.

Well, she'd never pleased Miguel's sister anyway, so there was no sense in worrying about pleasing her now. In fact, Dolores de Avero was among the least of her worries.

The Easter feast was delicious. Succulent pork roasts, ham and chicken, a variety of fresh vegetables, the famous "wrinkled potatoes" topped with a spicy *mojo picon* sauce—a Canary Island tradition—and a magnificent *flan* for dessert. Finally, the inevitable small cups of strong, sweet black coffee.

Carmen, forever the matchmaker, had seated Miguel and Pamela next to each other. Miguel studiously avoided watching her as she ate, but Pamela was sure that he'd noticed her difficulty swallowing. By the time they left the table, she felt as if she actually did have a fever. Maybe the trauma was enough to induce an elevated body temperature in an otherwise sound person. In any case, her face felt hot and flushed, and she had a raging headache.

She sought out Carmen, and whispered in her ear that she really didn't feel well and would like to be excused.

"I knew you were not well, Pamelita," Carmen said, almost triumphantly. "I said so to Dolores."

Carmen spoke in English; fortunately, most of her guests spoke only Spanish. Miguel was on the other side of the room, talking with a retired businessman and his wife, and Rafael had managed to disappear, evidently without attracting anyone's attention.

"Go and rest," Carmen prescribed. "I will come to see how you are very soon."

"You don't have to do that," Pamela protested. "I think if I could just sleep for a while I'd be fine," she added, though she knew this was anything but true. It would be a miracle if she ever went to sleep again.

In her room, Esperanza had drawn the shades against the sun, and it was blissfully cool. Pamela did drift off to sleep and slept the kind of sleep that comes with deep emotional exhaustion.

It was very quiet when she woke up. She went to the window and glanced out into the patio. It was empty. She glanced at the clock on the bedside table and saw it was nearly eleven. Early, by Spanish standards, but today's Easter feast had started much earlier.

Evidently, everyone had left. Or else they were still in the *sala*, and speaking very softly. Pamela was not about to investigate; there was the chance that Miguel had lingered, and she didn't think she could face him tonight.

She'd already seen the reproach in his eyes, had felt the sting of his anger.

She was still wearing her lace dress. Now she slipped it off, and shrugged into a pink, terry cloth robe.

When a knock came at the door, Pamela went cold. She was sure Miguel had lingered, certain that it was him. What she feared more than anything else was that he might pry out her secret. She was weak at the moment, physically and emotionally, and hardly up to coping with his questions.

But it wasn't Miguel, it was Grace. She was looking at her in that same anxious way that Carmen and Miguel had since her return to Arucas. Her voice betraying her concern, Grace asked, "Are you feeling any better, Pam? You've had an awfully rough time, I'd say."

Pamela looked at Grace and crumbled, the tears coming in floods. Grace led her over to the bed and held her while she cried. When the tears began to abate, she said, "There now, darling," as if she were the mother and Pamela a helpless child. "It can't be that bad!"

Pamela had no answer, because it was considerably worse. But she couldn't tell Grace that.

Grace said, "Look, Pam, I knew something was wrong when Miguel stormed out of the house. He looked like he was about to erupt!" She sighed, then added, "Come on...don't let this get you down so. All lovers have quarrels from time to time. You should hear Juan and me when we get started on something, and we've been married for years. Miguel will get over it."

So, Grace had diagnosed her problem as a lovers' quarrel. It suddenly occurred to Pamela that perhaps Miguel had come to the same conclusion. Her safest course would be to follow this lead until she could pull herself together and decide what to do about Rafael.

Miguel didn't appear at Carmen's house the next day, nor did he telephone. "Miguel is very busy," Carmen said at one point, as if she felt compelled to explain his actions . . . or lack thereof.

Pamela mumbled something about being sure that Miguel was extremely busy, and Grace gave Carmen a knowing look. They were still going along with the lovers' quarrel theory; Pamela indicated nothing to the contrary.

After *comida*, Juan packed the few things they'd brought to Arucas back into his car, and they set off for Las Palmas. Pamela had another splitting headache, but she didn't dare suggest that she go to bed immediately upon their arrival at the house; she couldn't bear to be alone with her dilemma.

Anyway, there was a distraction. That day's post had brought a letter from Charles Evans, the first word she'd had from him since writing him several weeks before, just after her arrival in the Canaries.

She'd tried to convey in her letter that the time had come to admit to each other that their romance was over. Now she remembered that she'd also expressed the usual—and almost always trite—sentiments about hoping their friendship would endure.

Charles, though, in his somewhat peremptory fashion, made it plain that he hadn't taken anything she'd said too seriously. "I've been on vacation in Mexico, doing some fantastic scuba diving off Cancun," he reported. "You'd love it, Pam. I've got to get you into scuba when you come back. There's a whole new world underwater."

Charles went on about the fascinating Mayan ruins in the Yucatan, and added, rather wistfully, that he'd kept thinking how much she would enjoy them, too.

That did touch her. In retrospect, there had been many good things about her relationship with Charles, and very little trauma. No trauma at all, in comparison to the emotional roller coaster ride with Miguel. Life with Charles would be very civilized, they'd have enough of everything, they'd be compatible . . . and there would be absolutely no spark!

But she didn't love Charles. She had never truly loved anyone, until now, and she doubted very much that there could ever be another man for her like Miguel.

Charles asked that she write back soon with the date of her return to the States, and finished with the words, "I want to plan something very special."

Pamela didn't want him to plan anything. She didn't want to go back to the States; she didn't want to stay in the Canaries. She wished she could escape to some place more remote than the moon, where she would suddenly become invulnerable.

She was sitting in the spillover room with Grace as she read the letter, and then put it down with a sigh.

Grace smiled. "More romantic problems?"

"Not exactly." Grace was acting as if all of this was fun and games. Maybe it was, to her. From her vantage point, it was probably easy to look upon so-called "love affairs" as valentines, all done up in frothy lace and red satin ribbons.

But Grace at least knew when to stop. She finished a letter she'd received herself, and said, "How about going for a walk? I ate so much at Carmen's yesterday I'm still uncomfortable."

"I don't think so, Grace." Pamela hedged. "I really should answer this letter."

"So quickly?" Grace asked demurely. "Very well then. I think I'll go for a stroll on the *paseo* myself. Juan is going to be occupied with business for the next couple of hours."

Pamela chided herself after Grace had left. She could have buried her problems for a while—tried to bury them, she amended—and gone along with her hostess.

She made a stab at trying to answer Charles's letter, but could think of nothing to say to him. Being alone was doing her no good at all. She tried to get back into her research, but she simply couldn't ignore the troublesome extraneous issues that were constantly impinging upon her concentration.

Finally, Pamela wandered down to the spillover room, thinking that perhaps Grace had come back and they could have a cup of tea together. Grace wasn't there, but Juan was.

He was wearing dark-rimmed reading glasses, which he flipped up to look at Pamela appraisingly. "Grace is right," he concluded. "You are off your feed, little one."

Juan had more of an accent that Miguel did, and usually it was amusing when he tried to use American slang. But nothing was funny today. Pamela's sense of humor had not only gone into hiding, she was afraid she'd lost it forever.

Nevertheless, she attempted to answer Juan with a light touch. "Honestly," she said, "you people are getting paranoid about me!"

"Are we?" Juan asked skeptically. "All right, Grace insists that you and Miguel have had a little spat, and that's your business. Now, how about some sangria? It's a very warm afternoon. I think sangria would go well just now, don't you?"

Pamela was willing to agree. It was relaxing to sit and sip sangria with Juan while he tactfully changed the subject and asked how her research was progressing.

Actually, she'd learned more than she'd realized. They talked about everything she'd covered, and finally she concluded, "It's such an economic merry-go-round, that's the problem. If desalinization plants could be built at strategic locations around the island, the water shortage would be solved. Banana growers could keep on growing bananas forever. There could be expansion almost everywhere. But I don't have to tell you, Juan, that the cost of constructing even one plant is enormous. The burden of assuming such a cost say, times five, would be completely overwhelming, if not impossible. There's no way that kind of money can be amassed without the help of a very strong economy... before the fact, not afterward, if you follow me."

"I follow you, Pamelita," Juan said grimly. "Although we are part of Spain, we are far enough away from Madrid. Our problems at times seem remote to the government. We have to face up to politics. Is there any end to facing up to politics in this world?"

He sighed. "Whenever I get into a discussion on this particular subject, I feel like I am lost in a maze, going around hopelessly. What surprises me is that more people do not share my concern. Even close friends shrug off the problem, as if all of a sudden it is going to start to rain buckets, and keep on raining. I suppose this is because the drought has been with us for so long that people have become accustomed to it. Except for those whom it touches directly, like Miguel, it is relatively easy to overlook. Especially for those who live in an area like Las Palmas, where it is easy to forget there is any water problem at all. Here, in the city, we do benefit from the one desalinization plant."

Pamela nodded. "I love Las Palmas, Juan," she said, reflectively. "I love Grand Canary...."

"And, perhaps, one of its inhabitants?" Juan asked astutely.

She tried to sidestep this, and laughed, "Juan, you know I've always been crazy about you!"

"Pamelita, you know it is not myself I am talking about," Juan returned, mocking her. "I think you have fallen in love with Miguel Rivero. Call me a busybody, if you wish, but I look upon you very much like a daughter, believe it or not."

Pamela smiled. "No one would have believed it, back when I was in college, and you and Grace rescued me from Glenn Babcock."

"True." Juan grinned. "Ah, it is still pleasant, at moments when I am depressed, to think that half of that college town pictured me as such a Casanova! But," he added ruefully, "that was a few years back, Pamelita."

"You still wouldn't have any trouble convincing people that you're an absolute rake!" Pam teased.

"Flatterer!" he accused. "Regardless, I do think of you as a daughter, Pamelita. And I do not like to feel that one of my countrymen could be breaking your heart."

"Miguel is not breaking my heart," Pamela said. And that, essentially, was true. Perhaps her heart might be broken in the final analysis. But if that happened, it would be due to circumstances beyond their control—the shadows on their sun—Rafael, Dolores, and Anita.

She added, carefully, "There are a few things I must straighten out, Juan, that's all."

"The lover in the States?" Juan asked quickly.

"You are absolutely incorrigible!" Pamela blustered. "Yes, I need to clarify things with Charles. And get a better grip on my work. And . . . yes, I do need to resolve a couple of things with Miguel, but . . ."

"But what, Pamelita?"

"As you say in Spanish, *poco a poco*," Pamela murmured, to Juan's delight. "I'm going to have to take things a step at a time."

"Always an excellent philosophy," Juan approved.

They smiled at each other, and Pamela began to feel more relaxed. Maybe all the odds weren't so insurmountable after all. She *did* have a good head on her shoulders, or so she'd been told. Maybe if she followed her own advice, and took it a step at a time....

The first step was to find out more about the house with the yellow door. She nearly asked Juan if he knew anything about the place, and would have if Grace hadn't returned from her walk just then and joined them.

Later, Pamela decided it was prudent that she hadn't brought up the subject of the yellow door with Juan. One question was apt to lead to another, and to the necessity of giving an answer she didn't want to give. The last thing in the world she wanted Juan Basilio to know was that she suspected Rafael Rivero of having stolen her jewelry. She could imagine Juan's fury, and the type of immediate action he would take. She could envision him talking to Miguel over the phone in thunderous tones. She could picture Miguel arriving on the scene, furious because she hadn't told him of her suspicions. And then Carmen would get into the act. And Grace. And Dolores.

It was too much to contemplate.

It finally occurred to her that Roberto might be the one person she could question in safety.

This immediately created a language problem, but Roberto did know a little English, more than Pamela realized at first because he was shy about his pronunciation. Anyway, she had a Spanish dictionary and a phrase book.

The next day, while Grace was working with Juan in his study, Pamela made her way to the kitchen, taking her dictionary with her. Evidently Octavia was out, because Roberto was alone. He was sitting at the kitchen table sipping coffee and scanning the daily newspaper.

He sprang to his feet when he saw her. *"Señorita!"* he exclaimed, not only startled to see her, but obviously chagrined. He'd taken off the thin black necktie he usually wore, and evidently felt as if he'd been caught out of uniform.

"Please, Roberto, sit down," Pamela said quickly, making motions to help convey her meaning. She thought of trying to say the sentence in Spanish, then opted for a slow English. "I would like to ask you a question," she said carefully.

Roberto concentrated on every syllable. "A question?" he repeated.

"Yes. The other day, when I was out walking, I saw a house in an alley not far from here. It had a bright-yellow door, and I wondered..."

Roberto shook his head, frustrated, and Pamela realized she'd gone way beyond him.

She started again, looking up a word at a time, and then trying to make phrases in her halting Spanish. *"Hay una casa, cerca de aquí,"* she managed. "This house," she went on, lapsing into English, "has a... *una puerta amarilla."*

"Una puerta amarilla?" Roberto echoed. "A yellow door?"

"Yes," Pamela nodded. "A yellow door."

Roberto looked at her as if she'd lost her mind. Then he scowled, and said a few rapid-fire words, ending with "Calle Alfredo."

Alfred Street, Pamela translated automatically. Was that the name of the street that ran by the alley? She had no idea, and wished she'd paid more attention when she'd followed Rafael.

"On the corner," she said. *"La esquina* . . . there is a store with newspapers." She pointed to the newspaper on the table.

Roberto's scowl deepened, and then he broke into a torrent of Spanish, obviously disturbed. Whereupon Pamela threw up her hands despairingly, unable to understand a single word.

Roberto nodded grimly, and reached for the dictionary. For the next few minutes, they struggled to communicate, and succeeded.

Pamela left the kitchen knowing that the house with the yellow door was occupied by a notorious gambling establishment run by people connected with international crime. In Roberto's opinion, it was a blot on the Las Palmas scene, and should be removed. But it was difficult, even for the police, to get the kind of proof they needed to close this place down.

Learning all of this—literally, word by word—had been exhausting. Roberto had finished, growling out the syllables, "Is not a place for you to go near, *señorita.*"

Pamela was more than willing to agree with him about that!

She was heavyhearted as she took her dictionary back to her room and stashed it away. She wondered if Roberto would tell Juan about an inquiry he must have thought was rather strange. She hoped not, of course, and actually doubted that he would. She'd managed to convey that she'd merely happened to see the house and was curious, that was all. Roberto had seemed mollified when she'd left him.

Pamela was hardly at peace with herself, though. Perhaps she was leaping to conclusions, but she felt convinced that the gambling house and the theft of her jewelry were connected . . . and somehow Rafael Rivero was involved.

Rafael had his problems, and she'd only be heaping trouble upon him if she spoke to Miguel, or anyone else, about her suspicions. Even if he were absolutely innocent of the thefts, or if she'd made a mistake in judgment and he hadn't gone to the gambling house at all that afternoon, Rafael would be hauled over the coals thoroughly until the truth came out.

And there was always the chance she could be wrong. So, after another night of fitful sleep, she decided that the only satisfactory way to solve the riddle was to ask Rafael himself.

Chapter Fourteen

It was strange—very strange—to be driving up the mountainside to Miguel's house by herself. Strange, frightening, and disconcerting as she cautiously steered Grace's aged Saab around a curve.

That morning, she'd told Grace she had to go up to Arucas for just a few hours. Grace had commented that it wasn't a good day for a visit because it was Carmen's bridge day. Now that Lent was over, Carmen and Dolores met with a number of other women for bridge once a week. This week, it was Maria Suarez's turn to play hostess to the bridge party. Grace said she knew that because, on Easter Sunday, Maria had suggested that she drive up and join them.

"I can play *at* bridge," Grace told Pamela. "But I'm not in their league. They're all real whizzes."

"I don't need to see Carmen," Pamela said hesitantly, wanting to explain as little as possible to Grace.

"And...I won't be very long," she went on lamely, hoping that Grace wouldn't pose too many questions. She added, "I hate to ask you to lend me your car, because I've never driven it, but..."

"Think nothing of it," Grace rejoined airily. "Juan says it isn't a car any longer, it's a heap. I tell him the scratches are just cosmetic. Beulah—that's my car's name—could do with a face job and some new chrome here and there, but her engine is as sound as..."

Grace paused, then smiled quizzically. "What's really sound these days?" she queried. "I think the planned obsolescence theory has infiltrated the entire world."

Pamela hadn't tried to answer that. She was content to let Grace assume that the reason she wanted to go to Arucas so unexpectedly was Miguel. Because she wanted to smooth over the rift between them that Grace had imagined.

Pamela pulled up in front of the outer wall of the Rivero hacienda, and her hands grew clammy as she contemplated what she was about to do. She knew that Dolores was out playing bridge, and that Miguel was off attending to business. Again, she'd enlisted Roberto's help. Using their own brand of communication, she had asked Roberto to find Miguel's number for her, which he did from a list the Basilios kept in a kitchen drawer. Then she asked him to dial the number—first making it clear that she did not want to speak to Miguel—and ascertain whether or not Miguel would be home that afternoon.

The servant who answered the phone assured Roberto that *Señor* Rivero would not be available until much later in the day. Roberto, hanging up the receiver, had turned to Pamela to say, "He has *un problema* at the *destilateria*, and is not at the house until very late."

Roberto managed his communication in reasonably understandable English, and Pamela answered, *"Muchas gracias."* She reflected wryly that if she and Roberto kept on the way they were going, they'd soon wind up speaking each other's languages.

Climbing out of Grace's car, she wished she had Roberto with her now. Her fingers were unsteady as she rang the bell at the gate—Carmen had simply hit the horn, she remembered—and when Ignacio Ramirez appeared, he looked stern and unyielding, as if he'd never seen her before.

Then, as he peered at her more closely, he recognized her, and it occurred to Pamela that he was probably nearsighted. "Ah," he said, "the American señorita who is a friend of Doña Carmen's. *Bienvenido.*"

He opened the main gate for her, and when Pamela drove into the wide courtyard that separated Miguel's hacienda from the outside world, she nearly turned Beulah around and sped out.

Ignacio had spoken to her in heavily-accented English, but now he reverted to Spanish. Pamela managed to understand that neither Dõna Dolores nor Don Miguel were at home.

She took her courage in hand. "And Rafael?" she asked.

"Sí, es aquí," Ignacio replied rather coolly, then turned away. Pamela surmised that he would go and get him.

Meantime, she was ushered through the wrought iron gate, the garden courtyard, the massive pinewood entrance, the interior patio and, finally, the *sala* which, void of people, looked huge and disconcertingly formal. When, a moment later, Rafael appeared in the doorway,

Pamela felt that he could easily have stepped down from one of the ancestor portraits hanging on the walls.

Only Rafael's dress was different. He wore tight-fitting black pants and an open-throated white shirt. But his jet-black hair, his beautifully chiseled Castilian features, and his arrogant posture were strictly characteristics inherited from his forebears.

"You wished to see me, *señorita*?" he asked politely, then added, as if this were difficult to believe, "That is what Ignacio told me."

He moved toward her as he spoke, his face like a cameo carved from ivory-colored marble, and Pamela saw that his eyes were afire in a way that suddenly frightened her. Rafael had remarkable self-control for his age, but his eyes were giving him away. They were like hot lava in an erupting volcano. But Pamela remained steadfast.

It had not occurred to her until this moment that Rafael could be dangerous. She'd been thinking of him as a boy scarcely beyond adolescence, a boy living with a widowed aunt who didn't have any rapport with him, and a father who didn't seem to understand him.

All along, she'd felt sympathy for Rafael, a sympathy she hadn't thoroughly defined. She'd actually been protecting him by keeping her secret.

Still speaking politely, Rafael said, "Ignacio suggested I ring for coffee or sherry, if either would suit you. Personally, I don't want anything just now. Do you?"

His tone was cordial, yet he was obviously bent on being rude. Very rude. This was not unexpected, but Pamela still didn't know how to reply.

She didn't have to. Surveying her closely, Rafael asked, "Why did you come here today, *señorita*?"

Suddenly, Pamela knew he knew.

She tried to invent a plausible story, and started to say that she'd driven up from Las Palmas in the hope of finding Miguel at home... or even Dolores. Finally, she stammered, "I left something here when... when I was here before."

Rafael's eyebrows rose, and Pamela wouldn't have thought that a boy his age could look so sardonic. His tone was as cold as steel and, at the same time, abrasive as he asked, skeptically, "You left something here, in this house?"

"No," she said quickly. "No, at Carmen de Moreno's."

"And you have come here to find it?"

"No. That is, Carmen isn't at home today. I thought..."

Rafael's lips curved in a taunting smile. "What is it you left at *Tía* Carmen's, *señorita*?" he asked suddenly. "Your emerald ring?"

Shocked, Pamela's knees began to buckle. To save herself, she sat down abruptly on the nearest chair.

Rafael watched her dispassionately. "You have gone very white," he observed. "You are perhaps going to faint?"

That did it. His caustic tone got to Pamela now, and she began to smolder. "I suppose that's exactly what you wish I'd do!" she challenged him.

"No. What I wish is that you stay in Las Palmas. Better, that you went back to the United States," Rafael said, faltering slightly over the words. Despite an occasional hesitation, Pamela was surprised at how good his English was. Carmen had said that he'd studied English in school, and that he was bright, but...

She tried to find her voice, actually searching around with her eyes as if she'd mislaid it someplace. "Look, Rafael..."

"Look, Rafael," he mimicked. "May I ask, *señorita*, exactly what you expected when you came here? Did you think I would welcome you?"

Pamela's answer came involuntarily. "You've never welcomed me!" she charged, flinging the words at him, and forgetting her fright. "Neither has your aunt. I would say that despite your polite Spanish surface you've both made me feel more *unwelcome* than I've felt in my entire life. Does that satisfy you?"

Rafael glared at her in silence for several interminable moments. Suddenly, Pamela didn't give a damn any longer. Perhaps it was adrenaline suddenly rushing to her brain. Whatever, Pamela felt an infusion of raw courage, and with it came the determination to keep this arrogant young Spaniard—this rebellious boy who happened to be Miguel's son—from intimidating her any longer.

"All right," she said, hissing the words from between clenched teeth. "Let's get down to the basics, and I will determine what satisfies me or does not! Of course you were not about to welcome me here, if you're as guilty as I think you are!"

She drew a long breath, then challenged Rafael defiantly. "Did you steal my jewelry, or didn't you?" she demanded.

Pamela saw Rafael close his eyes and shudder. She sensed the effort it was taking him to summon the strength to answer her. As she waited for him to speak, she began to realize that, until a couple of seconds ago, his act had been exactly that—an act. He'd been bluffing, putting up a front he couldn't maintain.

She felt unexpected pity for Rafael, and then asked herself indignantly, *Why should I feel sorry for this offensive, arrogant boy? Why should I think anything of him except that he's a thief, and I've found him out?*

Because he is Miguel's son.

The answer was clear-cut. But it wasn't the right answer. Maybe, under other circumstances, Rafael could have become special to her because he was Miguel's son. Right now, Rafael had to stand on his own. There were just the two of them here, with one issue squarely in the way.

Rafael opened his eyes, and Pamela saw that their fire had died. The bleakness on his face shocked her even more. She'd seen that same bleakness distort Miguel's countenance when he'd told her he didn't know whether or not he had a wife.

"All right," Rafael began. "You have come here to accuse me of stealing your things." Again he shuddered. "All right," he said again. "I stole them. Is that what you want to hear?"

"No!" she exploded, shouting the denial at him.

"Then why?" he asked. "Why did you come here?"

Pamela stood, her legs again steady. She said, "Because I had to know."

"So now you know," Rafael muttered. "Now you can tell my father, if you haven't already told him. You must have spoken to Juan Basilio. It surprises me that he didn't come here with you. Or did he? Is he perhaps outside, waiting to come to your rescue if I . . ."

"If you what, Rafael?"

"Does it matter, *señorita*? If I so much as lifted a finger at you, I would be accused of all sorts of...brutality. *¿Verdad?* But that is nothing compared to what will happen when my father hears your report. And when

Juan hears? He is not my godfather, but he should have been," Rafael finished, bowing his head pensively.

"No one knows that any of my jewelry was ever stolen," she said steadily.

Rafael looked up incredulously. "How can I believe that? Am I to think you came here today with no one knowing why you come—came?" he corrected himself, unconsciously. "That would not be bravery, *señorita*, it would be craziness. Am I to believe you would come here to face someone who might…strangle you, let us say, to keep from being found out? If so, you are insane."

"Perhaps," Pamela conceded. "At the least, it was somewhat foolish. But then you're not about to strangle me, are you, Rafael?"

He turned away from her and said, over his shoulder, "Please. For just a moment, please." After that moment, Rafael faced her again, and Pamela saw his eyes shimmering with unshed tears. "I stole your jewelry," he said. "You are right in what you suspect. And so now here we are. Go tell my father, *señorita*, and then go back where you came from. Will that satisfy you?"

He looked so vulnerable, Pamela wanted to cry for him. "No," she said softly.

"Then, *por Dios*, what do you want?" he asked, clearly confused.

"I think," Pamela said, reflecting on his question, "that right now I want to talk to you. And I don't think this is the place. Your father may finish with his business at the distillery sooner than he planned. I don't know when your aunt gets back from playing bridge, but I would hate to have her walk in on us. Is there somewhere else we could go?"

Rafael shrugged. "You came in a car, did you not?"

"Yes. Grace Basilio's car."

"So, we could go for a drive. Perhaps up Arucas Mountain. It would not be crowded at this hour of the day. It would be as good a place to talk as any I can think of."

Pamela thought of the steep drive up to the top of the mountain, and hesitated. But Grace's car was very easy to handle.

She could always ask Rafael to take the wheel if there were any problems, but realized she wasn't quite ready for that. Anyway, she didn't even know whether he was old enough to have a license.

She made a sudden decision. "Come on," she told him.

They left the house without Ignacio, or anyone else, seeing them go. And when they started down the road from the Rivero property to the main, two-lane highway, Pamela began to think she was an absolute fool.

She was even more convinced of this by the time she was halfway up the mountain. Thinking back to the way Miguel had negotiated this small endurance course so easily, she wondered if he was especially cool and competent, or if she'd just stretched her nerves to the limit.

Twice, she had to pull to the side to let "downhill" vehicles pass. Each time, the drivers had honked their horns not once, but a number of times, and it occurred to Pamela that maybe they were as nervous about negotiating hairpin turns as she was!

There were very few people at the summit, even fewer than there'd been on Easter Sunday morning. Clouds had temporarily blotted out the sun, unnerving Pamela even more. She felt she'd reached a pinnacle from which it would be all too easy to tumble off. Tumble off? How about pushed off? she asked herself, and shuddered.

Rafael said suddenly, "I don't see any waiters, so I will get us some coffee." The way he said it reminded Pamela so much of Miguel, it wrenched her heart. Nevertheless, she was more than ready to sit down at one of the outdoor tables, while Rafael disappeared inside the restaurant.

As they sat opposite each other at the small round table, a sense of total unreality began to creep over Pamela. What was she *doing* here, on a mountaintop in the Canary Islands, with a recalcitrant youth who had stolen her best jewelry? Was she losing her mind?

She could see now that she'd been overly sentimental about Rafael from the very beginning. It was difficult not to react to him with sympathy even now, as she watched him sip his coffee, his face remote, his dark eyes staring out at some point in space.

It would help if he didn't look so much like his father! Annoyed at her overreaction, she glared at Rafael. It was anger at herself, rather than him, that made her blurt, "Okay, why did you steal my jewelry?"

Rafael forced his eyes to meet hers, his mouth twisted, and he said bitterly, "I needed money."

Pamela hadn't expected such a direct answer. Especially not *that* answer. "Why?" she countered, equally blunt.

"Last winter, during the Christmas season, I went with friends—classmates—into Las Palmas," Rafael told her. "We met some men in the city. They took us to a place where there is gambling."

"A house with a yellow door?"

"How would you know that?" he demanded, staring at her. "You have told my father about your jewelry, haven't you?"

"I think you know that if I'd told your father anything about anything you wouldn't be sitting here now," Pamela retorted tersely. "I know there's a gambling establishment in an alley, not far from the *paseo*. One that does not have a good reputation."

"It is . . . not legal," Rafael amended. "In this country, gambling is controlled by the government. People my age are not permitted in casinos. So you see, when I go to Las Palmas with my friends at Christmas and we meet these men . . ."

He paused, remembering. "These men invite us," he continued, "and we go with them, everyone is very friendly. In this place, they teach us to play blackjack, and in the beginning everything is fine. Then I start to lose. My friends already want to get out. I think I must try to make back the money I have lost. They will not wait for me, so they go. Then I am by myself, and I only lose more and more . . ."

Rafael was speaking slowly, awkwardly, obviously translating from Spanish to English as he went along. But he was doing a lot better than she could have done under similar circumstances.

"What happened next?" she asked.

"It got very late. I was told to come back another time, and I would have a chance to win what I had lost. I was warned not to say anything to anyone about where I had been. There was no way I could find my friends. I did not know how I could get back to Arucas, so one of the men drove me . . ."

"And found out who you were, and where you lived?"

Rafael nodded. "Yes."

The only son of a wealthy, influential family. Probably all of the boys Rafael had been with that night fell into the same category. They'd most likely been spotted on their own in the city, and easily led to slaughter. Except that the other boys evidently had been lucky enough to quit before they fell into holes of their own digging. Not so with Rafael.

"You went back, of course," Pamela stated, rather than asked.

"Yes, and it became worse and worse, *señorita*. I lost more and more. It seemed impossible for me to win."

I can imagine, Pamela thought wryly.

"So they said to me that I must get the money and pay them, or they would go to my family. As it was, *Tía* Dolores was beginning to get suspicious about me. I would try to slip out of town into Las Palmas at times like today, when she plays bridge. But then, during Lent, she was at home or in church almost all of the time. I had to take more chances. Once, you will remember, she was about to call the police."

"Yes."

"Before then, I knew I must do something. You came to dinner, *señorita*, and I saw the jewelry you were wearing, and I knew emeralds were valuable. And...I thought it would be safe to steal from you. You are a stranger; I thought you would not be coming back to Arucas, and..."

"And," Pamela said steadily, "you did not like me anyway."

"Yes," Rafael admitted quietly. "I did not like you anyway."

Their eyes met and, to her surprise, Pamela saw a grudging admiration in Rafael's gaze.

"How did you get into Carmen's house late at night?" she asked. "Not just once, but twice? How could you know where I'd keep my jewelry?"

"*Tía* Carmen is my godmother," Rafael said simply. "Her house is like mine. Her kitchen doors are never locked. So, both times I entered by the kitchen door. I know the room in which *Tía* Carmen usually puts her guests. And you were there."

Rafael paused, and swallowed hard. Then he said, "On the first time, I found only your necklace."

"Pendant," Pamela corrected.

Rafael shrugged. "It was on top of the dresser. I had a small flashlight, but I did not see the ring. Then, you moved in your sleep. I was afraid you would wake up. I took the . . . pendant and I left very quickly. As soon as I could, I went with it to Las Palmas, and the men there were pleased. They said they would take off a sum from my debt with them. But they warned me it was still not enough.

"So . . . you came to Arucas at Easter and I saw you wearing the jewel I had stolen. I could not believe my eyes."

"Some of your friends run a booth in the Parque de Santa Catalina. Either that, or they sell to the man in the bazaar," Pamela informed Rafael. "That's where I found my pendant, where I bought it back. At quite a price, I might add."

"Yes," Rafael nodded. "I am sure they, too, robbed you. Anyway, when you returned to Arucas for Easter, I did not dare to take the pendant again. But . . . I did, as you know, go into your room at *Tía* Carmen's late that night and . . . I took your ring."

"And you gave it to the men in the gambling place?"

Rafael shook his head. "No. I have not been able to go to Las Palmas. *Tía* Dolores watches me like she suspects me of something. Even my father has been around more than usual. So, I have had no chance. And now . . ."

Again, Rafael met her eyes. "The ring is in my room, in my house," he said. "I will return it to you."

"And I suppose you will ask for my silence in return?" Pamela suggested.

"Your silence?"

"I suppose the deal is that you will give me back my ring if I say nothing to your father about this? Obviously, the reason you went through this whole thing in the first place is because you didn't want to risk having your father approached by these gamblers."

"What does that matter to you?" Rafael asked roughly. "You are like all the other women my father meets. You are American, yes. But I begin to think that doesn't make so much difference. You still look at him in the same way all the others do, with eyes that tell the whole story."

All the other women? Pamela gritted her teeth, consumed by a massive dose of jealousy.

Just how many women had paraded around the Rivero house, within Rafael's memory, gazing adoringly at his father?

"Well?" Rafael challenged. "You are in love with him, are you not?"

"Suppose I am?" Pamela hurled back.

"It is nothing to me, *señorita*," he said defiantly. "Nothing. I am, anyway, at the...end of my rope. Those men in Las Palmas are going to come to my father when I fail to give them more money, or more jewelry. So, he is going to find out, one way or another. And God knows what he will do to me then."

Pamela asked slowly, "Have you ever thought of telling your father about this problem yourself?"

Rafael laughed shortly. "I am not entirely insane," he advised her.

"It's easy to see," she said, "that you are very bitter about your father. I don't know why, and it's none of my business. I have known your father for only a short time. However, I think I know him well enough to say that if you told him, he would first be very angry. But then he would try to help you."

Rafael smiled derisively. "My father has never tried to help me, *señorita*," he informed her. "And I am not crazy enough to think he might start now. He will feel I have disgraced him, and my family. And I suppose that is true enough. So, he will consider it his duty to punish me as severely as possible. I can assure you he will enjoy every moment of that punishment."

"Come on, Rafael," Pamela protested. "You don't know what you're saying."

"Yes, I know what I am saying," Rafael contradicted her. "But whatever happens does not really matter, *señorita*. Nothing could make things worse than they are."

Briefly, very briefly, Pamela glimpsed a very hurt and bewildered boy. Regardless of everything, her heart went out to him. His arrogance, his bravado, his aloofness were all cloaks hiding deep pain.

"I think you should give your father a chance, Rafael."

He looked at her bitterly. "There is no chance for me with my father," he said soberly. "My father hates me. He has always hated me."

Pamela stared at him, shocked.

"What I say is true," he told her. "I remind my father of *her*."

"Your mother?" Pamela managed.

"Yes, my mother," Rafael repeated, then got up and stood very straight. "So, there is nothing more for us to say. We may as well go back."

Chapter Fifteen

Rafael was right; they'd said everything there was to say to each other—for the moment. But they were not finished with each other. Before they reached the Rivero's house, Pamela was determined to bring at least part of their problem to resolution.

Unfortunately, the mountain road was so treacherous that she wasn't able to think about anything except driving. Just remembering to honk her horn when she approached a curve was a chore.

By her side, Rafael was silent, slumped back against the seat. Pamela darted a glance at him, and saw that his eyes were closed. Emotional weariness? she wondered. In any event, she couldn't blame him for shutting his eyes if her driving was making him half as nervous as it was herself.

Pamela thought she'd never get to the base. She felt a rush of relief to see the main two-lane road ahead of her, and automatically made a right turn, then sank back, relaxing. Funny, how one's concepts changed, depending upon circumstances. She'd thought *this* road was something of a challenge, coming from Las Palmas. Now it seemed like a superhighway.

She drove, lost in a maze of thoughts. Glancing again at Rafael, she saw the steady rise and fall of his chest. He'd actually fallen asleep. If she'd needed any indication to suspect he was exhausted, that was it.

Somehow, she had to help Rafael and Miguel work out this tangled mess between them. Rafael had been wrong to steal from her, there was no doubt about that. Yet there were extenuating circumstances, not all of them having to do with his gambling debt.

He'd admitted, in response to her prodding, that he didn't like her. Obviously, she was another in a long line of women interested in his father, many of them no doubt gold diggers. Though she winced at the thought of being classed with such company, Pamela could see how such a parade might have a destructive effect upon a young, impressionable, motherless boy. The women must have appeared, to Rafael, as potential stepmothers. And he already had his Aunt Dolores to contend with.

It wasn't that Pamela was trying to make excuses for him, she insisted to herself as she drove along. *Of course* he'd had no right to steal from her, and should be punished. But she shrank from imagining the kind of punishment Rafael indicated his father would inflict.

Was Miguel really so heartless? Did he really hate his own son because Rafael reminded him of the wife who'd deserted him? Actually, Rafael looked very much like Miguel. Was his temperament more like Anita's?

There was no way to answer these questions. The miles passed, and suddenly Pamela realized she'd been driving for quite a while; she should have come to the road to Miguel's house before now.

Suddenly, she saw the road ahead, bearing off the highway. She swerved onto it almost too quickly, glad that she hadn't missed Miguel's turn after all.

But her relief was short-lived. As the road began to climb and twist, growing narrower every second, she realized she was lost. There was no place at all to turn around.

When the car jounced over one especially hard bump, Rafael woke up. He rubbed his eyes dazedly, then peered out the window. *"Dios!"* he exclaimed. "Where are you taking us?"

"I thought I was taking you home," Pamela said tightly.

"But we are driving away from Arucas." Rafael complained. "You have already come a long way. Did you have no concept you had made a mistake?"

"No, I did not." Pamela gritted her teeth once more. She'd been thinking about *him*, damn it! If anyone was responsible for her mistake it was Rafael, she thought, and then admitted she was being unfair.

"When you came off the mountain to the main road, which way did you turn?" Rafael asked.

"Right," Pamela said, concentrating on yet another hairpin bend. She couldn't believe that she'd got into such a rugged area so quickly. But the road was little more than a narrow lane at this point, hugging a deep ravine.

"You should have turned left," Rafael pointed out.

"Great!" Pamela hissed. "You should have been awake when I needed you to give me some directions."

"This way," Rafael said practically, "we will not get anywhere. And, before long, it will be dark...."

"Tell me about it," Pamela snapped.

"I *am* telling you about it, *señorita*. You must find a place to turn around."

"Could you suggest a likely site?"

"Often, there are places at the sides of these roads, where you can turn around," Rafael said.

"Okay, then," she agreed. "Keep your eyes out."

But there evidently were no turnarounds on this road. It was all Pamela could do to keep her mind off the frightening drop just inches beyond her wheels on the right. The ravine appeared to be hundreds and hundreds of feet deep. They'd plainly never heard of guardrails in the Canaries, Pamela thought dismally. Not that a guardrail would make that much difference if she were to lose control and slam into it.

Another bend appeared, and Pamela was about to blow her horn when she fancied she heard the horn of a car approaching from above. It could be her imagination playing tricks on her, but there was no way of telling, because the curve ahead was completely blind.

Pamela panicked, and could think only of the ravine looming to her right, and how a passing car would almost surely force Grace's Saab off the edge. Now, she couldn't keep herself from staring toward the ravine; it was enough to make her lose control. Thinking only of getting away from that gaping chasm—thinking of imminent disaster—she swerved, and rammed the car hard into the side of the mountain.

There was blackness, and then slowly there was light, but there was no sense of time at all. Days, even years, could have passed. Pamela was caught in limbo, in a nether realm filled with agonizing pain. Pain tortured her body in not one, but a number of places, and her head ached intolerably. Also, strangely enough, there was warm water—very warm water—dripping continuously. Pamela carefully moved her hand toward her head, intending to brush the water from her face. Instead she encountered a damp cloth.

She opened her eyes to find Rafael peering down at her anxiously. He was holding a large handkerchief that was dripping wet.

"I am sorry the water is so warm," he said. "I got it out of the car radiator."

Pamela smiled weakly. "That was ingenious," she managed. She knew, only too well, that a person was not apt to stumble across a brook or running stream on Grand Canary.

Rafael crouched down next to her. "There will be help coming, sooner or later," he said.

"How do you know that?"

"Not many cars use this road . . ." he began.

"Now I realize that," Pamela agreed cynically.

"A man came by with his *burro* and a small wagon. But it was too small to carry even you," Rafael told her. "So, we are lucky. He will find a place where he can summon help for us."

"Eventually?"

Rafael managed a tiny grin. "Yes, eventually. In the meantime, I . . . dragged you in here."

Pamela became aware that she was lying in the shelter of a cave. There wasn't any rock, just hard-packed dirt walls, and an equally hard dirt floor.

"I could not leave you in the road," Rafael explained. "This . . . was safer. It is a cave used by the Guanches a very long time ago. Do not worry. It is strong."

"I'm not worried about that. I'm more worried about whether anyone will ever find us."

"They will find us," Rafael said confidently, then fell silent.

Pamela managed to glance toward him, and saw a strange, brooding expression on his face. "What is it?" she asked sharply.

"We were lucky," Rafael said simply. "You had the thought to turn the car toward the mountain, when you felt it going out of control. With my mother, the car went the other way. Into a deep ravine, not too far from here."

"What?"

Rafael nodded. "When my mother ran away, long ago, she did not get very far. They . . . crashed. It is so thickly covered with bushes, where the car fell, that the place cannot be seen from the road. But . . . my grandmother knew where it was. The mother of my mother, you understand. People from the hills came to tell her, because one of them saw the accident and told the others. She was a woman of—how should I say it?—of religious influence. She pledged them to silence."

"Your grandmother never told your father this?" It was incredible, beyond reason or comprehension.

Rafael shook his head. "She hated my father," he stated. "She hated him because he never loved my mother. He married her only because she was pregnant . . . with me. My father at that time was young and . . ."

Rafael's English suddenly failed him. *"Joven y impetuoso,"* he finished. Young and impetuous.

Pamela closed her eyes, waves of emotional as well as physical pain enveloping her. Hot tears stung her eyelids.

"How long have you known this?" she asked Rafael.

"Since three years, a little more than three years," he answered. "As my grandmother was dying, she told me what had happened to my mother. She pledged me to silence. She made me take a vow."

"My God, Rafael..." It was dim in the cave, and would soon be dark outside, but right now that didn't matter. What mattered—more than anything Pamela could remember—was the enormity of what Rafael had just told her.

"How could you have kept this from your father?" she demanded. "How _could_ you?"

Rafael shook his head dully.

"You know that all these years your father has continued to search for your mother, all over the world. You know..."

"Yes," Rafael said. "Yes, I know."

Pamela saw the spasm of pain that shook him. Physical pain. Pure, wrenching, physical pain.

"Rafael," she cried. "You're hurt!"

He nodded, and managed the faintest of smiles. "Yes," he admitted. "Yes...I think my arm is broken."

And with that he passed out.

By the time help arrived, Pamela was delirious with fatigue. The next few hours were hazy for her.

She realized that she was in a hospital. She tried to communicate with the nurse who seemed to have been put on guard duty next to her bed, but the nurse didn't understand English. After a minute, the nurse muttered something rather desperately and left the room. Shortly thereafter, a young, dark-haired doctor came in. Following on his heels came Miguel.

Miguel's face was a mask in which his eyes burned like live coals. Pamela shrank away from the sight of him, tried to say something, couldn't think of what to say, and fell silent.

Miguel confined his conversation to a dialogue with the doctor. This evidently concluded, he turned to Pamela. "You must spend the night here as a precaution," he reported tersely. "Your injuries do not appear to be serious, but they want to be sure. You are badly bruised, but there are no bones broken. You have a slight concussion. But on the whole, you have been very fortunate."

"And Rafael?" she asked.

She saw Miguel's eyelids flicker as he heard his son's name, but his voice was emotionless. "Rafael has a broken arm, but there seems to be nothing else wrong. I am taking him home with me tonight. I will call for you in the morning."

With that, Miguel turned and strode out of the room.

Pamela was too proud to call after him. Too proud to let the nurse see her cry. She suffered in a sort of frozen silence through the next few hours, then they gave her something to help her sleep, and the night passed.

When Miguel came for her the next morning, Pamela was ready and waiting to leave. He insisted that he was going to get a wheelchair for her, but she told him icily that she was entirely capable of walking under her own power. With that, she shrugged off his assistance.

Miguel settled her into his car, then took his place behind the wheel. He started to drive, but before he reached the end of the hospital parking lot, he pulled to the side and shut off the motor.

"All right," he said. "You have put the fear of God into me, you have caused me to suffer... unmercifully. Now don't you think you owe it to me to tell me what you were doing on a back road in a borrowed car with my son?''

As he confronted her, Pamela could see that even though he was making a tremendous effort to keep his mask in place, it was beginning to crumble. She looked at him, her lower lip began to tremble, and she couldn't hold back the tears.

"You are such a fool!" she blurted accusingly. "Such an arrogant, stubborn fool. Exactly like a grown-up version of Rafael!"

"*Rafael?*" he echoed, thunderstruck by her statement. "Rafael?" he said again, then laughed bitterly. "I would say that Rafael and I have very little in common."

"On the contrary, you are ridiculously much alike," Pamela informed him. "In all the wrong ways."

"The wrong ways?"

"Yes, the wrong ways," she repeated impatiently. "Stubborn, unyielding, hot-tempered, unforgiving... do you want me to go on?"

For a moment, Pamela thought she'd pushed him too far. Then Miguel said reflectively, "No, I don't want you to go on. Maybe someday I'll ask you a few more questions along those lines, but right now..."

Miguel drew a deep breath. "Do you have *any* idea how much I love you?" he demanded.

His question was a jolt, her answer shaky. "I...I guess I thought I did," she stammered.

"Thought!" he scoffed. "Can you begin to imagine how I felt when Grace called last night and said you had borrowed her car to drive up here, and you hadn't returned? Then Ignacio informed me that you had been here, and that evidently you and Rafael had gone off together? And then, hours later, there came a call from the police that some... some man from the hills with a donkey cart had come in to report that you were in a Guanche cave miles from anywhere. With that, my heart stopped beating. I nearly went out of my mind with worry and..."

"Rafael was wonderful," Pamela cut in shortly.

"What?"

"I said Rafael was wonderful. His arm was broken, though I didn't know it at the time. The pain must have been terrible, but he still managed to dip his handkerchief in water from the car radiator and wash my face. At that moment, it was almost like having you there."

"I don't think I understand," Miguel said darkly.

He was scowling, but as he surveyed Pamela more closely, his expression changed to one of deep concern. Slowly, he shook his head. "What I want more than anything in the world is to take you in my arms and convince you of my love for you. But I can't do that just now, can I, *querida*? Even a hug, I am afraid, would cause you to yelp with pain. So I shall take you home."

It didn't occur to Pamela that by "home" Miguel meant anything other than Grace's house, or perhaps, Carmen's. But when they turned off the highway onto the "right" road, she knew she was mistaken. He was taking her to his house. To Dolores's house.

Inadvertently, she reacted. "No."

"No?" Miguel echoed.

"I can't go to your house. You should know that."

He kept his eyes on the road. "And why not?"

"You should know that, too. I would not be welcome. Dolores..."

"The house does not belong to Dolores," Miguel said evenly. "It belongs to me. Perhaps you didn't realize that."

"It doesn't matter. Dolores..."

"Like all of us, Dolores has just had a bad night," Miguel stated. "It would be charitable of you to give her another chance, Pamelita."

They were virtually at his gate, and Pamela was too tired, and too weak to argue with him.

Ignacio was waiting for them by the garage, while Dolores, Carmen and Ignacio's wife, Maruca, were all anxiously standing at the entrance to the garden courtyard.

For the next fifteen minutes, Pamela was exposed to a constant murmur, mostly in Spanish, as the women fussed over her. Then she lay in a wide bed covered with a beautiful hand-embroidered spread, having been cautioned to rest so that she would heal quickly. But tired though she was, rest was impossible.

After a while, Maruca arrived with chicken broth and toasted homemade bread. Pamela could hear the echo of voices in the distance, and knew that Miguel and the others must be having their *comida* in the dining room.

Then she heard a sound at her door, and looked up to see Rafael standing on the threshold. His eyes were jet black and enormous as he stared across the room at her, and his face looked chalky, almost as white as the sling that supported his arm in a heavy cast.

Pamela saw him moisten his lips. "My father told me that you were all right. But...I had to be sure."

She saw him reach, with his good hand, into his trousers pocket. Then he came over to the bed and, thrusting out his hand said, "Here."

Pamela found herself gaping at her emerald ring.

"I am sorry, *señorita*," Rafael said, his voice low. "I am very sorry. I...want you to know that. I want you to know, too, that I understand you must tell my father. I will not blame you."

"Rafael..." Pamela hesitated, wanting to be sure to say the right words. "I don't want to tell your father."

"What are you saying?"

"I want *you* to tell your father," she persisted. "I want you to tell him exactly what happened, and how it happened. I think he'll understand. After all, he was young once himself...."

"Was he really?" a sardonic voice behind Rafael asked dryly.

Miguel stood in the doorway, his hands in his pockets, inscrutably surveying the scene.

"So," he said, strolling forward. "What is it I am expected to understand because I was young once myself...incredible though that may seem?"

Pamela said hotly, "I don't think much of eavesdropping."

"I wasn't cavesdropping," Miguel said calmly. "I was coming to see how you were."

He sat down on the edge of her bed as if he belonged there, while Pamela glared at him. "It would seem that there are things you should tell me, Rafael," he said.

Rafael answered in swift Spanish, and Miguel heard him out. Then he told his son, "I think you can manage in English...and that we should, for Pamela's benefit. It seems she has risked a great deal, maybe even her life, to save you from...something. I think I have a right to know why."

Rafael stood silent, his lips compressed, his stance mutinous. His eyes sparkled with resentment.

"I think that I would rather you called the police," he announced, turning away. "I think I would prefer to tell them."

"Talk some sense, Rafael!" Pamela advised impatiently. "Anyway, as far as I'm concerned, the police have nothing to charge you with."

"Are you saying to me . . . ?"

"That I refuse to say anything about anything?" Pamela interjected. "Yes, that's what I'm saying."

Rafael shook his head, as if he couldn't believe this. Then he faced his father, and said defiantly, "I stole her pendant, and her ring, from *Tía* Carmen's house because I gambled in Las Palmas and I owe a lot of money. I was . . . threatened, unless I somehow raised it."

His voice sounding hoarse, Rafael continued, "She bought her own necklace back, in the Parque de Santa Catalina. I gave her the ring, just now. Even so . . . I did steal it. And if she had not come here yesterday, I would have taken it to Las Palmas and given it to those men."

"And you think they would have wiped out your debt to them?" Miguel asked caustically.

"No," Rafael conceded. "No, I know they wouldn't."

"So!" Miguel said sharply. "At least you have some sense. But how in God's name were you such an idiot to . . . ?"

Pamela cut in. "Does it occur to you," she asked Miguel, "that Rafael has just been very brave?"

Miguel had been glaring at his son, but now he swung around to glare at her. Then his face softened, and he asked quietly, "And what do you call bravery, Pamelita?"

She hesitated, then she said, slowly, "Facing up to you, to begin with. Having the courage to admit he's done something very wrong. Trying to make amends. Also, yesterday, helping someone as Rafael helped me, even though he must have been going through hell with his arm. If he'd left me lying in the middle of that road, even though it isn't used very often..."

"Please!" Miguel implored, reaching out a hand as if he could stop what she was saying by force, if necessary. "That is not something I even want to think about. But...you are right." He faced his son. "You *have* been brave, Rafael. And I am glad I have been lucky enough to find this out. I doubt I ever would have learned it directly from you.

"But," Miguel added, "there is one thing I hope you appreciate. If Pamela were not so generous, you might indeed be arrested...and find yourself facing a prison term."

"I know that," Rafael said, still staring at the floor. "But I may still have a prison term. I owe the money..."

"You owe those people nothing!" Miguel stated harshly. "They are criminals, operating outside the law, taking advantage of boys like yourself who are too young to know any better." Suddenly, he smiled. "As you suggest, Pamelita, I was once young myself."

Pamela could not repress a smile. She suddenly remembered Miguel telling her how, as a youth, he'd wanted to go to Madrid to "play around a little" and also study the piano. She remembered, much more recently, that Miguel had demonstrated his own fondness for gambling in the casino at the other end of the island. True, Miguel did not risk money he couldn't afford to lose, but discretion and maturity had come with the years. She could imagine how he must have been when he was Rafael's age, he and his son had a lot more in common than he realized.

Miguel said levelly, "You may like to know that though I don't condone what Rafael has done—somehow he must atone for it—I can understand how it could happen.''

Pamela nodded. She desperately wanted to say that there was one way Rafael could, indeed, atone for what he'd done. He could break the vow he'd made to his grandmother. He could reveal the terrible secret he'd harbored so long from his father.

She couldn't say this to Rafael in front of Miguel, though, without violating Rafael's confidence. So she let them both go, Rafael leaving the room first, and Miguel following a minute later.

Carmen came in as soon as Miguel had left, and reported, among other things, that Grace and Juan had telephoned. ''Grace says that you must not worry about the car,'' Carmen said. ''Juan told her it is a blessing to be rid of it, and that they are lucky that you were not hurt severely.''

Late in the afternoon, Dolores appeared with a glass of sherry. ''I do not think this would hurt you,'' she said, handing the glass to Pamela. ''Miguel tells me that you are not on any medication.''

''Perhaps a couple of aspirin before I go to bed for the night, that's all,'' Pamela agreed.

Dolores was trying to be friendly, but it was still very difficult for Pamela to relate to this woman. She wondered if anything had been said to Dolores about Rafael's problems. Did she know about the gambling or the theft?

By the time Dolores left her room, Pamela was certain that Rafael's secret was known only to Miguel and herself—and the men who ran the gambling ring.

It was the next morning before she had a chance to talk to Rafael alone. By then, she'd examined her bruises in dismay. They were large and ugly, and would take weeks to fade. But at least they *would* fade, and would probably be less painful with each passing day.

She dressed carefully in some loose and comfortable clothes that Carmen loaned her. Then she slowly made her way out onto the patio. There was no one around at the moment, so she progressed to the kitchen. She found Rafael there, eating a large slice of sweet bread, liberally spread with butter.

Maruca promptly offered Pamela anything she might like, conveying the offer primarily by means of sign language. Pamela refused, in much the same fashion, having finished breakfast in her room not long before.

Then she turned to Rafael. "I wonder... could we manage to talk, just by ourselves, do you think?"

Rafael couldn't repress a smile. "Another car ride, *señorita*?" he teased her.

His humor surprised her, especially under the circumstances, and his smile was enchanting.

"Definitely not another car ride. How about a walk?"

"That will be rather difficult for you. Are you not in much pain now?"

"Well, it's my arms and shoulders that hurt the most," Pamela told him. "My legs are okay."

"Have you seen yet how bananas grow?" Rafael asked.

"Not really."

"Then I will show you that."

They went out through a kitchen door, emerging next to a service gate in the rear wall. The banana fields began almost immediately on the other side of the wall and, as he led Pamela down a path that wove through row after row of tall bushes laden with fruit, Rafael said, "The bananas grow in large clusters, upside down. That is their flower. That big, red blossom. Or would you say it is pink?''

"A very dark pink, I'd call it.''

"Many of the stalks have been covered with those blue plastic bags. That is done as the harvest approaches. The idea is to conserve as much moisture as possible.''

"Did I ever tell you that your English is very good, Rafael?'' Pamela complimented him.

"I have many times heard my father talk in English to people about the business,'' Rafael said modestly. "So, I have remembered his words.'' He turned and faced his new student. "What is it you want to talk to me about, *señorita*?'' he asked abruptly.

"Do you suppose you could call me something other than *señorita*?'' she suggested. "Pamela, perhaps?''

Rafael smiled slightly. "I think I would prefer to call you Pamelita, as my father and *Tía* Carmen do.''

"Then please do.''

"Okay, Pamelita, what is it you wish to talk to me about?''

She looked at him, standing tall and straight before her—too thin, so young, so vulnerable.

"Rafael,'' she began shakily, knowing she was treading on dangerous ground, "I know how... well, how important a vow is. Especially a promise you make to someone you love, when they are dying.''

A wary gleam crept into Rafael's dark eyes.

"But,'' Pamela continued steadily, "sometimes a deathbed promise can be terribly unfair to the people who live on. It can keep them from fulfilling their own destinies. Do you know what I mean?''

"I think so,'' he admitted.

"It can cause someone who may not *want* to hurt someone, to do exactly that.'' She paused, and gathered her courage. "You have been doing a great wrong, Rafael, and you will continue to, unless you tell your father what really happened to your mother."

Rafael said stubbornly, "I loved my grandmother, Pamelita. It is not my fault that she and my father hated each other. Her family was different from the Riveros. More simple people, if you know what I mean?"

"Yes." Pamela nodded. "I can imagine."

"My mother," he said, "I remember very little, almost not at all. Like I saw her once in a dream, and then she was gone. So, I cannot say what was right and what was wrong about what she did."

"You're not supposed to have to say that, Rafael!" Pamela blurted. "You were a little child. You had nothing to do with anything those people did. Even when you made that promise to your grandmother, you were so young...."

"Yes," he agreed. "But not so young that I didn't know what a promise was. A solemn vow, before God. Certainly before my grandmother."

"God would not ask you to keep that promise," Pamela said, and wondered if Rafael would consider her blasphemous for saying so.

"Perhaps you are right," he murmured.

"This is the one way you can truly make up for getting in trouble in Las Palmas, and for taking my jewelry," Pamela said. "You would be doing the greatest thing you could ever do for your father. So think about it, Rafael, okay?"

"I will think about it," Rafael said gravely.

They turned, by unspoken consent, and started back to the house. At the gate, Rafael paused with his hand on the latch. "It is true that I did not like you in the beginning. But now, Pamelita, I like you very much indeed."

Chapter Sixteen

When Pamela called Las Palmas on the phone in Miguel's library and asked someone to come and get her, Grace said quickly, "Either Juan or I will be there for you before noon, Pam. Don't worry about a thing."

Miguel had left the house before Pamela got up that morning. And when she told Dolores that she had to get back to the city—she'd used the excuse of being far behind in her research—Miguel's sister actually seemed regretful. She had to give Dolores points. She'd made every effort to be pleasant, this time. Pamela had an idea that this gratitude somehow involved Rafael, but she couldn't imagine why.

Grace tried to make small talk on the drive back to Las Palmas. Pamela was thankful that at least for now, Grace wasn't asking any awkward questions.

Grace lightly dismissed the fact that her car was now a good-for-nothing junk heap. "What matters is that neither you nor Rafael were seriously injured," she said, then added quietly, "It was bad enough as it was, Pam. Miguel was absolutely frantic after the police called. He started out to try to find you himself, but they convinced him it would be best if he waited at the hospital."

"He was concerned about Rafael," Pamela said reasonably.

"I'm sure he was concerned about Rafael," Grace agreed. "But he was *hellishly* concerned about you! I wish you'd stop underestimating the effect you have on that man." She paused deliberately, then said, "Incidentally, your Charles Evans has been phoning on a daily basis."

"What?"

"Would you believe it, it seems you made the papers in the States?"

"What are you saying, Grace?" Pamela asked wearily.

"Exactly what you just heard, darling. Some correspondent in Las Palmas evidently found out that my car had been wrecked on a remote mountain road. They checked with the hospital in Arucas and found out that you were the driver. So there was a *very* small item in the *New York Times* to the effect that an American scientist had been injured while on a research project on Grand Canary. And that was you, Pam, my dear! Juan was absolutely delighted. He's always said you were going to be famous."

"I don't think it's funny," Pamela said sourly.

"Well, it's a nice aftermath," Grace disagreed. "Evidently, this Charles person never misses a word in the

Times. He was agitated, let me tell you. As a matter of fact, it was all I could do to persuade him not to take the first plane to Las Palmas."

"Oh, please . . ." Pamela protested.

"He has an important case coming up in court and, since I convinced him you were all right, I don't think he'll fly over," Grace said quickly. "It wouldn't be a bad idea, though, for you to give him a call."

Pamela put a call through to Charles Evans that evening at about ten-thirty, completely forgetting about the five-hour time difference between Las Palmas and New York. It was five-thirty in the afternoon in Manhattan, and Charles had just got home from work. He was obviously irritable, and it took him a few long seconds to realize it was really Pamela on the phone.

At first, he was pleased to verify for himself that she was alive and well. He sounded angry, he said, because he'd just been stuck in a maddening rush hour jam on the subway. Then he began to reproach her, and insisted that she give him the date of her return to New York. Gradually, the conversation disintegrated, and by the time she hung up Pamela was sorry she'd called him in the first place. She decided to join Juan and Grace for a nightcap upstairs in the solarium.

As she trudged up the stairs, Pamela was still feeling tired and achy from the accident, but mostly she felt disheartened. Her bridges were burned with Charles; there was no doubt of that after tonight's dialogue. Once he thought over what they'd said to each other, she was sure he'd begin to come to that same conclusion. They were people who ultimately, perhaps, might be very good friends. But lovers again? Never.

Still, it wasn't Charles who was causing her to feel as if her whole life had been chopped into splinters. Nor was it the accident, or Rafael.

It was, of course, Miguel. He'd seemed so *angry* with her yesterday.

True, maybe he'd been frantic when he'd heard about the accident . . . because of Rafael, as well as because of her. Actually, he'd been surprisingly understanding as they'd extracted the painful admission of Rafael's gambling escapade and the later thefts. Even so, beneath the surface, something had simmered deep inside. Before she and Miguel could truly get together, something would have to give.

Pamela was brooding as she walked into the solarium, and was not even remotely prepared to face Miguel. He got slowly to his feet as she entered. The sight of him was a shock.

She was seeing Miguel as he would look twenty years from now. At least twenty years from now. His face appeared to have become lined overnight, his brow was furrowed, and there were dark circles under his eyes. His hair hadn't been combed very carefully, and even his clothes looked rumpled.

He said, without preamble, "Grace tells me you were talking to your friend in New York?"

"Yes, I was," Pamela stated, wondering why she had to feel so defensive about her answer. Damn it, did the sparks always have to fly?

"I hope it was an enjoyable conversation," he said, with suspicious mildness.

"It wasn't," she assured him, lifting her chin in preparation to do verbal battle.

Juan and Grace exchanged significant glances, and Juan said, "I have some work I must finish before I can call it a night. And Grace has promised to help me."

"Liars," Miguel accused, smiling at them. "But thank you, anyway." He waited until Grace and Juan had started down the stairs, then turned toward Pamela. Tension stretched like a tight steel cable across the ten feet that separated them.

Pamela tried to look at him. Instead, she gave her attention to the panorama that was spread out before her. The city glittered with lights, and on the Playa de Las Canteras the colors reflected from the *paseo* streamed across the sand, sending silvery ribbons over the dark water beyond.

Overhead, the sky was even darker than the water, and the stars were diamond-brilliant, the crescent moon a white metal sliver. Pamela even fancied that she could smell a gardenia . . . and was startled when a gardenia, so incredibly fragrant, so everlastingly reminiscent of Miguel, was thrust into her hand.

"A small peace offering?" he suggested. "A very small peace offering, perhaps? Oh God," he confessed. "I have been so angry with you, Pamela."

"I know." Her voice trembled, and she fought a brief battle for control. "What I don't understand," she managed to stammer, "is why?"

"Don't you remember that we made a promise? Don't you remember that? No secrets."

"*You* made a promise," she said gently.

"It was my impression that you . . . agreed with me, *querida*."

"No," she said, shaking her head slightly. "I couldn't make you that promise. Not just then."

"Because of Rafael?"

"Yes."

Miguel sighed again. "Sit down, will you. So will I. I need to put some distance between us, otherwise I will go completely crazy. And you're still all battered and bruised..."

"I'm getting better."

He laughed. "Is that an invitation?"

"No," Pamela said steadily. "No, there are too many things to settle between us first."

After a moment, he nodded solemnly. "I agree. So first of all, Pamelita, I must tell you that I owe you a debt I can never hope to repay, even if I lived for a thousand years."

She frowned. "I don't know what you're talking about."

"Rafael...told me about his mother."

Such a simple statement, with so many complex emotional overtones! Pamela felt a chill as she looked up to meet Miguel's midnight gaze. Rafael had done what she prayed he would, but it was impossible to tell from Miguel's expression whether or not his awful burden had been lifted.

"He came to my office this morning shortly after I got to work. This time, he had the principal's permission to leave school." Miguel closed his eyes tightly and shuddered. "He told me—because of you."

The lump in Pamela's throat made it almost impossible for her to speak. Still, she managed to say, "Yes...we talked."

Something indefinable flashed across Miguel's face. "This afternoon, workers from my plantation combed the ravine where they crashed. They found the car. And..."

He didn't have to finish the sentence. Pamela knew what he was going to say, and her eyes filled with tears. She ached for him, yearned to console him, and could only begin to imagine what he was going through. "Oh my darling, my darling..." Forgetting everything except her love for him, she bridged the distance between them and threw her arms around him, ignoring her physical hurt because his emotional hurt was so much greater.

Miguel nestled her head against his shoulder with one arm, and gently encircled her waist with the other. "Yes, they were there in the car," he whispered, "where they have been all these years. Anita, and her lover...less than twelve kilometers from where I live. Can you believe that?"

Pamela answered by clutching him more tightly.

"And so now," he added heavily, "there will have to be a proper funeral, to satisfy everyone. Not me, certainly. But there are other families involved, and there is Rafael. So, that will be the end of a very sorry chapter, Pamelita."

"Yes, it will," she whispered.

After a moment, Miguel said, "Rafael says he told you I never loved his mother."

Pamela's mouth was dry. "Yes, that is what he said."

"Well, Rafael was right. It's true, I never loved his mother, though I don't know what my admitting it will make you think of me. I was young and...and crazy. And she was a very pretty girl. One thing led to another. We were not as wise as people are in the States. Anita became pregnant. Her mother went to my father. There was no discussion of anything except my marrying her.

"From the first day, as you might imagine, it was a disaster. But from such an unhappy union there did come Rafael. Only I never could reach him, not even when he was a small child. There was Dolores, on one side, trying to make him into the son she never had herself. And his grandmother on the other side, hating me with every fiber of her body and exerting her influence on Rafael even though he was too young to know what was happening.

"But now, finally... because of you, maybe there is a chance for Rafael and me to have a decent relationship. You have reached him in a way no one else ever has. Not even Carmen, though she adores him and they are reasonably close."

Pamela stood and moved toward the windows again. Looking out over the glittering lights and the water she asked, skeptically, "What about that parade of women who have traipsed through your house?"

Miguel's eyebrows arched, and he looked totally puzzled. "What women are you talking about?"

"Rafael said there have always been women," Pamela reported, "even though I got the impression that it was, perhaps, more a question of their pursuing you than of your pursuing them."

"So!" Miguel exclaimed. "That little devil..."

"Don't blame Rafael," Pamela said quickly. "Anyway, it's true, isn't it?"

"Yes, I suppose it's true," he conceded, but he was grinning. "But that was mainly due to Dolores. Even before I attained my legal freedom, she tried to play matchmaker. She has wanted me to get married so that she could escape her own reins."

"You mean, she wants to leave your house?" Pamela asked incredulously.

"Oh, yes," Miguel answered easily. "She grew tired of being my housekeeper a long time ago. For a few years, early in her marriage, Dolores and her husband lived in Madrid. She developed a taste for city life, and would much prefer to have a place of her own here in Las Palmas, where she could shop to her heart's content, and lunch with her lady friends, and always have some interesting place to go. She has put up with Arucas," Miguel finished evenly, "because she has a fetish for doing penance. You would think that Dolores was a very sinful person, when the fact is I doubt she has ever seriously sinned in her entire life. Except, perhaps, in her attitude, occasionally. I found a great deal of fault with the way she treated you. In retrospect, I think there was nothing directed against you personally. I believe she was afraid that it might be disastrous if I were attracted to a woman from such a different culture. Even so..."

"Your sister was merely formal toward me," Pamela defended her.

"She was merely slightly colder than ice," Miguel countered. "But Rafael told her in the hospital that you had done something very great for him. He would not say much more than that, but he told Dolores he would forever be thankful to you."

"Rafael said that?"

"Yes."

Pamela shook her head. "I have to admit that surprises me."

"It surprised me, too. But it had a definite effect on Dolores. She was not just charitable when I took you home from the hospital, Pamelita. She was trying, in her way, to be friendly to you. She really hopes to be your friend one day."

Miguel broke off, and stared at Pamela bleakly. "Hell," he said. "How do any of us know what will happen *any* day, as far as our relationships with one another go?"

Pamela hesitated, then told him, "You have a way of posing questions to which there are no possible answers—rhetorical questions, Miguel. You wanted to know what that meant, remember? Anyway, no one can tell anything about tomorrow. About what's going to happen tomorrow, that is. The future is blocked with clouds we can't see through, but if you're speaking of enduring relationships, that's something else again."

"Yes?"

"Yes."

Miguel joined her, to stare out over Las Palmas by night. "Sometimes the stars seem so near to me," he said thoughtfully. "At other times, they seem so far away. Like happiness, they are elusive. One reaches out for silver, and grasps only dust."

He swung around to face Pamela. "Sometimes I tried to grab happiness where I found it," he admitted. "Usually, the dust left on my fingers was not anything close to stardust." The question came suddenly. "Why did you bring up the fact that I have known a few women...or, as you put it rather succinctly, that a few women had evidently attempted to pursue me over the years?"

"Well..." Pamela began. She stopped; although Miguel still sounded very serious, there was laughter in his eyes. No fireflies, not yet. Just the glint of laughter.

The hard knot that had lodged in her throat, a knot she'd almost become accustomed to, was starting to dissolve. She hadn't been sure if she'd ever see that wonderful, shining laughter in Miguel's jet-black eyes again. So much had happened, but now...

"*Querida,*" Miguel said, and now she had no doubt that he was teasing her, "you have been somewhat reticent with me in discussing your past, you know. You were free to admit that there have been men, that there is a man in the States."

"I've been trying to break off with him," Pamela murmured.

"I can understand why he would not let you go easily."

"I feel the same about any woman who had designs on you," Pamela pointed out.

"I take it that's a compliment? Pamelita, why are you looking like that?" Miguel chuckled. "Can I permit myself to believe that Rafael's comments actually made you jealous?"

Miguel was enjoying this repartee with her, having fun at her expense.

Catching on, she smiled at him, carefree. "Rafael's comments made me jealous as hell!" she admitted.

To her chagrin, Miguel's smile faded and he stared at her incredulously. "Do you mean that?"

"You better believe it!"

"I'd *like* to believe it." He drew a deep breath, and she saw how unsteady he was, despite his recent attempts at raillery. He looked unsure of himself in a boyish, vulnerable way. "Pamelita, I drove down here tonight because I couldn't wait until tomorrow."

"What do you mean?"

"When I made that promise to you that there would never again be secrets between us, I meant it. As far as I am concerned, I will never hold back from you again."

"Well, I'm now free to make you that same promise," Pamela declared. She was studying every line in Miguel's handsome face, and was about to speak again when he cut her off.

"Look," he said. "Everyone you have met here on Gran Canaria, even briefly, is crazy about you. Carmen dotes on you; I think one day you will have a good friend in Dolores. You have reached Rafael in a way no one else ever has."

"Yes?"

"Well... what I am trying to say, I suppose, is that I know our worlds are far apart, in so many ways. I have lived in both, after all. I could make a list a mile long of all the differences...."

"And?"

"I would be very naive if I didn't take them into consideration," Miguel said simply. "I would be ignoring reality if I didn't wonder if it could work between you and me."

"For Rafael's sake?" Pamela asked provocatively.

"For Rafael's sake, hell!" Miguel exploded, glaring at her. "Although I intend to do everything to better things between Rafael and myself, I have no intention of asking anyone, especially you, to be my son's surrogate mother!"

Pamela became acutely aware of the gardenia's sweet scent. The dark night, the warm air, the silver of a moon, and the radiance of the stars all enveloped her. Desire flamed within her.

Miguel read her correctly, but he shook his head gently. "No," he said. "You are driving me crazy, Pamelita. But then...you usually do drive me crazy. This time, though..."

He paused, and after a moment when he didn't continue she prodded, "Yes?"

"It is too serious this time, *querida*. We are not that much for bullfighting in the Canaries."

"Bullfighting?" Pamela echoed incredulously.

Miguel laughed. "I do not wonder that you look as if you think I have totally taken leave of my senses! But there is, in the *corrida*, in the bullfight, a certain element of...veracity. It is called the moment of truth. For the matador, it is the overwhelming moment of the struggle. He is poised over the bull, his sword precisely aimed, ready for the kill. And then he faces the moment when he will know whether there is to be triumph...or defeat."

He shook his head. "I am saying this poorly," he told her. "Though you will scoff at me, my English *does* fail me on those occasions when I need it the most. I could say this so much better to you in Spanish."

Pamela shook her head, puzzled and more than a little impatient with him. The only thing she could think of was the effect he was having on her. The only thing she was sure of was that she wanted him forever and ever. Yet at a moment when he should be sweeping her into his arms, he was solemnly discoursing on a Spanish tradition that she had always found abhorrent.

"I honestly don't understand what you're getting at, Miguel."

"In each life, there is that moment of truth," he told her. "For the bullfighter, it is one thing. For most of us it is something entirely different. But for each of us, it must be faced. It cannot be avoided. Do you follow me?"

"I'm not sure."

"For us to make a commitment to each other—that is a moment of truth, Pamelita. For me, probably my once in a lifetime moment of truth. I have never before committed myself to any woman. Not in this way."

"All right, then," she stated. "I have never before committed myself to any man. Not in this way."

"For you," Miguel murmured, "I suppose it must be admitted the commitment may be the greater one. Because I am asking you to come to where I live, join my ways with yours. Undoubtedly, to make compromises . . ."

Pamela suddenly remembered something Juan Basilio had said to her. Juan had spoken of compromise, and had said that those who failed to compromise only succeeded in thwarting their own personal growth.

She was facing her own moment of truth, and a decision that would change her life. Miguel had not come out and said so, but what he was asking was if it was possible for her to join her life with his. To compromise, forever.

Not wanting to rush this, wanting him to know how sure she was, she spoke slowly. "I'm used to being my own person, Miguel."

He shook his head reprovingly. "Pamelita, do you think you really need to tell me that?"

"Well . . . whatever I might enter into with you would have to be with the understanding that I *am* my own person, that I have my own career. . . ."

To her amazement, he broke out laughing. "Tell me," he chided, recovering, "Can you think of a better place than these Canary Islands for a hydrologist to pursue her career? My God, lady, we cry out for answers to our perpetual water problems. If, by your knowledge, you could start us on even a beginning, that in itself would be a miracle. But," he continued slowly, "although I respect your career, although I respect *you*, although I would never want you to be anything but what you are, *querida*, I must admit that where you are involved, I am not nearly so concerned with my island's problems as I am with my own."

Miguel faced Pamela; his eyes looked darker and deeper than night to her. His voice was so low she had to strain to hear him. "I have thought about this a great deal. And I do not see how I can possibly go on any longer without you."

Pamela looked up at him, and the world became a very tiny place. It was *their* world, hers and Miguel. A globe of clay, thrust into their hands. It was up to them to shape it.

It was also time to stop counting the differences, time to start considering the far more important things they shared. Most important of all, a love that would strengthen and grow as time passed, a love that would triumphantly surmount the small obstacles that were bound to be tossed in its path.

Pamela looked up at Miguel; everything she felt for him showed in her eyes. *"Te quiero."*

His smile tore her heartstrings. "I am going to say this in English," he whispered, "but the expression is entirely Spanish. My house, my country, and myself, are yours forever. Do you believe me, Pamelita? *Mi corazón?"*

Pamela started to answer him...not that it was a question that needed an answer. But she couldn't; Miguel was effectively sealing her lips with his.

It was night. The sky outside was still as dark as Miguel's eyes. But Pamela had no doubt that, once morning came, she was going to see the sun shining in a blue sky. The shadow on the sun would be gone.

Silhouette Special Edition

COMING NEXT MONTH

FIRE AT DAWN—Linda Shaw
As New Orlean's finest tried to put ghetto doctor Brittany Schellenegger behind bars, rugged police detective Hammer Curry intervened to save her...and soon two hearts were captive in a dangerous enthrallment.

THE SHOWGIRL AND THE PROFESSOR—Phyllis Halldorson
Carefree Reno showgirl Sunshine Smith wanted tutoring in math, and intellectual professor Chad Fitzhugh III was happy to give her *very* private lessons. But theirs was a case of opposites attracting in a nearly disastrous collision.

HONORABLE INTENTIONS—Kate Meriwether
Though anti-nuke lobbyist Libbie Greer and Army lieutenant Cole Matthews fiercely clashed on political issues, even more explosive was their sudden, unbidden, impossible passion.

DANGER IN HIS ARMS—Patti Beckman
For globetrotter Dusty Landers and ex-CIA agent Mack O'Shea, life was a series of exciting escapades. Still, constant adventure left little time for leisure...and less for loving.

THEIR SONG UNENDING—Anna James
When plane failure stranded conservative investment counselor Logan Addison and flamboyant entertainer Justine Hart on a romantic island paradise, calamity rapidly led to desire. All too soon, though, grim reality threatened to shatter their unlikely new love.

RETURN TO EDEN—Jeanne Stephens
When she learned that her childhood idol had wed her on the rebound, Mia had had the sense to flee the sham marriage. Now David was pursuing her in earnest, but how could she give her whole heart to the man who'd once broken it in two?

AVAILABLE NOW:

FOR NOW, FOREVER
Nora Roberts

SHADOW ON THE SUN
Maggi Charles

ROSE IN BLOOM
Andrea Edwards

THE EXECUTIVES
Monica Barrie

GOLDEN FIRESTORM
Anne Lacey

OBJECT OF DESIRE
Jennifer West

Silhouette Intimate Moments

MARCH MADNESS!

Get Intimate with
Four Very Special Authors

Silhouette Intimate Moments has chosen March as the month to launch the careers of three new authors—Marilyn Pappano, Paula Detmer Riggs and Sibylle Garrett—and to welcome top-selling historical romance author Nancy Morse to the world of contemporary romance.

For years Silhouette Intimate Moments has brought you the biggest names in romance. Join us now and let four exciting new talents take you from the desert of New Mexico to the backlots of Hollywood, from an Indian reservation in South Dakota to the Khyber Pass of Afghanistan.

Coming in March from Silhouette Intimate Moments:

SACRED PLACES: Nancy Morse
WITHIN REACH: Marilyn Pappano
BEAUTIFUL DREAMER: Paula Detmer Riggs
SEPTEMBER RAINBOW: Sibylle Garrett

ATTRACTIVE, SPACE SAVING BOOK RACK

Display your most prized novels on this handsome and sturdy book rack. The hand-rubbed walnut finish will blend into your library decor with quiet elegance, providing a practical organizer for your favorite hard-or soft-covered books.

Only $9.95

Approximately 16" x 8" when assembled

Assembles in seconds!

To order, rush your name, address and zip code, along with a check or money order for $10.70* ($9.95 plus 75¢ postage and handling) payable to *Silhouette Books*.

Silhouette Books
Book Rack Offer
901 Fuhrmann Blvd.
P.O. Box 1325
Buffalo, NY 14269-1325

Offer not available in Canada.

*New York residents add appropriate sales tax.

BKR-2R

**Coming February
from Special Editions—
The final book in Nora Roberts's sensational
MacGregor Series**

For Now, Forever

The MacGregor Series, published in 1985, followed the lives and loves of the MacGregor children. We were inundated with fan mail—and one request stood out: Tell us about Daniel and Anna's romance!

For Now, Forever is that Story...

Anna is a proud, independent woman determined against all odds to be a surgeon. Daniel is ambitious and arrogant, a self-made tycoon who wants a woman to share his home and raise his children. Together they battle each other and their feelings as they try to make their own dreams come true.

Look for *Playing the Odds*, *Tempting Fate*, *All the Possibilities* and *One Man's Art*, all to be reissued in February in a special Collectors Edition.

Don't miss them wherever paperbacks are sold.